JUPITER'S LEGACY ®

MARK MILLAR · FRANK QUITELY
WRITER • CO-CREATORS • ARTIST

PETER DOHERTY
COLOURS • LETTERS • DESIGN

ROB MILLER
DIGITAL ART ASSISTANT

NICOLE BOOSE
EDITOR

DREW GILL
PRODUCTION

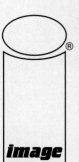

IMAGE COMICS, INC.
Robert Kirkman – Chief Operating Officer
Erik Larsen – Chief Financial Officer
Todd McFarlane – President
Marc Silvestri – Chief Executive Officer
Jim Valentino – Vice-President

Eric Stephenson – Publisher
Ron Richards – Director of Business Development
Jennifer de Guzman – Director of Trade Book Sales
Kat Salazar – Director of PR & Marketing
Corey Murphy – Director of Retail Sales
Jeremy Sullivan – Director of Digital Sales
Emilio Bautista – Sales Assistant
Branwyn Bigglestone – Senior Accounts Manager
Emily Miller – Accounts Manager
Jessica Ambriz – Administrative Assistant
David Brothers – Content Manager
Jonathan Chan – Production Manager
Drew Gill – Art Director
Meredith Wallace – Print Manager
Addison Duke – Production Artist
Vincent Kukua – Production Artist
Tricia Ramos – Production Assistant
IMAGECOMICS.COM

JUPITER'S LEGACY. First printing, April 2015. Published by Image Comics, Inc. Office of publication: 2001 Center Street, Sixth Floor, Berkeley, CA 94704. Copyright © 2013, 2014, 2015 Millarworld Limited & Frank Quitely Ltd. All rights reserved. Originally published in single-magazine form as JUPITER'S LEGACY #1-5. "Jupiter's Legacy," the Jupiter's Legacy logo, and all character likenesses herein are trademarks of Millarworld Limited & Frank Quitely Ltd unless expressly indicated. "Millarworld" and the Millarworld logos are trademarks of Millarworld Limited. "Image" and the Image Comics logos are registered trademarks and copyrights of Image Comics, Inc. All rights reserved. No part of this publication may be reproduced or transmitted, in any form or by any means (except for short excerpts for journalistic or review purposes) without the express written permission of Millarworld Limited, Frank Quitely Ltd., or Image Comics, Inc. All names, characters, events, and locales in this publication are entirely fictional. Any resemblance to actual persons (living or dead) or events or places, without satiric intent, is coincidental. Printed in the USA. For information regarding the CPSIA on this printed material call: 203-595-3636 and provide reference # RICH-612684. Representation: Law Offices of Harris M. Miller II, P.C. (rightsinquiries@gmail.com).
ISBN: 978-63215-310-4.

CHAPTER 1

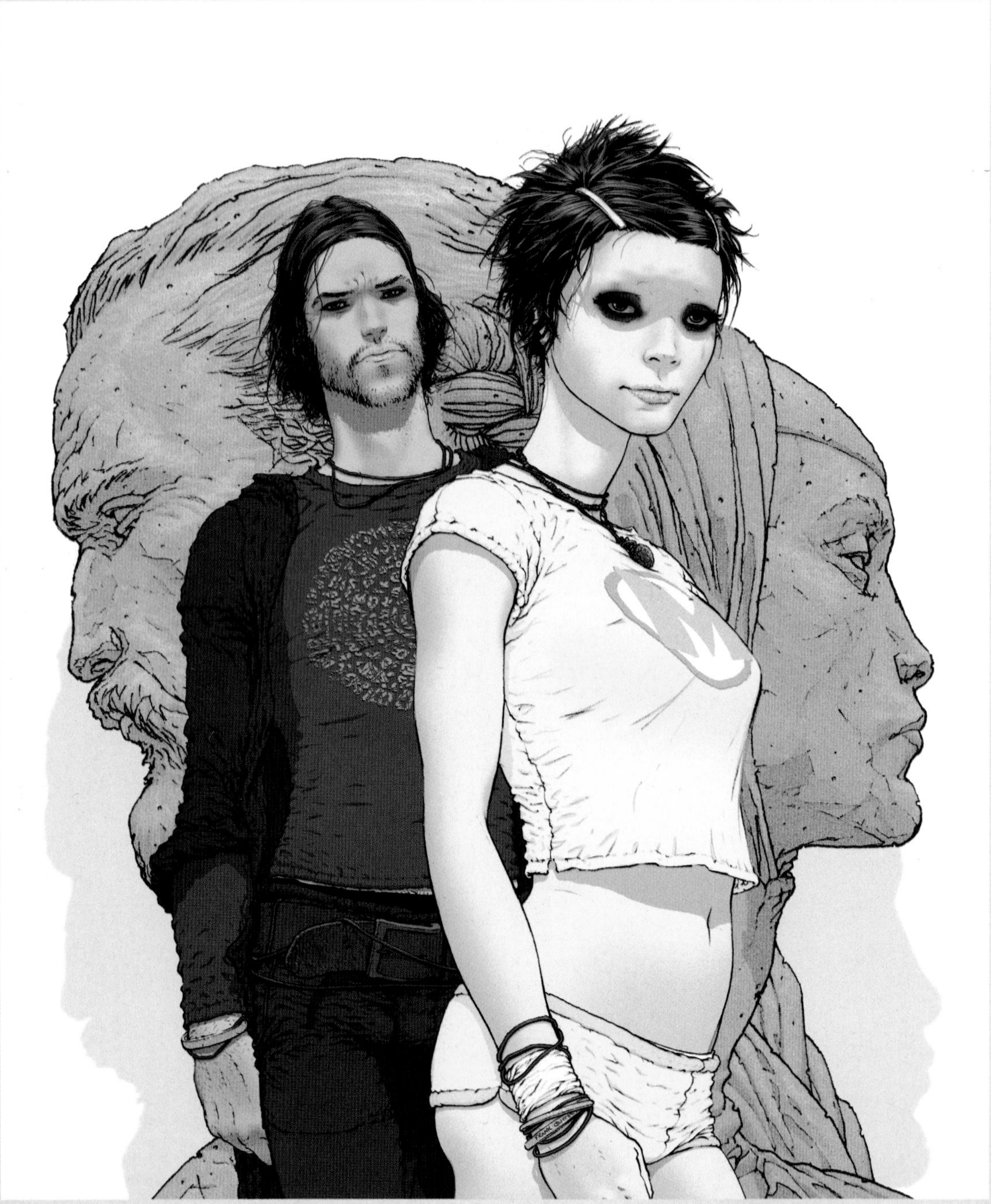

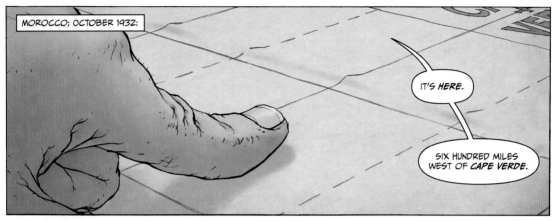

MOROCCO; OCTOBER 1932:

IT'S *HERE.*

SIX HUNDRED MILES WEST OF *CAPE VERDE.*

THIS IS WHERE I WANT YOU TO *TAKE* US, CAPTAIN BORGES. THIS IS WHERE THE *ISLAND* IS.

WELL, I'M NOT A MAN TO TURN DOWN FREE MONEY, MISTER SAMPSON, BUT I'M NOT IN THE HABIT OF WASTING PEOPLE'S TIME *EITHER.*

I'VE SAILED THOSE WATERS MY ENTIRE LIFE AND I PROMISE YOU NOW THERE ARE NO ISLANDS IN THOSE PARTS FOR *A HUNDRED MILES.*

TRUST ME, BUDDY. IF *SHELDON* SAYS THERE'S AN ISLAND ON THAT SPOT YOU CAN PRETTY MUCH BET THE FARM ON IT.

OH *REALLY?* WHAT MAKES YOU SO *SURE?*

HE SAW IT IN A DREAM.

AND THE REST OF YOU ARE *COMFORTABLE* WITH THIS?

ENTIRELY COMFORTABLE.

ONE THING WE'VE LEARNED OVER THE YEARS IS THAT IF MY BROTHER GETS AN *IDEA* IN HIS HEAD THERE'S NO POINT TRYING TO TALK HIM *OUT* OF IT, CAPTAIN.

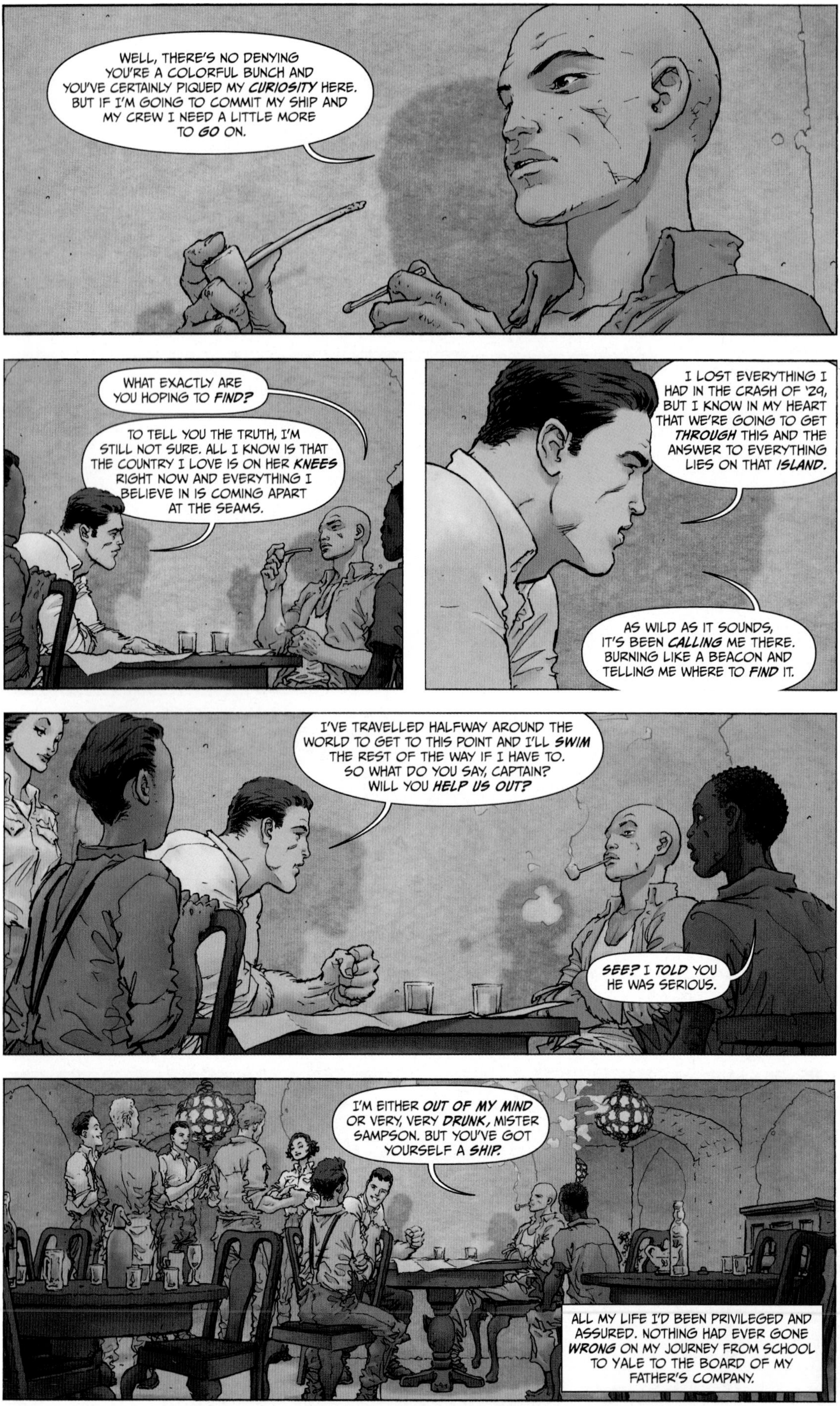
WELL, THERE'S NO DENYING YOU'RE A COLORFUL BUNCH AND YOU'VE CERTAINLY PIQUED MY CURIOSITY HERE. BUT IF I'M GOING TO COMMIT MY SHIP AND MY CREW I NEED A LITTLE MORE TO GO ON.
WHAT EXACTLY ARE YOU HOPING TO FIND?
TO TELL YOU THE TRUTH, I'M STILL NOT SURE. ALL I KNOW IS THAT THE COUNTRY I LOVE IS ON HER KNEES RIGHT NOW AND EVERYTHING I BELIEVE IN IS COMING APART AT THE SEAMS.
I LOST EVERYTHING I HAD IN THE CRASH OF '29, BUT I KNOW IN MY HEART THAT WE'RE GOING TO GET THROUGH THIS AND THE ANSWER TO EVERYTHING LIES ON THAT ISLAND.
AS WILD AS IT SOUNDS, IT'S BEEN CALLING ME THERE. BURNING LIKE A BEACON AND TELLING ME WHERE TO FIND IT.
I'VE TRAVELLED HALFWAY AROUND THE WORLD TO GET TO THIS POINT AND I'LL SWIM THE REST OF THE WAY IF I HAVE TO. SO WHAT DO YOU SAY, CAPTAIN? WILL YOU HELP US OUT?
SEE? I TOLD YOU HE WAS SERIOUS.
I'M EITHER OUT OF MY MIND OR VERY, VERY DRUNK, MISTER SAMPSON. BUT YOU'VE GOT YOURSELF A SHIP.
ALL MY LIFE I'D BEEN PRIVILEGED AND ASSURED. NOTHING HAD EVER GONE WRONG ON MY JOURNEY FROM SCHOOL TO YALE TO THE BOARD OF MY FATHER'S COMPANY.

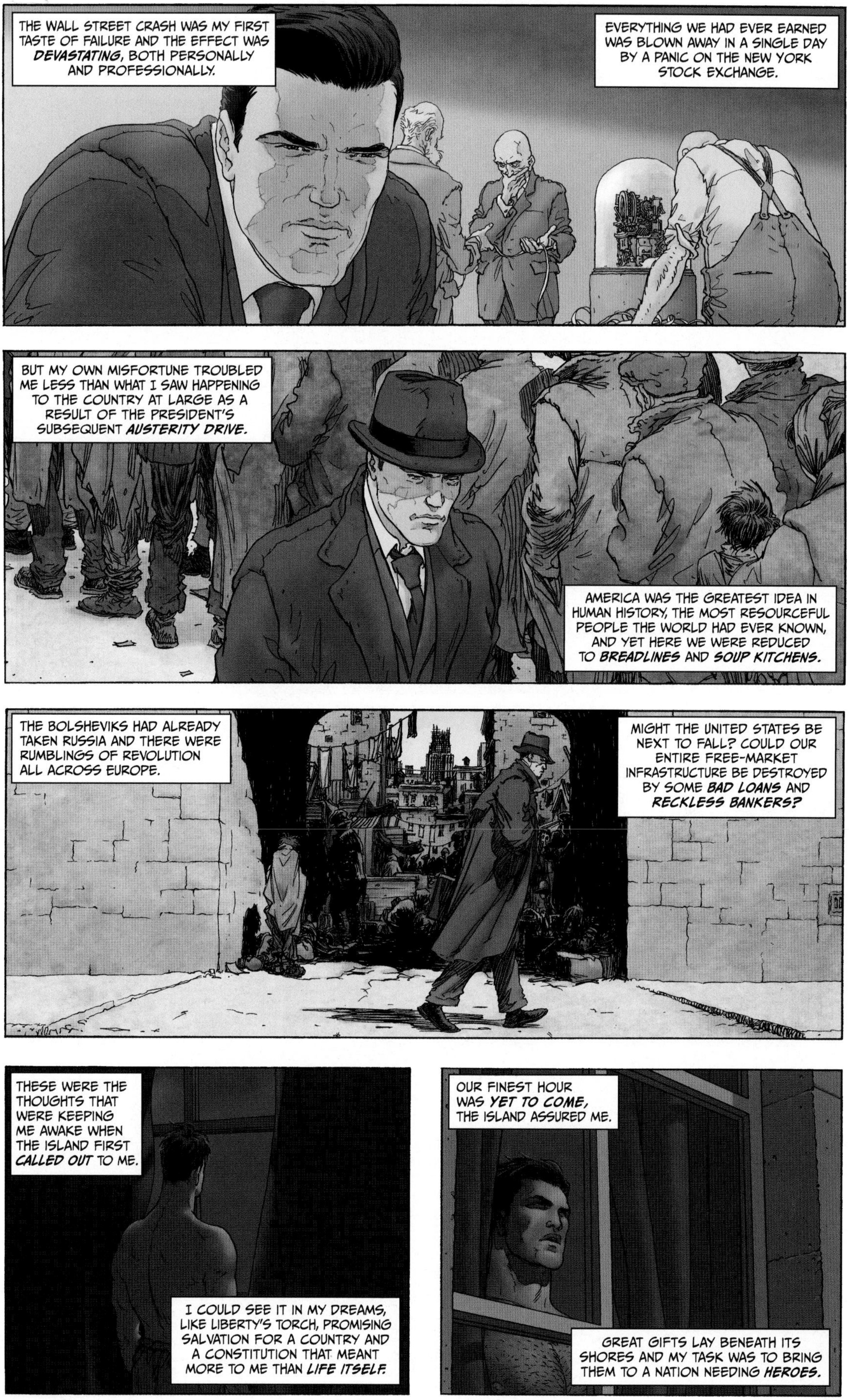
THE WALL STREET CRASH WAS MY FIRST TASTE OF FAILURE AND THE EFFECT WAS *DEVASTATING*, BOTH PERSONALLY AND PROFESSIONALLY.
EVERYTHING WE HAD EVER EARNED WAS BLOWN AWAY IN A SINGLE DAY BY A PANIC ON THE NEW YORK STOCK EXCHANGE.
BUT MY OWN MISFORTUNE TROUBLED ME LESS THAN WHAT I SAW HAPPENING TO THE COUNTRY AT LARGE AS A RESULT OF THE PRESIDENT'S SUBSEQUENT *AUSTERITY DRIVE.*
AMERICA WAS THE GREATEST IDEA IN HUMAN HISTORY, THE MOST RESOURCEFUL PEOPLE THE WORLD HAD EVER KNOWN, AND YET HERE WE WERE REDUCED TO *BREADLINES* AND *SOUP KITCHENS.*
THE BOLSHEVIKS HAD ALREADY TAKEN RUSSIA AND THERE WERE RUMBLINGS OF REVOLUTION ALL ACROSS EUROPE.
MIGHT THE UNITED STATES BE NEXT TO FALL? COULD OUR ENTIRE FREE-MARKET INFRASTRUCTURE BE DESTROYED BY SOME *BAD LOANS* AND *RECKLESS BANKERS?*
THESE WERE THE THOUGHTS THAT WERE KEEPING ME AWAKE WHEN THE ISLAND FIRST *CALLED OUT* TO ME.
I COULD SEE IT IN MY DREAMS, LIKE LIBERTY'S TORCH, PROMISING SALVATION FOR A COUNTRY AND A CONSTITUTION THAT MEANT MORE TO ME THAN *LIFE ITSELF.*
OUR FINEST HOUR WAS *YET TO COME,* THE ISLAND ASSURED ME.
GREAT GIFTS LAY BENEATH ITS SHORES AND MY TASK WAS TO BRING THEM TO A NATION NEEDING *HEROES.*

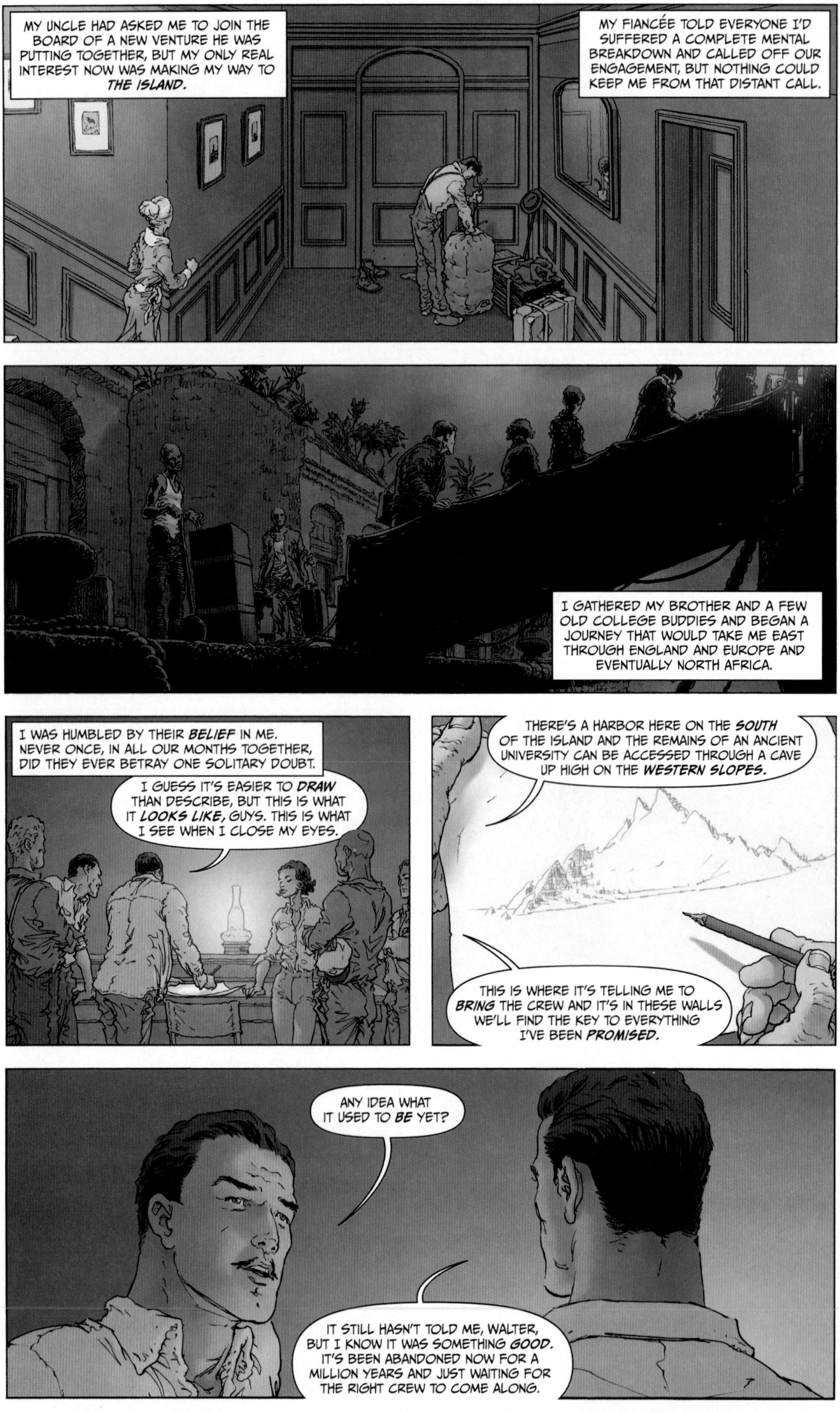
MY UNCLE HAD ASKED ME TO JOIN THE BOARD OF A NEW VENTURE HE WAS PUTTING TOGETHER, BUT MY ONLY REAL INTEREST NOW WAS MAKING MY WAY TO *THE ISLAND.*
MY FIANCÉE TOLD EVERYONE I'D SUFFERED A COMPLETE MENTAL BREAKDOWN AND CALLED OFF OUR ENGAGEMENT, BUT NOTHING COULD KEEP ME FROM THAT DISTANT CALL.
I GATHERED MY BROTHER AND A FEW OLD COLLEGE BUDDIES AND BEGAN A JOURNEY THAT WOULD TAKE ME EAST THROUGH ENGLAND AND EUROPE AND EVENTUALLY NORTH AFRICA.
I WAS HUMBLED BY THEIR *BELIEF* IN ME. NEVER ONCE, IN ALL OUR MONTHS TOGETHER, DID THEY EVER BETRAY ONE SOLITARY DOUBT.
I GUESS IT'S EASIER TO *DRAW* THAN DESCRIBE, BUT THIS IS WHAT IT *LOOKS LIKE,* GUYS. THIS IS WHAT I SEE WHEN I CLOSE MY EYES.
THERE'S A HARBOR HERE ON THE *SOUTH* OF THE ISLAND AND THE REMAINS OF AN ANCIENT UNIVERSITY CAN BE ACCESSED THROUGH A CAVE UP HIGH ON THE *WESTERN SLOPES.*
THIS IS WHERE IT'S TELLING ME TO *BRING* THE CREW AND IT'S IN THESE WALLS WE'LL FIND THE KEY TO EVERYTHING I'VE BEEN *PROMISED.*
ANY IDEA WHAT IT USED TO *BE* YET?
IT STILL HASN'T TOLD ME, WALTER, BUT I KNOW IT WAS SOMETHING *GOOD.* IT'S BEEN ABANDONED NOW FOR A MILLION YEARS AND JUST WAITING FOR THE RIGHT CREW TO COME ALONG.

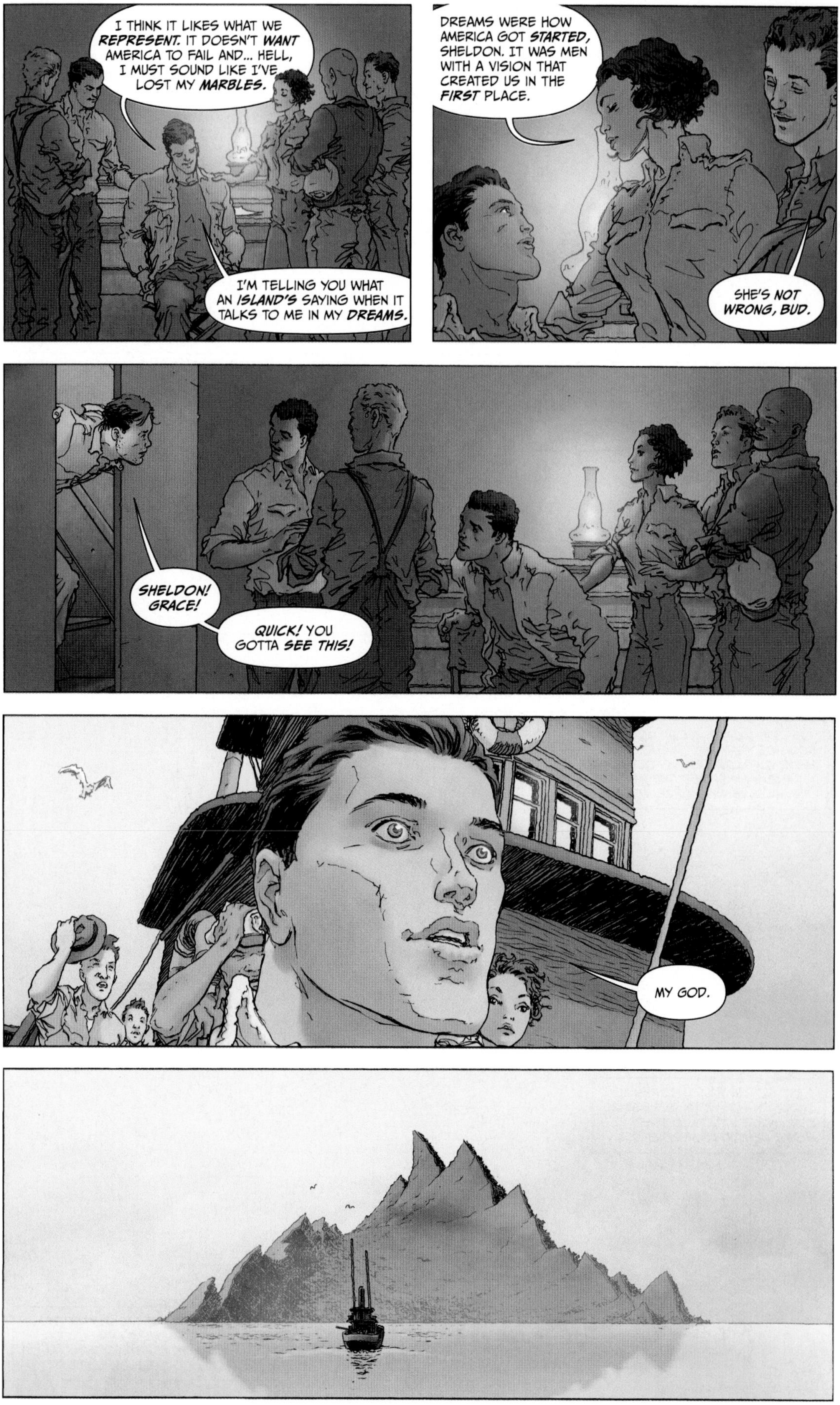
I THINK IT LIKES WHAT WE REPRESENT. IT DOESN'T WANT AMERICA TO FAIL AND... HELL, I MUST SOUND LIKE I'VE LOST MY MARBLES.
I'M TELLING YOU WHAT AN ISLAND'S SAYING WHEN IT TALKS TO ME IN MY DREAMS.
DREAMS WERE HOW AMERICA GOT STARTED, SHELDON. IT WAS MEN WITH A VISION THAT CREATED US IN THE FIRST PLACE.
SHE'S NOT WRONG, BUD.
SHELDON! GRACE!
QUICK! YOU GOTTA SEE THIS!
MY GOD.

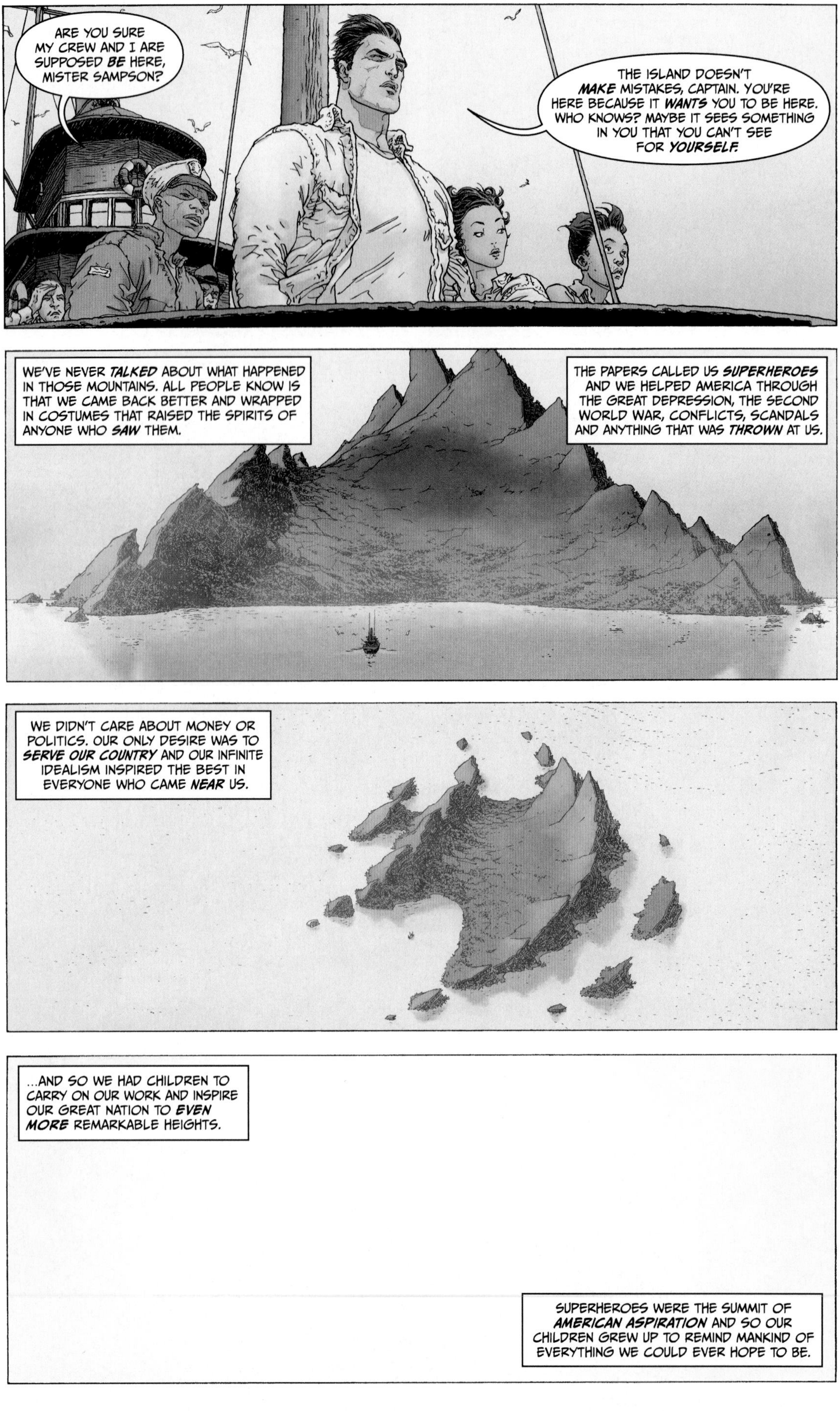
ARE YOU SURE MY CREW AND I ARE SUPPOSED *BE* HERE, MISTER SAMPSON?
THE ISLAND DOESN'T *MAKE* MISTAKES, CAPTAIN. YOU'RE HERE BECAUSE IT *WANTS* YOU TO BE HERE. WHO KNOWS? MAYBE IT SEES SOMETHING IN YOU THAT YOU CAN'T SEE FOR *YOURSELF.*
WE'VE NEVER *TALKED* ABOUT WHAT HAPPENED IN THOSE MOUNTAINS. ALL PEOPLE KNOW IS THAT WE CAME BACK BETTER AND WRAPPED IN COSTUMES THAT RAISED THE SPIRITS OF ANYONE WHO *SAW* THEM.
THE PAPERS CALLED US *SUPERHEROES* AND WE HELPED AMERICA THROUGH THE GREAT DEPRESSION, THE SECOND WORLD WAR, CONFLICTS, SCANDALS AND ANYTHING THAT WAS *THROWN* AT US.
WE DIDN'T CARE ABOUT MONEY OR POLITICS. OUR ONLY DESIRE WAS TO *SERVE OUR COUNTRY* AND OUR INFINITE IDEALISM INSPIRED THE BEST IN EVERYONE WHO CAME *NEAR* US.
...AND SO WE HAD CHILDREN TO CARRY ON OUR WORK AND INSPIRE OUR GREAT NATION TO *EVEN MORE* REMARKABLE HEIGHTS.
SUPERHEROES WERE THE SUMMIT OF *AMERICAN ASPIRATION* AND SO OUR CHILDREN GREW UP TO REMIND MANKIND OF EVERYTHING WE COULD EVER HOPE TO BE.

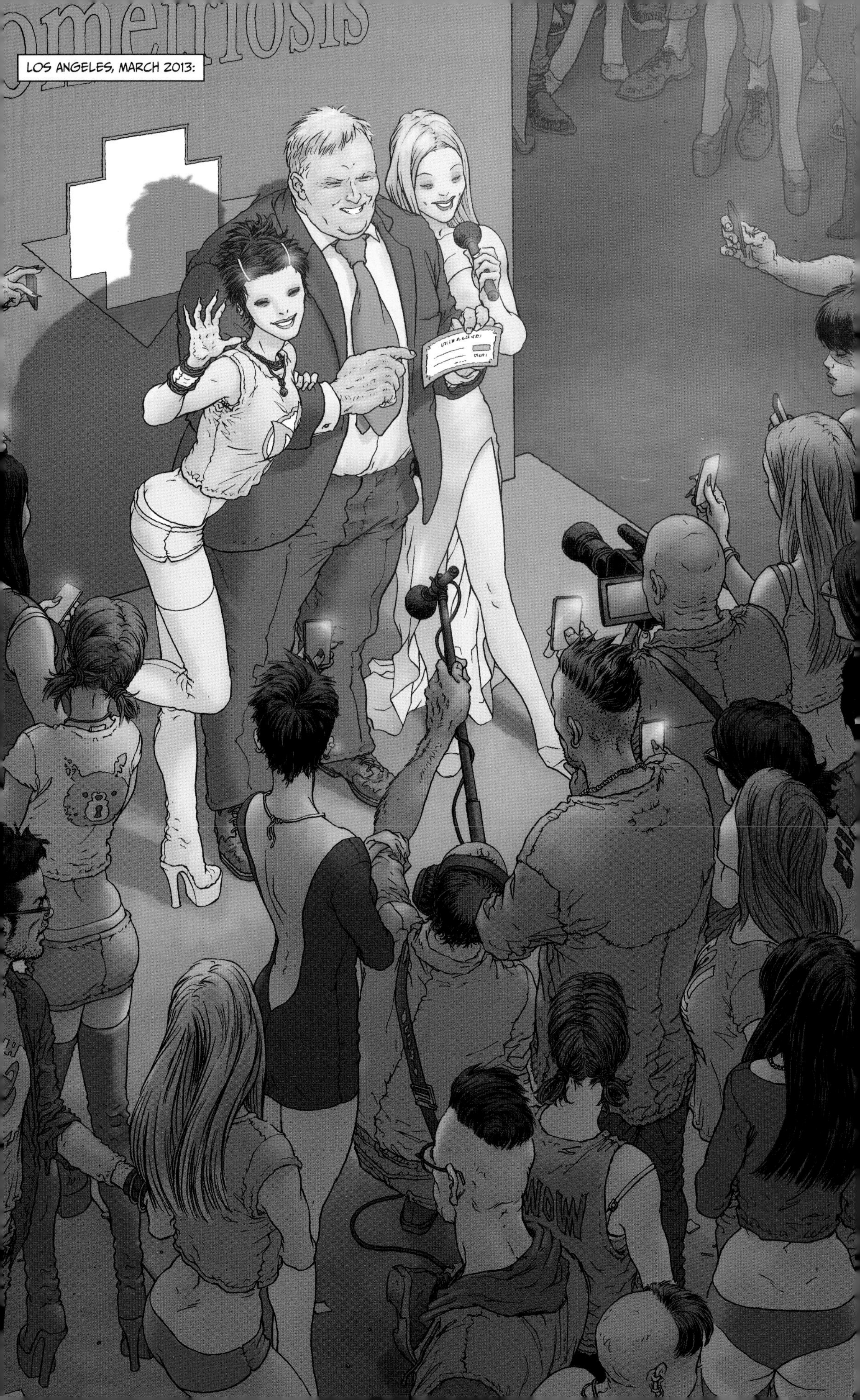
LOS ANGELES, MARCH 2013:

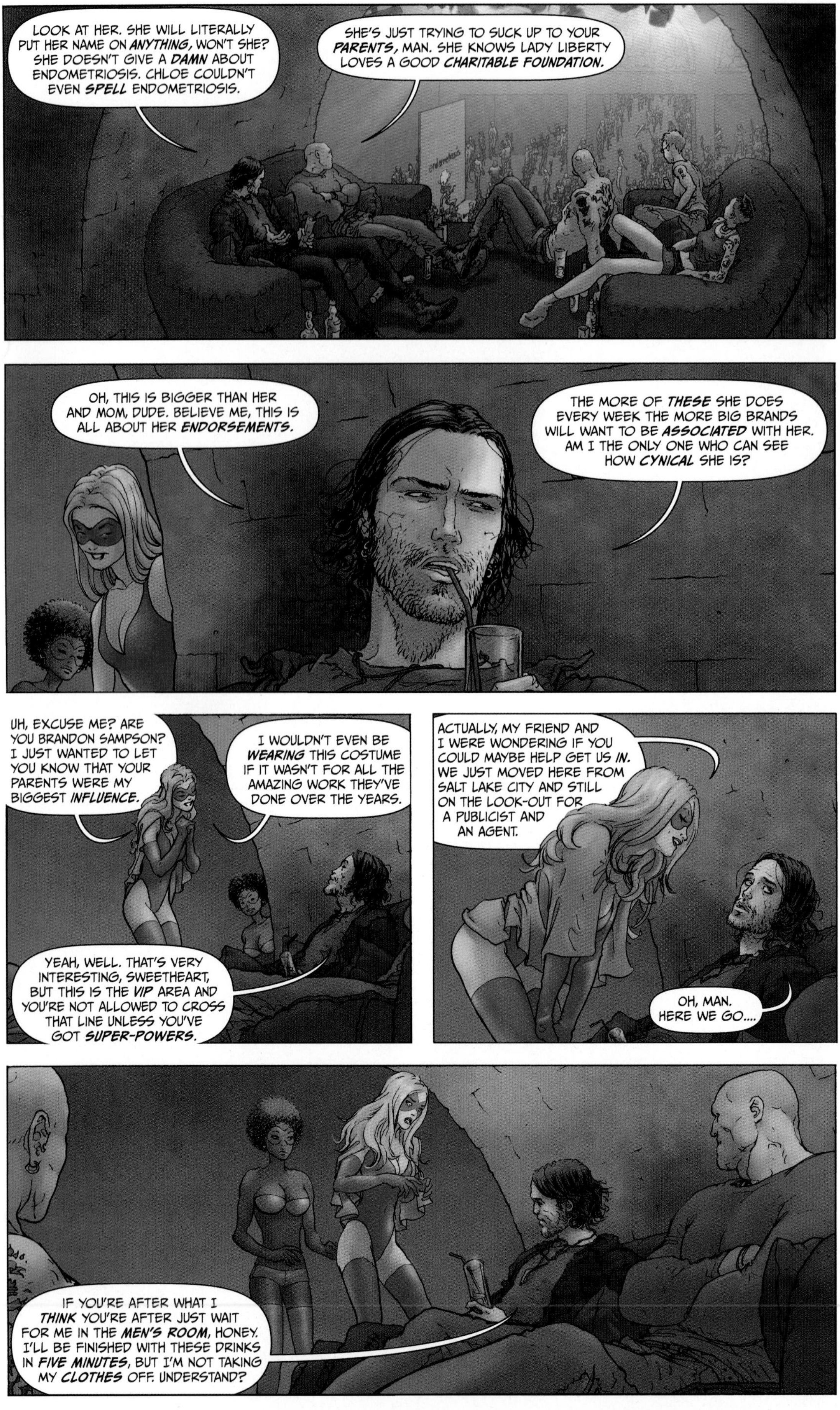
LOOK AT HER. SHE WILL LITERALLY PUT HER NAME ON ANYTHING, WON'T SHE? SHE DOESN'T GIVE A DAMN ABOUT ENDOMETRIOSIS. CHLOE COULDN'T EVEN SPELL ENDOMETRIOSIS.
SHE'S JUST TRYING TO SUCK UP TO YOUR PARENTS, MAN. SHE KNOWS LADY LIBERTY LOVES A GOOD CHARITABLE FOUNDATION.
OH, THIS IS BIGGER THAN HER AND MOM, DUDE. BELIEVE ME, THIS IS ALL ABOUT HER ENDORSEMENTS.
THE MORE OF THESE SHE DOES EVERY WEEK THE MORE BIG BRANDS WILL WANT TO BE ASSOCIATED WITH HER. AM I THE ONLY ONE WHO CAN SEE HOW CYNICAL SHE IS?
UH, EXCUSE ME? ARE YOU BRANDON SAMPSON? I JUST WANTED TO LET YOU KNOW THAT YOUR PARENTS WERE MY BIGGEST INFLUENCE.
I WOULDN'T EVEN BE WEARING THIS COSTUME IF IT WASN'T FOR ALL THE AMAZING WORK THEY'VE DONE OVER THE YEARS.
YEAH, WELL. THAT'S VERY INTERESTING, SWEETHEART, BUT THIS IS THE VIP AREA AND YOU'RE NOT ALLOWED TO CROSS THAT LINE UNLESS YOU'VE GOT SUPER-POWERS.
ACTUALLY, MY FRIEND AND I WERE WONDERING IF YOU COULD MAYBE HELP GET US IN. WE JUST MOVED HERE FROM SALT LAKE CITY AND STILL ON THE LOOK-OUT FOR A PUBLICIST AND AN AGENT.
OH, MAN. HERE WE GO....
IF YOU'RE AFTER WHAT I THINK YOU'RE AFTER JUST WAIT FOR ME IN THE MEN'S ROOM, HONEY. I'LL BE FINISHED WITH THESE DRINKS IN FIVE MINUTES, BUT I'M NOT TAKING MY CLOTHES OFF. UNDERSTAND?

OH MY GOD. WHAT MAKES YOU THINK YOU CAN *TALK* TO PEOPLE LIKE THAT?

YOU THINK BECAUSE YOUR DAD'S THE *UTOPIAN* YOU'RE *BETTER* THAN EVERYONE ELSE?

LEAVE IT, KENDRA. THE GUY'S AN *IDIOT.* LET'S GO TALK TO SOMEBODY ELSE.

YOUR LOSS, LADIES

YOU *OKAY,* MAN?

NOT REALLY. I JUST GOT WORD THAT OMEGA AND SAMSUNG HAVE CANCELLED MY CONTRACTS. THEY'RE SAYING IT'S THE DOWNTURN, BUT I THINK THEY FORGET I'VE GOT SUPER-HEARING.

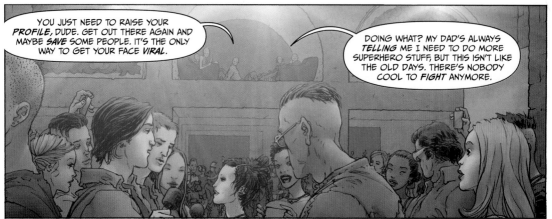

YOU JUST NEED TO RAISE YOUR *PROFILE,* DUDE. GET OUT THERE AGAIN AND MAYBE *SAVE* SOME PEOPLE. IT'S THE ONLY WAY TO GET YOUR FACE *VIRAL.*

DOING WHAT? MY DAD'S ALWAYS *TELLING* ME I NEED TO DO MORE SUPERHERO STUFF, BUT THIS ISN'T LIKE THE OLD DAYS. THERE'S NOBODY COOL TO *FIGHT* ANYMORE.

ALL THE GREAT BATTLES ARE WELL AND TRULY *OVER.* ALL THE BEST VILLAINS DIED *TEN* OR *TWENTY* YEARS AGO. MY PARENTS NEED TO REALIZE THEY WERE LIVING IN A *GOLDEN AGE.*

UH, *EXCUSE* ME?

I DON'T MEAN TO INTERRUPT, BUT MY FRIEND ASKED ME TO LET YOU KNOW SHE'S WAITING IN *THE MEN'S ROOM* WHEN YOU'RE READY.

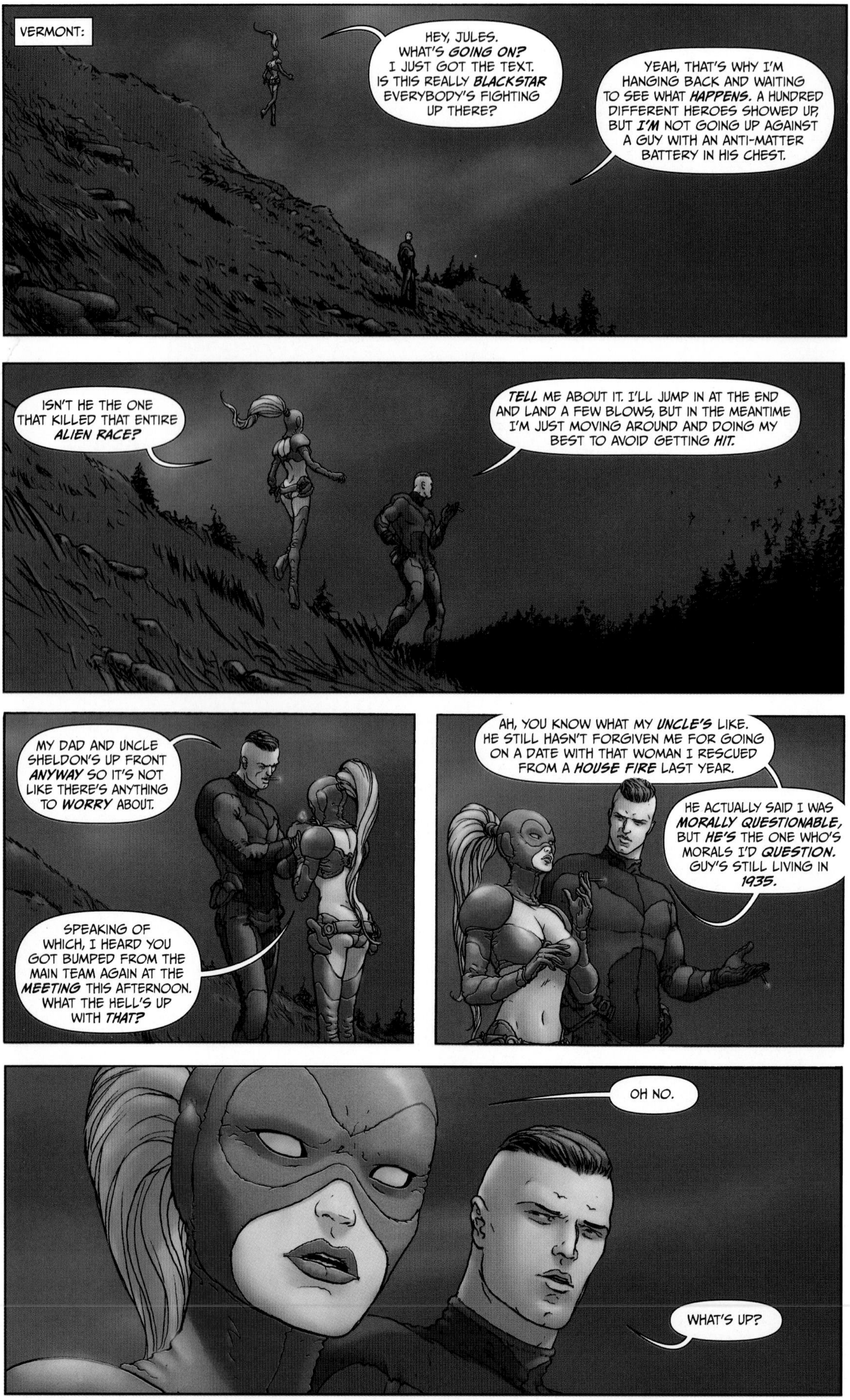
VERMONT:
HEY, JULES. WHAT'S GOING ON? I JUST GOT THE TEXT. IS THIS REALLY BLACKSTAR EVERYBODY'S FIGHTING UP THERE?
YEAH, THAT'S WHY I'M HANGING BACK AND WAITING TO SEE WHAT HAPPENS. A HUNDRED DIFFERENT HEROES SHOWED UP, BUT I'M NOT GOING UP AGAINST A GUY WITH AN ANTI-MATTER BATTERY IN HIS CHEST.
ISN'T HE THE ONE THAT KILLED THAT ENTIRE ALIEN RACE?
TELL ME ABOUT IT. I'LL JUMP IN AT THE END AND LAND A FEW BLOWS, BUT IN THE MEANTIME I'M JUST MOVING AROUND AND DOING MY BEST TO AVOID GETTING HIT.
MY DAD AND UNCLE SHELDON'S UP FRONT ANYWAY SO IT'S NOT LIKE THERE'S ANYTHING TO WORRY ABOUT.
SPEAKING OF WHICH, I HEARD YOU GOT BUMPED FROM THE MAIN TEAM AGAIN AT THE MEETING THIS AFTERNOON. WHAT THE HELL'S UP WITH THAT?
AH, YOU KNOW WHAT MY UNCLE'S LIKE. HE STILL HASN'T FORGIVEN ME FOR GOING ON A DATE WITH THAT WOMAN I RESCUED FROM A HOUSE FIRE LAST YEAR.
HE ACTUALLY SAID I WAS MORALLY QUESTIONABLE, BUT HE'S THE ONE WHO'S MORALS I'D QUESTION. GUY'S STILL LIVING IN 1935.
OH NO.
WHAT'S UP?

MOVE!

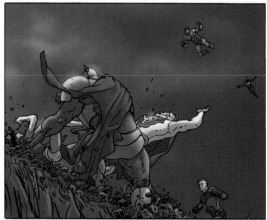

WHAT ARE YOU *WAITING* FOR, WALTER? *GET IN HIS HEAD* AND *CLOSE HIM DOWN!*

I'M TRYING MY BEST, BUT HIS DEFENSES ARE *INCREDIBLE.* IMAGINE A LOCK WITHIN A LOCK INSIDE A THOUSAND OTHER LOCKS! IT'S ALL ABOUT FINDING *THE CORRECT KEY!*

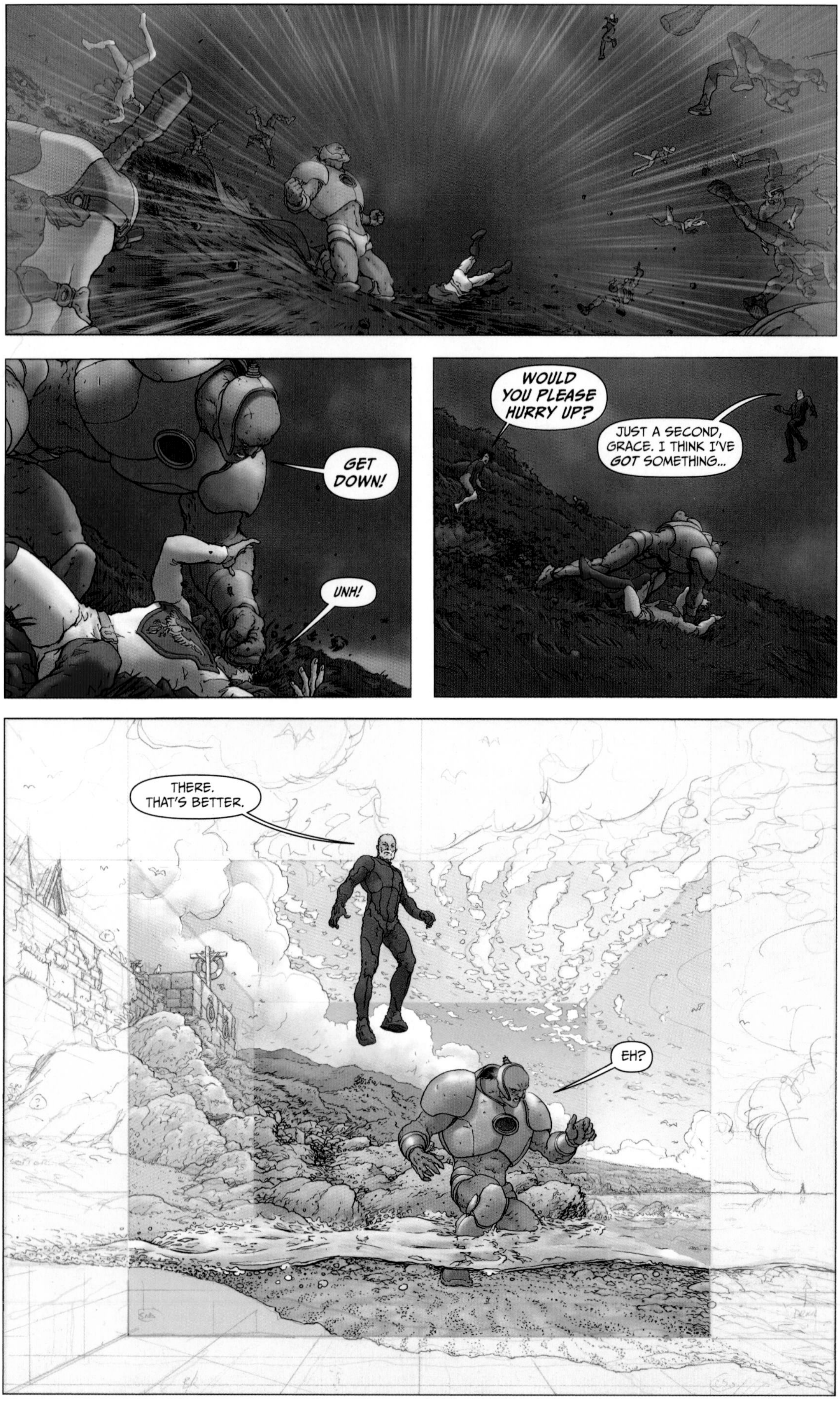
GET DOWN!
UNH!
WOULD YOU PLEASE HURRY UP?
JUST A SECOND, GRACE. I THINK I'VE GOT SOMETHING...
THERE. THAT'S BETTER.
EH?

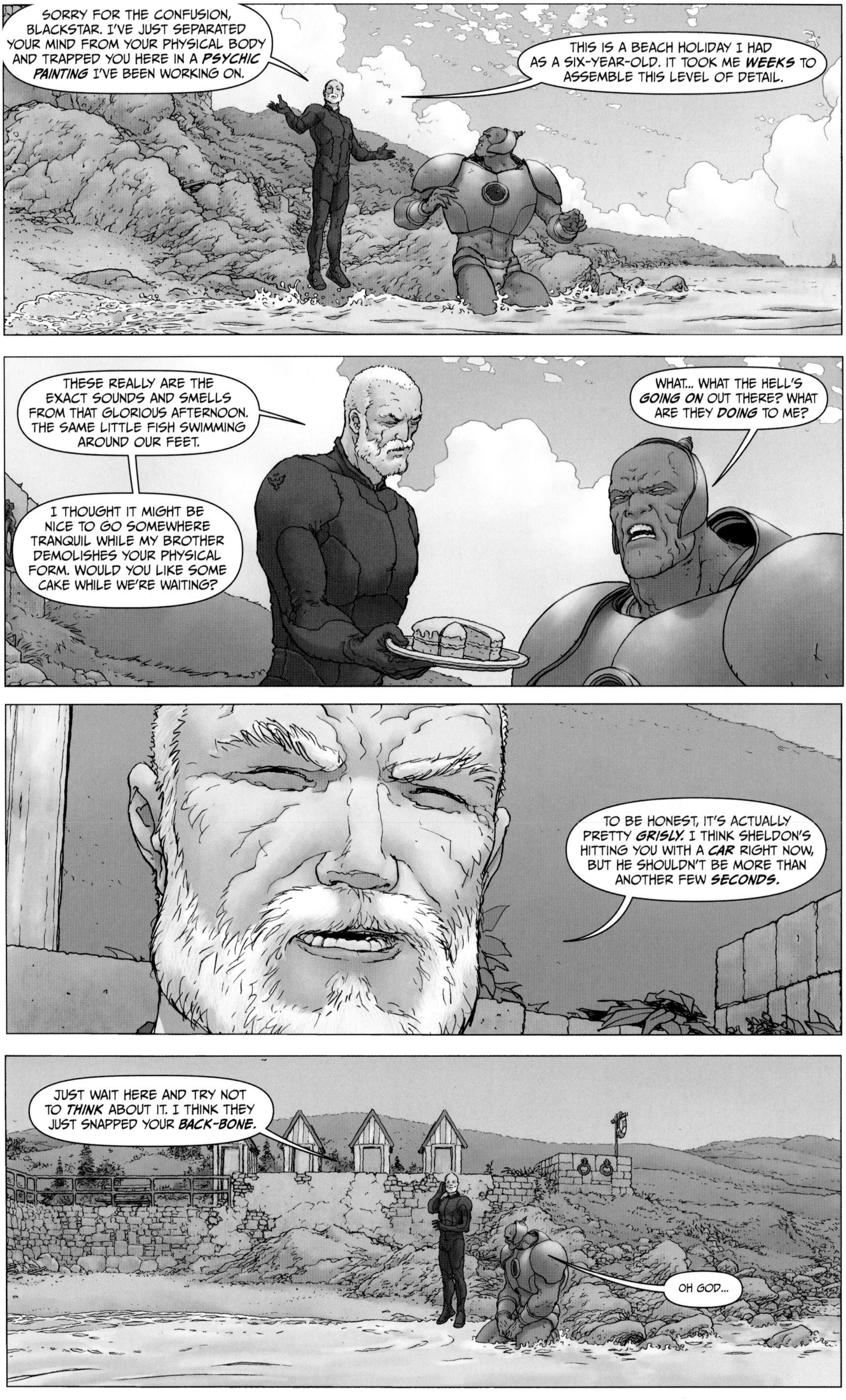
SORRY FOR THE CONFUSION, BLACKSTAR. I'VE JUST SEPARATED YOUR MIND FROM YOUR PHYSICAL BODY AND TRAPPED YOU HERE IN A PSYCHIC PAINTING I'VE BEEN WORKING ON.
THIS IS A BEACH HOLIDAY I HAD AS A SIX-YEAR-OLD. IT TOOK ME WEEKS TO ASSEMBLE THIS LEVEL OF DETAIL.
THESE REALLY ARE THE EXACT SOUNDS AND SMELLS FROM THAT GLORIOUS AFTERNOON. THE SAME LITTLE FISH SWIMMING AROUND OUR FEET.
I THOUGHT IT MIGHT BE NICE TO GO SOMEWHERE TRANQUIL WHILE MY BROTHER DEMOLISHES YOUR PHYSICAL FORM. WOULD YOU LIKE SOME CAKE WHILE WE'RE WAITING?
WHAT... WHAT THE HELL'S GOING ON OUT THERE? WHAT ARE THEY DOING TO ME?
TO BE HONEST, IT'S ACTUALLY PRETTY GRISLY. I THINK SHELDON'S HITTING YOU WITH A CAR RIGHT NOW, BUT HE SHOULDN'T BE MORE THAN ANOTHER FEW SECONDS.
JUST WAIT HERE AND TRY NOT TO THINK ABOUT IT. I THINK THEY JUST SNAPPED YOUR BACK-BONE.
OH GOD...

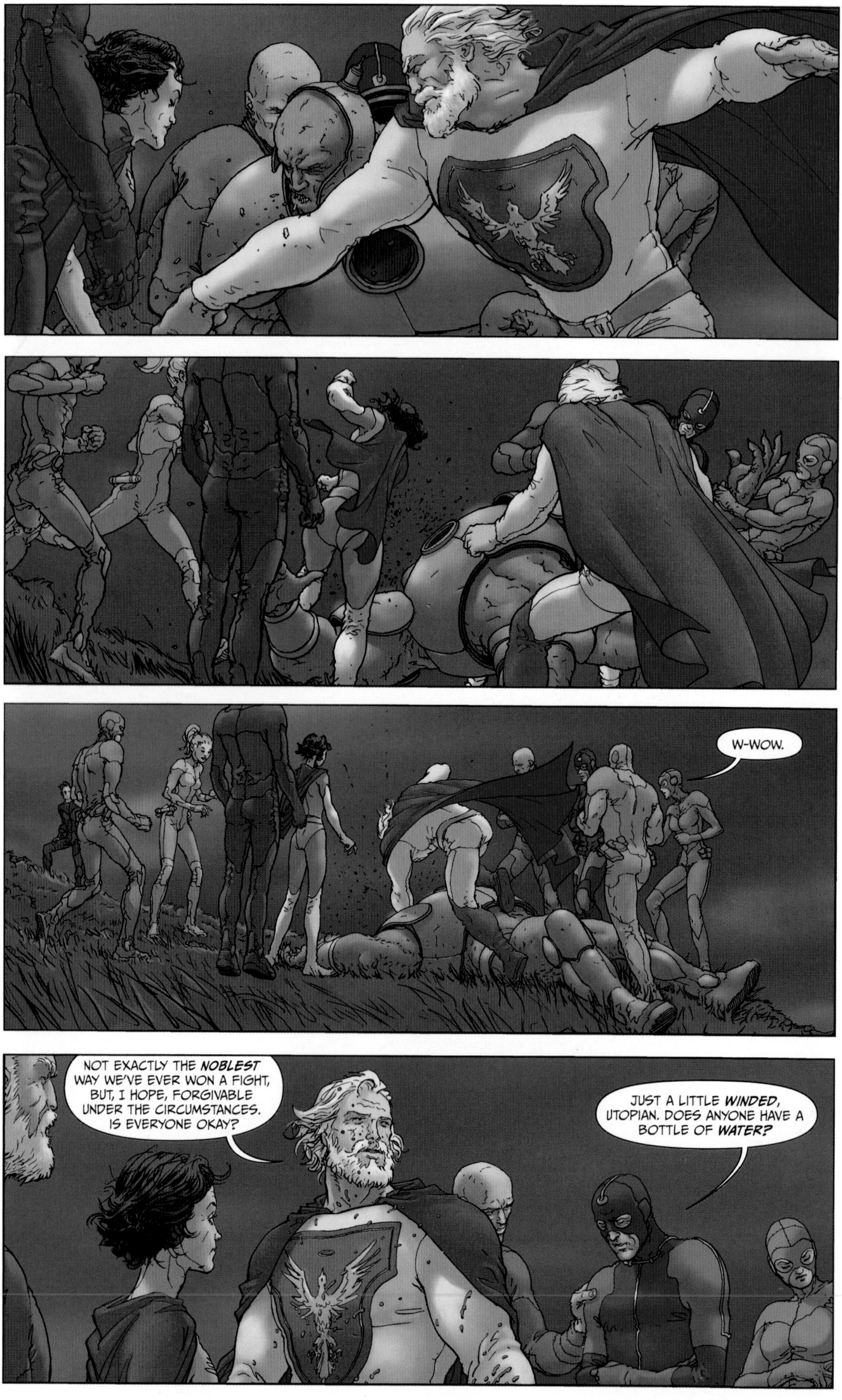
W-WOW.
NOT EXACTLY THE NOBLEST WAY WE'VE EVER WON A FIGHT, BUT, I HOPE, FORGIVABLE UNDER THE CIRCUMSTANCES. IS EVERYONE OKAY?
JUST A LITTLE WINDED, UTOPIAN. DOES ANYONE HAVE A BOTTLE OF WATER?

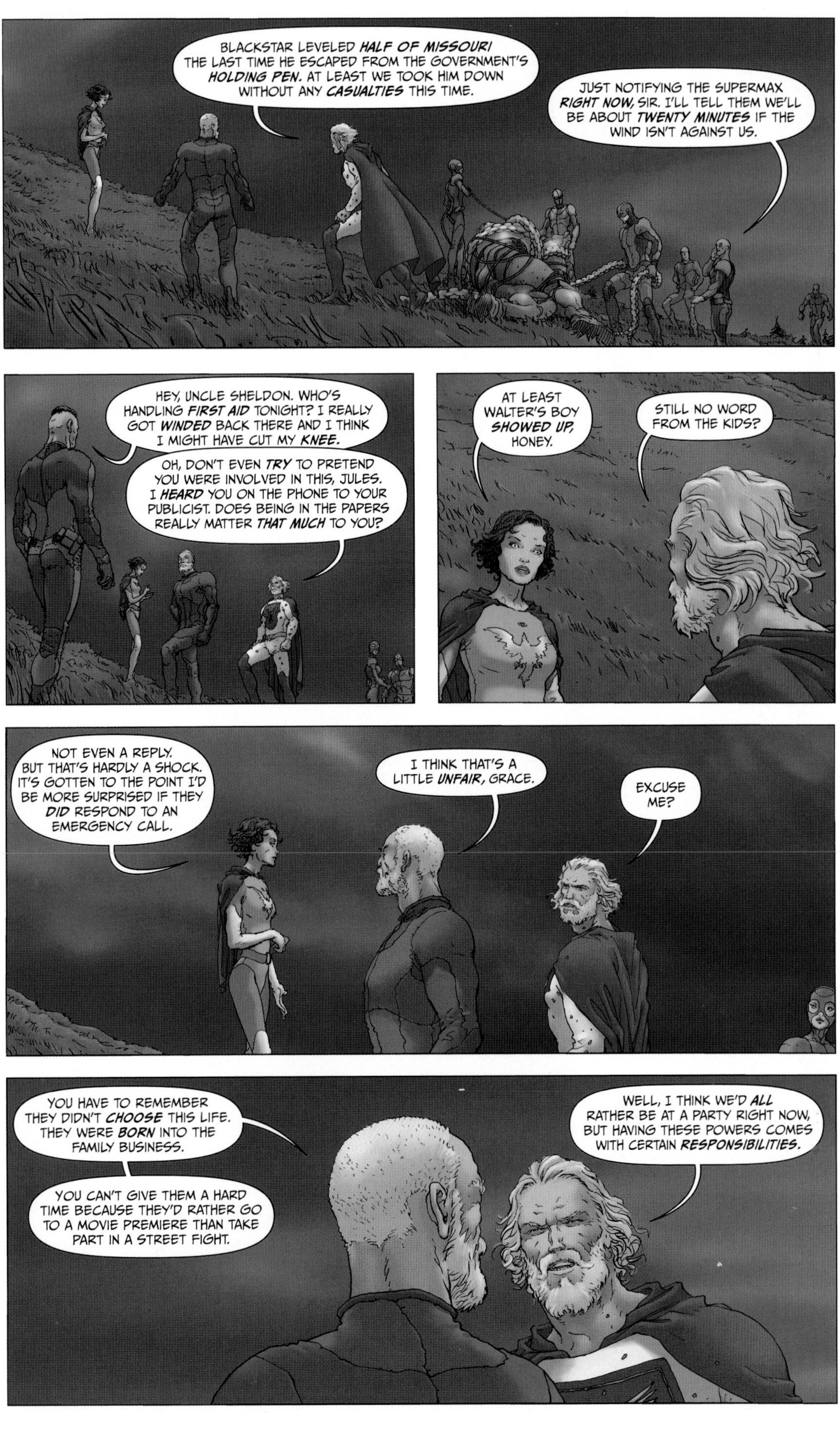
BLACKSTAR LEVELED HALF OF MISSOURI THE LAST TIME HE ESCAPED FROM THE GOVERNMENT'S HOLDING PEN. AT LEAST WE TOOK HIM DOWN WITHOUT ANY CASUALTIES THIS TIME.
JUST NOTIFYING THE SUPERMAX RIGHT NOW, SIR. I'LL TELL THEM WE'LL BE ABOUT TWENTY MINUTES IF THE WIND ISN'T AGAINST US.
HEY, UNCLE SHELDON. WHO'S HANDLING FIRST AID TONIGHT? I REALLY GOT WINDED BACK THERE AND I THINK I MIGHT HAVE CUT MY KNEE.
OH, DON'T EVEN TRY TO PRETEND YOU WERE INVOLVED IN THIS, JULES. I HEARD YOU ON THE PHONE TO YOUR PUBLICIST. DOES BEING IN THE PAPERS REALLY MATTER THAT MUCH TO YOU?
STILL NO WORD FROM THE KIDS?
AT LEAST WALTER'S BOY SHOWED UP, HONEY.
NOT EVEN A REPLY. BUT THAT'S HARDLY A SHOCK. IT'S GOTTEN TO THE POINT I'D BE MORE SURPRISED IF THEY DID RESPOND TO AN EMERGENCY CALL.
I THINK THAT'S A LITTLE UNFAIR, GRACE.
EXCUSE ME?
YOU HAVE TO REMEMBER THEY DIDN'T CHOOSE THIS LIFE. THEY WERE BORN INTO THE FAMILY BUSINESS.
YOU CAN'T GIVE THEM A HARD TIME BECAUSE THEY'D RATHER GO TO A MOVIE PREMIERE THAN TAKE PART IN A STREET FIGHT.
WELL, I THINK WE'D ALL RATHER BE AT A PARTY RIGHT NOW, BUT HAVING THESE POWERS COMES WITH CERTAIN RESPONSIBILITIES.

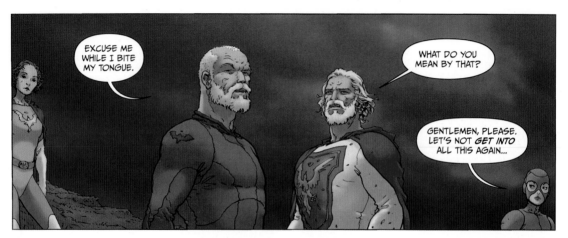

EXCUSE ME WHILE I BITE MY TONGUE.

WHAT DO YOU MEAN BY THAT?

GENTLEMEN, PLEASE. LET'S NOT *GET INTO* ALL THIS AGAIN...

NO, *LET'S.* AMERICA'S *COLLAPSING,* THE EURO-ZONE'S *BLEEDING TO DEATH,* THE GLOBAL ECONOMY'S HANGING BY A *THREAD* AND WE'RE STILL JUST OUT THERE *WRESTLING* LIKE *CHILDREN.*

DON'T YOU THINK WE COULD HELP MORE *DIRECTLY?* DOESN'T THIS GIVE YOU A HORRIFIC SENSE OF IMPOTENCE?

YOU'RE NOT AN *ECONOMIST,* WALTER. WHAT ARE YOU GOING TO DO? JUST BECAUSE YOU CAN FLY DOESN'T MEAN YOU KNOW HOW TO BALANCE A *BUDGET.*

YOU NEED TO ACCEPT THAT WE'RE *PUBLIC SERVANTS* AND HAVE A LITTLE FAITH IN THE GOVERNMENT WE'VE *ELECTED.*

OH, MY DEAR, SWEET BROTHER. IT'S THE POLITICIANS WHO ARE MESSING IT UP. DON'T YOU UNDERSTAND? PEOPLE ARE *PLEADING* FOR SOMEONE TO STEP IN AND FIX THIS CHAOS.

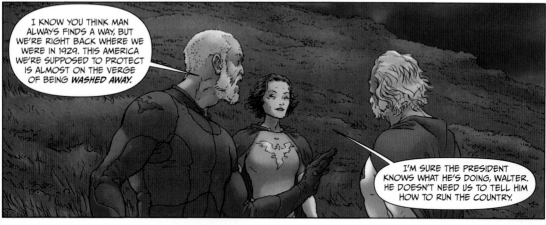

I KNOW YOU THINK MAN ALWAYS FINDS A WAY, BUT WE'RE RIGHT BACK WHERE WE WERE IN 1929. THIS AMERICA WE'RE SUPPOSED TO PROTECT IS ALMOST ON THE VERGE OF BEING *WASHED AWAY.*

I'M SURE THE PRESIDENT KNOWS WHAT HE'S DOING, WALTER. HE DOESN'T NEED US TO TELL HIM HOW TO RUN THE COUNTRY.

OH, OF COURSE. BECAUSE THEY'RE SO MUCH SMARTER THAN WE ARE. THAT'S WHY THEY LET THE BANKS RUN WILD LIKE THEY DID IN '29 AND STARTED ALL THOSE *WARS* WE COULDN'T AFFORD.

I SAW A FOOD LINE IN *LOS ANGELES* THIS MORNING, GRACE. HOW BAD DOES IT HAVE TO GET BEFORE WE FINALLY ADMIT THAT THE SYSTEM *DOESN'T WORK* ANYMORE?

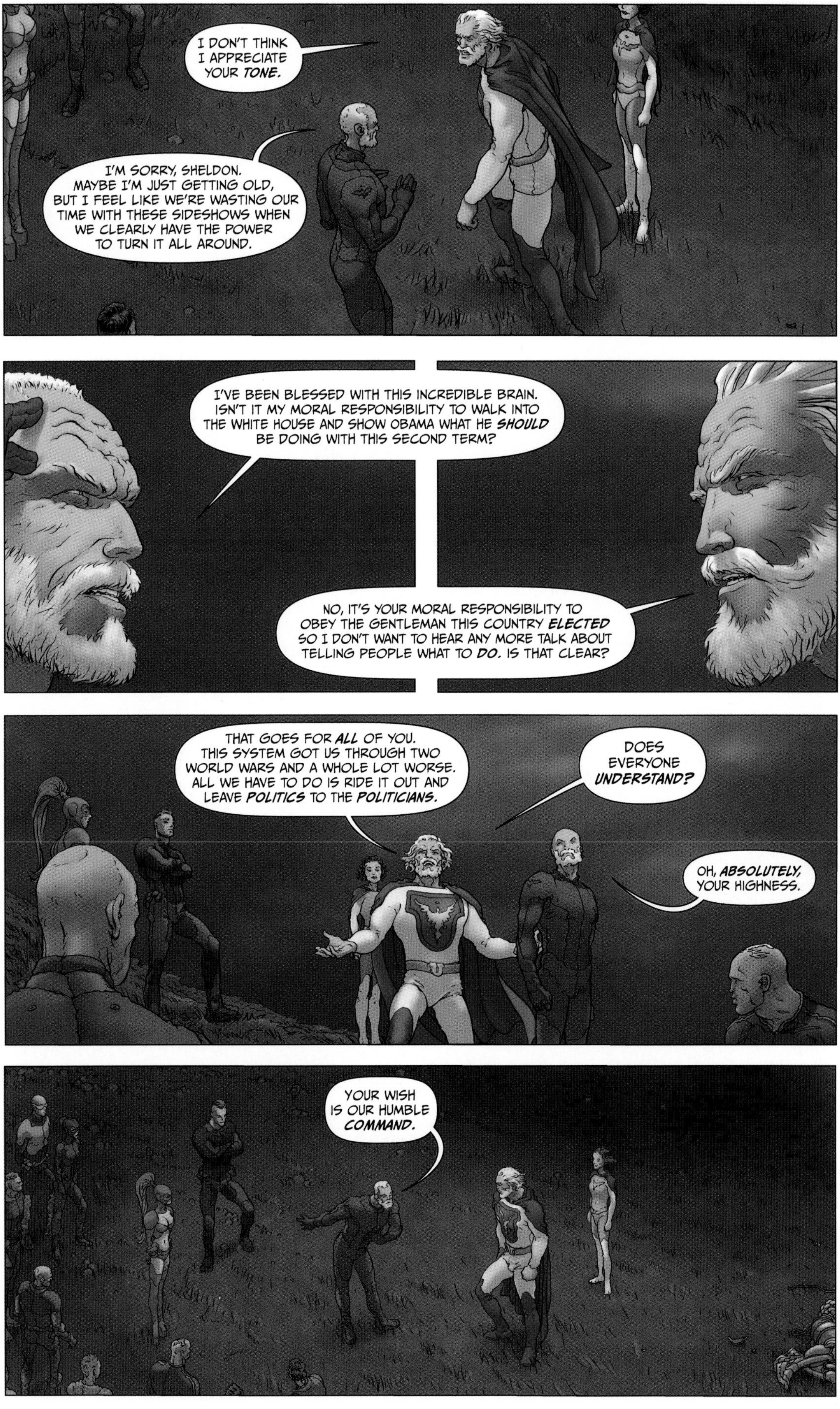
I DON'T THINK I APPRECIATE YOUR *TONE.*
I'M SORRY, SHELDON. MAYBE I'M JUST GETTING OLD, BUT I FEEL LIKE WE'RE WASTING OUR TIME WITH THESE SIDESHOWS WHEN WE CLEARLY HAVE THE POWER TO TURN IT ALL AROUND.
I'VE BEEN BLESSED WITH THIS INCREDIBLE BRAIN. ISN'T IT MY MORAL RESPONSIBILITY TO WALK INTO THE WHITE HOUSE AND SHOW OBAMA WHAT HE *SHOULD* BE DOING WITH THIS SECOND TERM?
NO, IT'S YOUR MORAL RESPONSIBILITY TO OBEY THE GENTLEMAN THIS COUNTRY ***ELECTED*** SO I DON'T WANT TO HEAR ANY MORE TALK ABOUT TELLING PEOPLE WHAT TO *DO.* IS THAT CLEAR?
THAT GOES FOR ***ALL*** OF YOU. THIS SYSTEM GOT US THROUGH TWO WORLD WARS AND A WHOLE LOT WORSE. ALL WE HAVE TO DO IS RIDE IT OUT AND LEAVE ***POLITICS*** TO THE ***POLITICIANS.***
DOES EVERYONE ***UNDERSTAND?***
OH, ***ABSOLUTELY,*** YOUR HIGHNESS.
YOUR WISH IS OUR HUMBLE ***COMMAND.***

4 AM, LOS ANGELES:

WAS SHE *MAD* AT YOU?

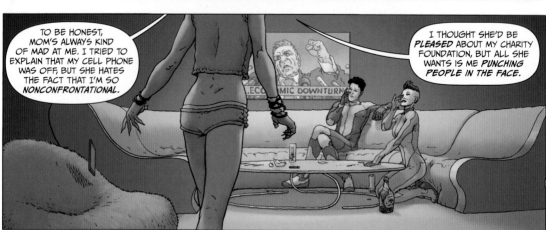

TO BE HONEST, MOM'S ALWAYS KIND OF MAD AT ME. I TRIED TO EXPLAIN THAT MY CELL PHONE WAS OFF, BUT SHE HATES THE FACT THAT I'M SO *NONCONFRONTATIONAL.*

I THOUGHT SHE'D BE *PLEASED* ABOUT MY CHARITY FOUNDATION, BUT ALL SHE WANTS IS ME *PUNCHING PEOPLE IN THE FACE.*

HOW CAN I HURT ANOTHER LIVING BEING? I'M A BUDDHIST AND A VEGETARIAN. I'M NOT GOING TO HURT SOMEONE BECAUSE THEY CONTRADICT OUR *BELIEF SYSTEM.*

OH, POOR, LITTLE *RICH GIRL.* COME AND MAKE IT ALL GO AWAY WITH LIONEL'S MAGIC NOSE POWDER.

WE GOT THIS STUFF FROM AN OFF-WORLD DEALER, CHLOE. YOU'LL *LOVE* IT. I'M MORE MESSED UP THAN THAT TIME WE DROPPED ACID IN THE MARIANAS TRENCH.

FINANCIAL CRISIS DEEPENING

EVERYONE THINKS IT MUST BE GREAT WHEN YOUR PARENTS ARE FAMOUS SUPERHEROES, BUT THEY REALLY HAVE *NO IDEA.*

I'LL NEVER BE AS COOL AS DAD OR AS BEAUTIFUL AS MOM. LOOK AT ME: I'M LIKE THE WORST ASPECTS OF BOTH OF THEM. I EVEN HAVE UGLY FEET .

OH, DARLING. GET OVER YOURSELF.

WIDESPREAD UNEMPLOYMENT

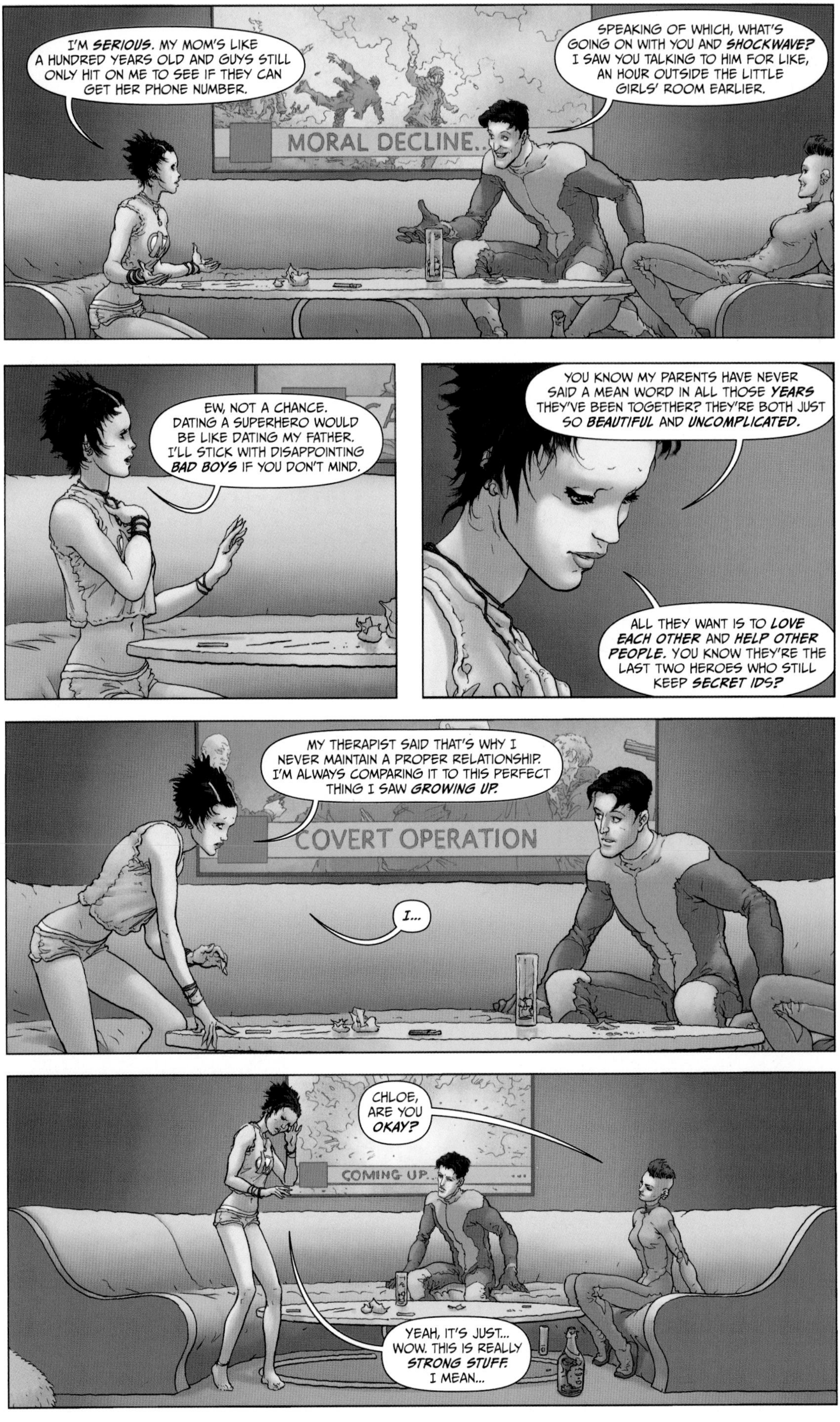

I'M SERIOUS. MY MOM'S LIKE A HUNDRED YEARS OLD AND GUYS STILL ONLY HIT ON ME TO SEE IF THEY CAN GET HER PHONE NUMBER.
SPEAKING OF WHICH, WHAT'S GOING ON WITH YOU AND SHOCKWAVE? I SAW YOU TALKING TO HIM FOR LIKE, AN HOUR OUTSIDE THE LITTLE GIRLS' ROOM EARLIER.
MORAL DECLINE...
EW, NOT A CHANCE. DATING A SUPERHERO WOULD BE LIKE DATING MY FATHER. I'LL STICK WITH DISAPPOINTING BAD BOYS IF YOU DON'T MIND.
YOU KNOW MY PARENTS HAVE NEVER SAID A MEAN WORD IN ALL THOSE YEARS THEY'VE BEEN TOGETHER? THEY'RE BOTH JUST SO BEAUTIFUL AND UNCOMPLICATED.
ALL THEY WANT IS TO LOVE EACH OTHER AND HELP OTHER PEOPLE. YOU KNOW THEY'RE THE LAST TWO HEROES WHO STILL KEEP SECRET IDS?
MY THERAPIST SAID THAT'S WHY I NEVER MAINTAIN A PROPER RELATIONSHIP. I'M ALWAYS COMPARING IT TO THIS PERFECT THING I SAW GROWING UP.
COVERT OPERATION
I...
CHLOE, ARE YOU OKAY?
COMING UP...
YEAH, IT'S JUST... WOW. THIS IS REALLY STRONG STUFF. I MEAN...

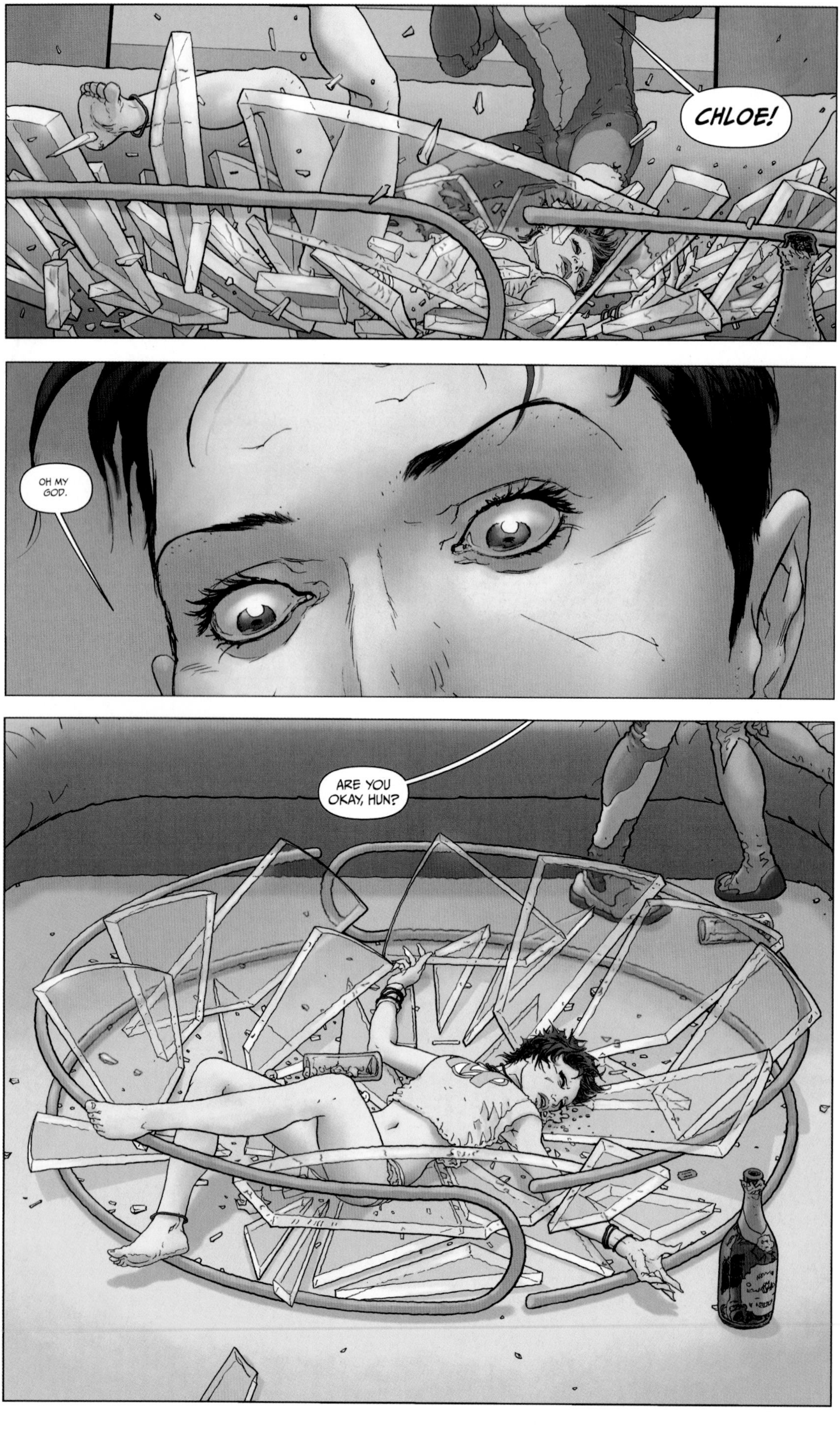
CHLOE!
OH MY GOD.
ARE YOU OKAY, HUN?

CHAPTER 2

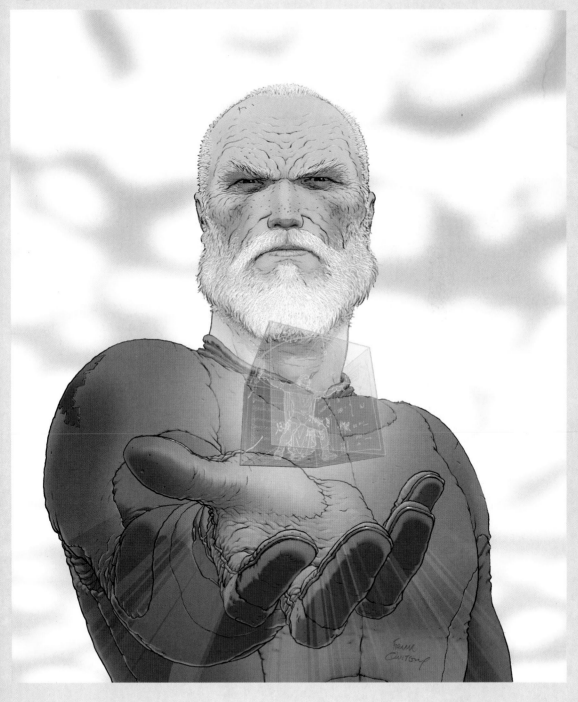

THE BAY AREA:

DAD'S GOING TO *LOVE* THIS. THIS IS EXACTLY THE KIND OF THING HE'S ALWAYS *TELLING* ME *I* SHOULD BE DOING.

HE SAYS WHEN I DON'T HAVE *SUPERVILLAINS* TO FIGHT I SHOULD BE OUT THERE DRUMMING UP BUSINESS AND *LOOKING* FOR WAYS TO HELP PEOPLE.

WELL, IT DOESN'T GET MUCH MORE AWESOME THAN *THIS*, HUH?

ABSOLUTELY.

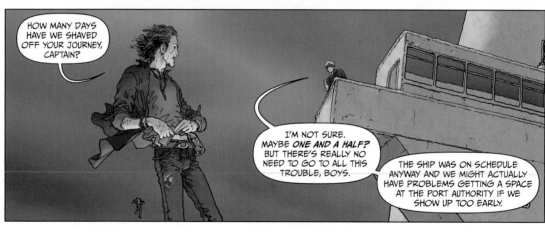

HOW MANY DAYS HAVE WE SHAVED OFF YOUR JOURNEY, CAPTAIN?

I'M NOT SURE. MAYBE *ONE AND A HALF?* BUT THERE'S REALLY NO NEED TO GO TO ALL THIS TROUBLE, BOYS.

THE SHIP WAS ON SCHEDULE ANYWAY AND WE MIGHT ACTUALLY HAVE PROBLEMS GETTING A SPACE AT THE PORT AUTHORITY IF WE SHOW UP TOO EARLY.

NO TROUBLE AT ALL, SIR. OUR PLEASURE. JUST TELL THE CREW TO SIT BACK AND RELAX AND WE'LL HAVE YOU IN SAN DIEGO IN A LITTLE OVER TWO HOURS.
MAN, I STILL CAN'T BELIEVE HOW MUCH WE PUT AWAY BACK THERE. I MUST HAVE HAD ABOUT FIFTY SHOTS.
HOW MUCH DID YOU DRINK, BRANDON? I SAW YOU HAVE TWENTY WITH THAT KENDRA GIRL, BUT YOU MUST HAVE DONE ANOTHER FIFTY WHEN WE GOT TO THE ROXY.
DUDE, WOULD YOU SHUT UP? I CAN'T COUNT AND DO TELEKINESIS AT THE SAME TIME. YOU'RE TOTALLY PUTTING ME OFF.
H-HEY!
SEE WHAT YOU MADE ME DO? YOU'RE THROWING IT ALL OFF-BALANCE TALKING AND THINKING AT THE SAME TIME.
NOW TRY TO KEEP THE SHIP HORIZONTAL. WE NEED TO GET BOTH SIDES LINED UP.
SHIT!
GET OUT OF THE WAY!
WHAT ARE YOU DOING? YOU'RE FLIPPING IT!
WHAT?

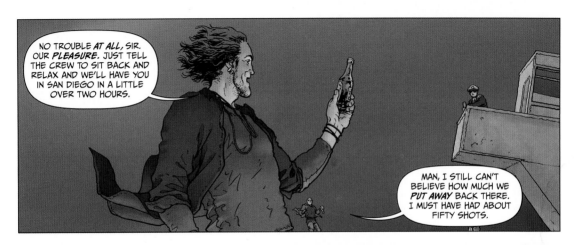

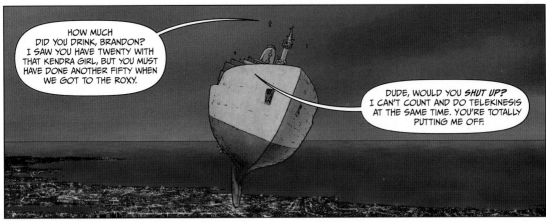

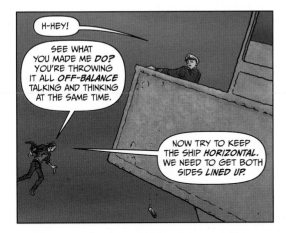

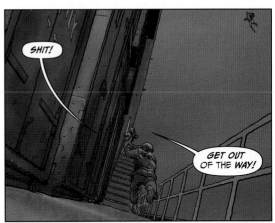

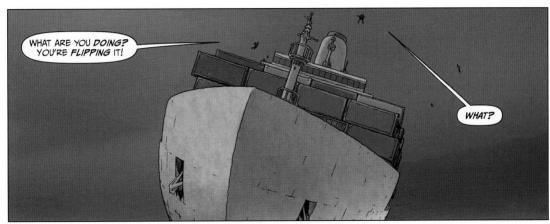

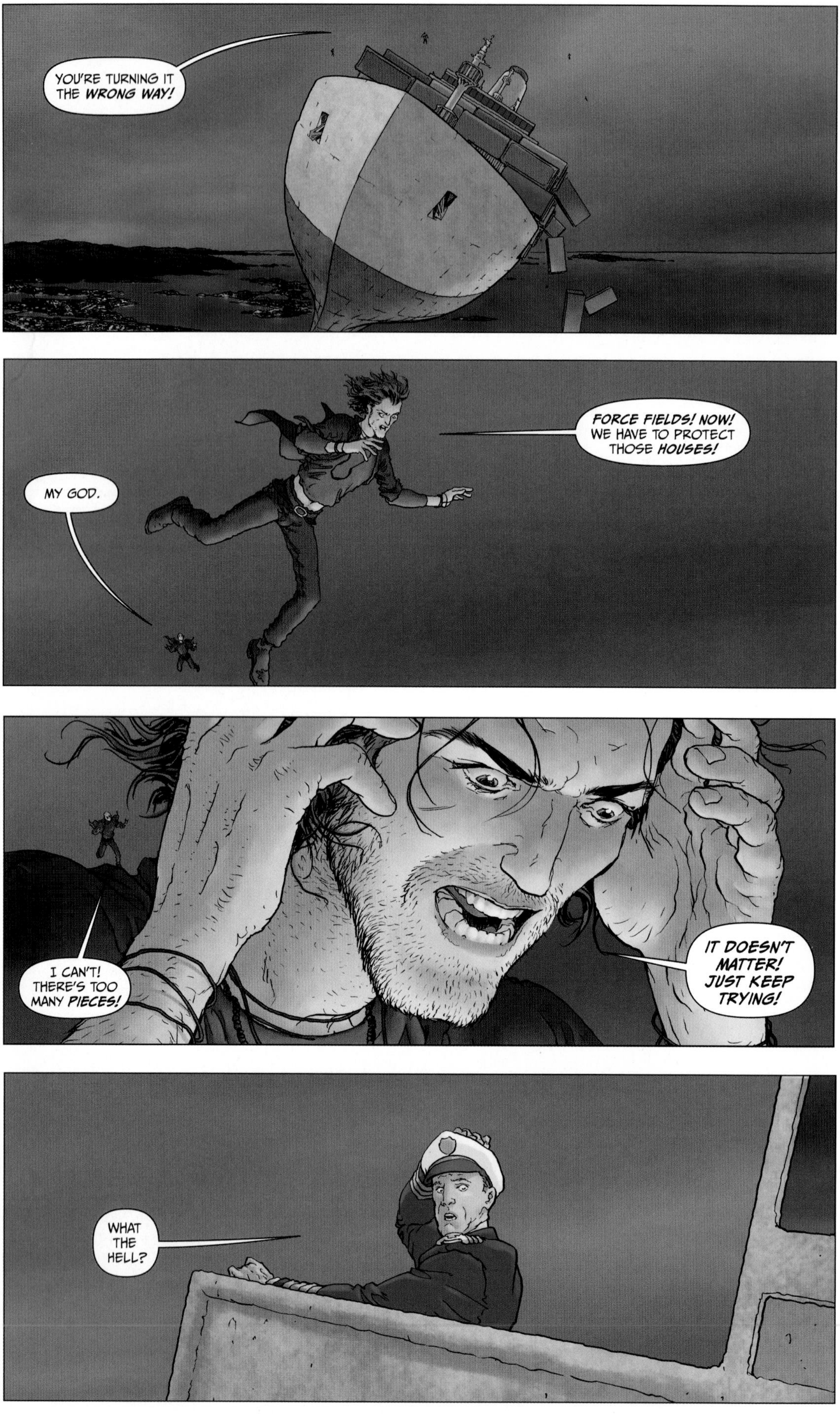
YOU'RE TURNING IT THE *WRONG WAY!*
FORCE FIELDS! NOW! WE HAVE TO PROTECT THOSE *HOUSES!*
MY GOD.
I CAN'T! THERE'S TOO MANY *PIECES!*
IT DOESN'T MATTER! JUST KEEP TRYING!
WHAT THE HELL?

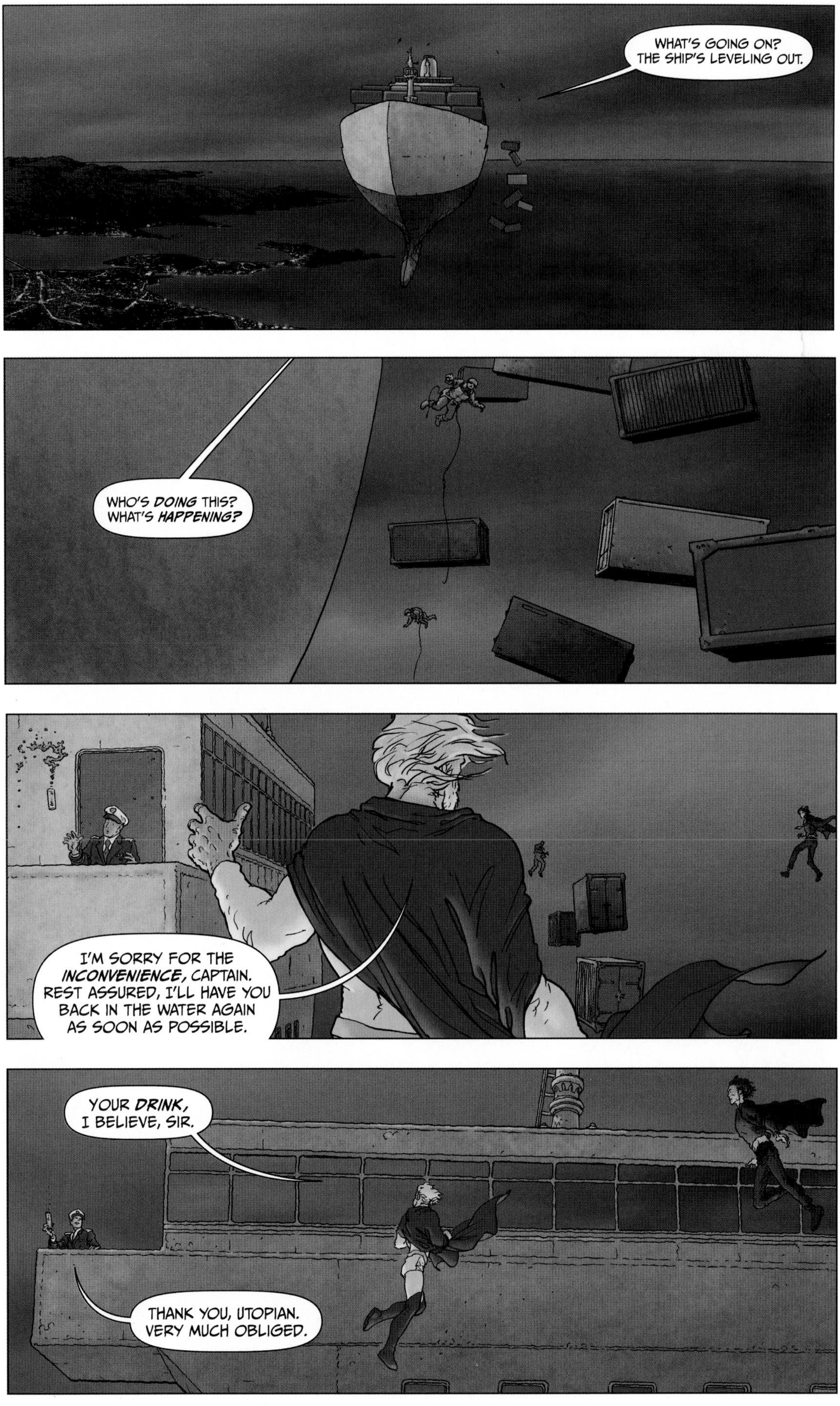
WHAT'S GOING ON? THE SHIP'S LEVELING OUT.
WHO'S DOING THIS? WHAT'S HAPPENING?
I'M SORRY FOR THE INCONVENIENCE, CAPTAIN. REST ASSURED, I'LL HAVE YOU BACK IN THE WATER AGAIN AS SOON AS POSSIBLE.
YOUR DRINK, I BELIEVE, SIR.
THANK YOU, UTOPIAN. VERY MUCH OBLIGED.

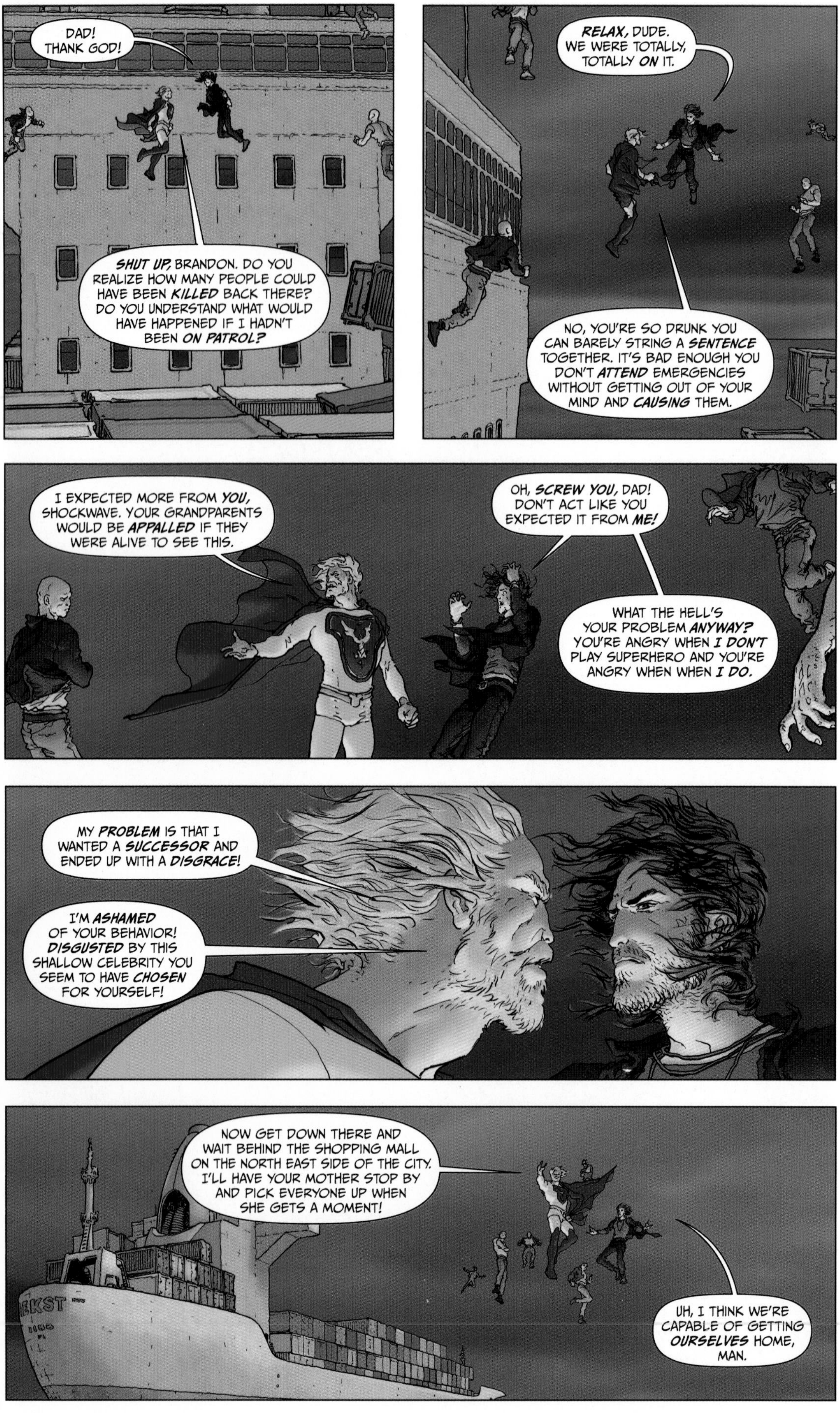
DAD! THANK GOD!
SHUT UP, BRANDON. DO YOU REALIZE HOW MANY PEOPLE COULD HAVE BEEN KILLED BACK THERE? DO YOU UNDERSTAND WHAT WOULD HAVE HAPPENED IF I HADN'T BEEN ON PATROL?
RELAX, DUDE. WE WERE TOTALLY, TOTALLY ON IT.
NO, YOU'RE SO DRUNK YOU CAN BARELY STRING A SENTENCE TOGETHER. IT'S BAD ENOUGH YOU DON'T ATTEND EMERGENCIES WITHOUT GETTING OUT OF YOUR MIND AND CAUSING THEM.
I EXPECTED MORE FROM YOU, SHOCKWAVE. YOUR GRANDPARENTS WOULD BE APPALLED IF THEY WERE ALIVE TO SEE THIS.
OH, SCREW YOU, DAD! DON'T ACT LIKE YOU EXPECTED IT FROM ME!
WHAT THE HELL'S YOUR PROBLEM ANYWAY? YOU'RE ANGRY WHEN I DON'T PLAY SUPERHERO AND YOU'RE ANGRY WHEN WHEN I DO.
MY PROBLEM IS THAT I WANTED A SUCCESSOR AND ENDED UP WITH A DISGRACE!
I'M ASHAMED OF YOUR BEHAVIOR! DISGUSTED BY THIS SHALLOW CELEBRITY YOU SEEM TO HAVE CHOSEN FOR YOURSELF!
NOW GET DOWN THERE AND WAIT BEHIND THE SHOPPING MALL ON THE NORTH EAST SIDE OF THE CITY. I'LL HAVE YOUR MOTHER STOP BY AND PICK EVERYONE UP WHEN SHE GETS A MOMENT!
UH, I THINK WE'RE CAPABLE OF GETTING OURSELVES HOME, MAN.

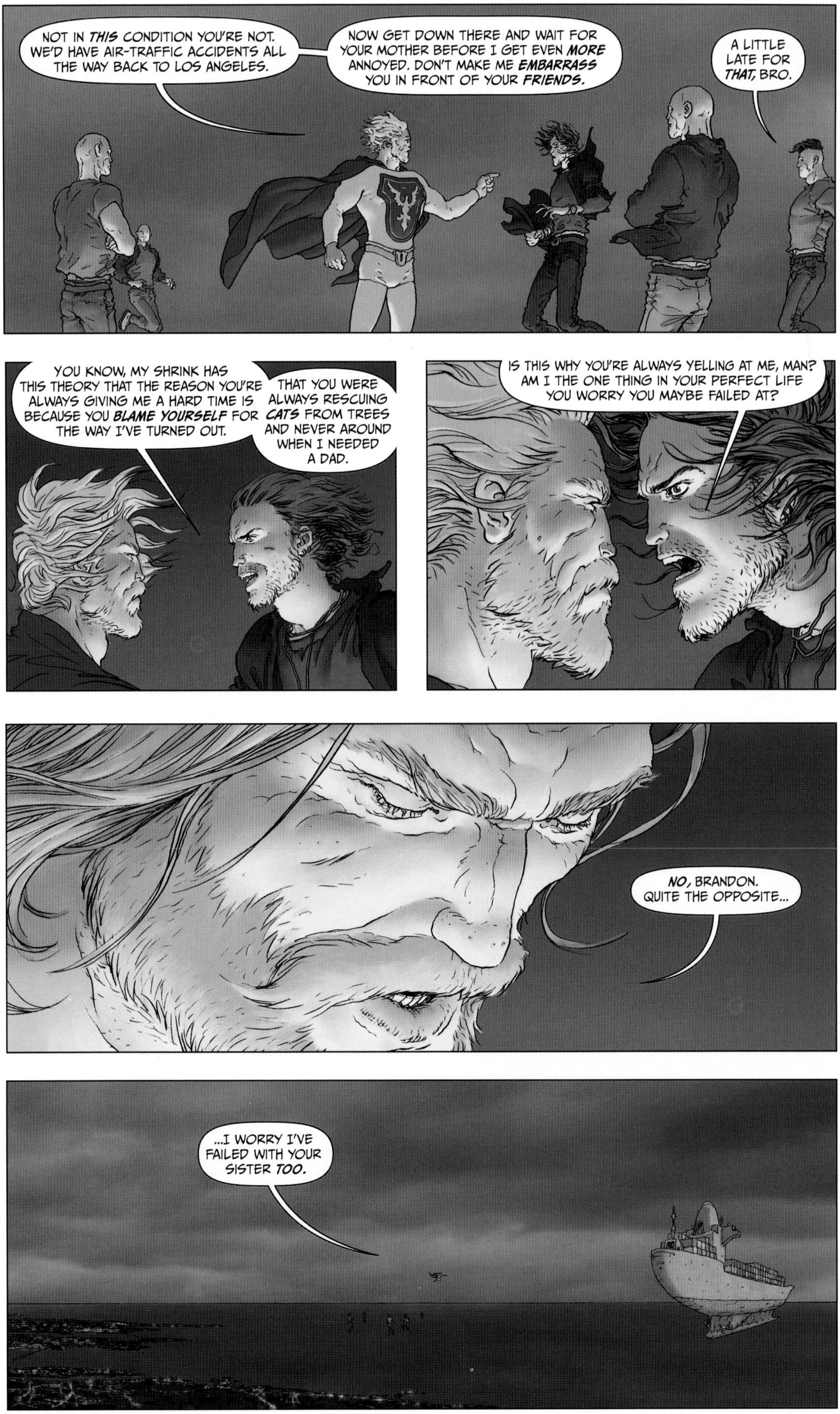
NOT IN *THIS* CONDITION YOU'RE NOT. WE'D HAVE AIR-TRAFFIC ACCIDENTS ALL THE WAY BACK TO LOS ANGELES.
NOW GET DOWN THERE AND WAIT FOR YOUR MOTHER BEFORE I GET EVEN *MORE* ANNOYED. DON'T MAKE ME *EMBARRASS* YOU IN FRONT OF YOUR *FRIENDS.*
A LITTLE LATE FOR *THAT,* BRO.
YOU KNOW, MY SHRINK HAS THIS THEORY THAT THE REASON YOU'RE ALWAYS GIVING ME A HARD TIME IS BECAUSE YOU *BLAME YOURSELF* FOR THE WAY I'VE TURNED OUT.
THAT YOU WERE ALWAYS RESCUING *CATS* FROM TREES AND NEVER AROUND WHEN I NEEDED A DAD.
IS THIS WHY YOU'RE ALWAYS YELLING AT ME, MAN? AM I THE ONE THING IN YOUR PERFECT LIFE YOU WORRY YOU MAYBE FAILED AT?
NO, BRANDON. QUITE THE OPPOSITE...
...I WORRY I'VE FAILED WITH YOUR SISTER *TOO.*

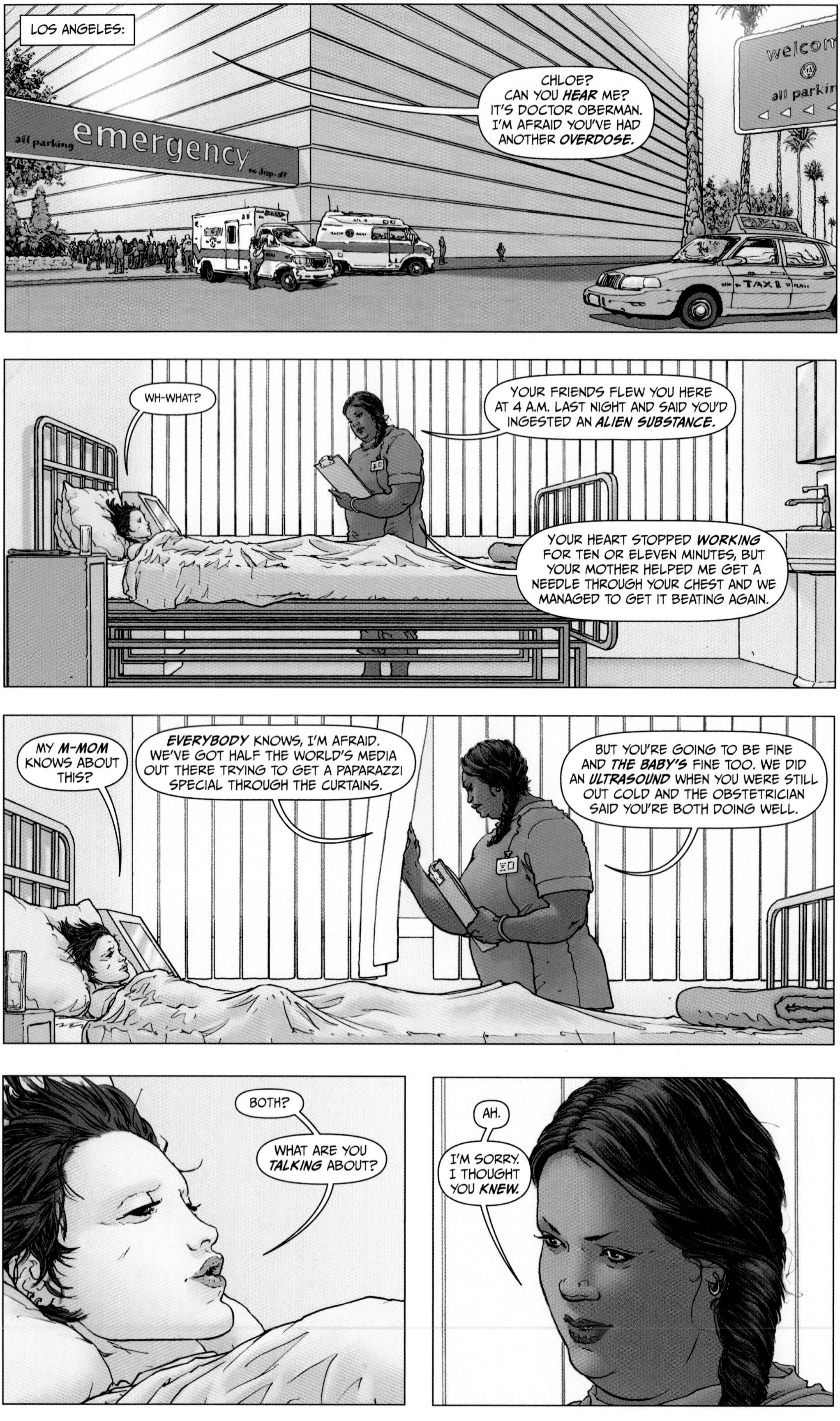
LOS ANGELES:
welcom
all parkin
all parking emergency no drop-off
CHLOE? CAN YOU *HEAR* ME? IT'S DOCTOR OBERMAN. I'M AFRAID YOU'VE HAD ANOTHER *OVERDOSE.*
TAXI
WH-WHAT?
YOUR FRIENDS FLEW YOU HERE AT 4 A.M. LAST NIGHT AND SAID YOU'D INGESTED AN *ALIEN SUBSTANCE.*
YOUR HEART STOPPED *WORKING* FOR TEN OR ELEVEN MINUTES, BUT YOUR MOTHER HELPED ME GET A NEEDLE THROUGH YOUR CHEST AND WE MANAGED TO GET IT BEATING AGAIN.
MY *M-MOM* KNOWS ABOUT THIS?
EVERYBODY KNOWS, I'M AFRAID. WE'VE GOT HALF THE WORLD'S MEDIA OUT THERE TRYING TO GET A PAPARAZZI SPECIAL THROUGH THE CURTAINS.
BUT YOU'RE GOING TO BE FINE AND *THE BABY'S* FINE TOO. WE DID AN *ULTRASOUND* WHEN YOU WERE STILL OUT COLD AND THE OBSTETRICIAN SAID YOU'RE BOTH DOING WELL.
BOTH?
WHAT ARE YOU *TALKING* ABOUT?
AH.
I'M SORRY. I THOUGHT YOU *KNEW.*

WE RAN A COMPREHENSIVE SET OF BLOODS AND URINALYSIS WHEN THEY BROUGHT YOU IN AND IT WAS THE FIRST THING THAT GOT FLAGGED UP.

I APOLOGISE YOU HAD TO FIND OUT THIS WAY, BUT WE ESTIMATE YOU'RE PROBABLY AROUND *ELEVEN WEEKS.*

OH MY GOD. ARE YOU SURE? I MEAN, COULDN'T THIS BE SOME KIND OF *MIX-UP?*

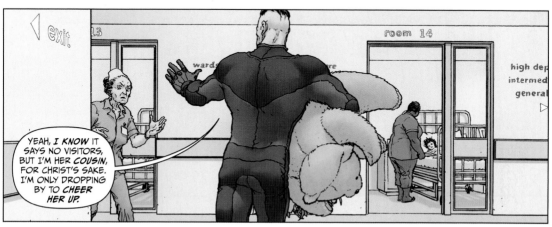

YEAH, *I KNOW* IT SAYS NO VISITORS, BUT I'M HER *COUSIN,* FOR CHRIST'S SAKE. I'M ONLY DROPPING BY TO *CHEER HER UP.*

CHLOE, WOULD YOU MIND *EXPLAINING* TO THIS POKER-FACED *HARPY* THAT THE WORLD WON'T END BECAUSE I'M HERE OUTSIDE *VISITING HOURS?*

NOT *NOW,* JULES. PLEASE. THIS IS ISN'T A *GOOD TIME...*

OH, *COME ON.* WHAT THE HELL'S *THE MATTER* WITH YOU? I TOOK THE TIME TO BUY YOU A GIFT. AT LEAST HAVE THE MANNERS TO...

I SAID NOT NOW JULES!

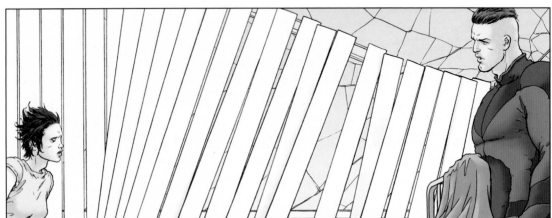

WELL, *SCREW* YOU.

IT'S OKAY, IT'S OKAY. WE'VE GOT PEOPLE HERE IF YOU NEED TO *TALK IT OVER*. YOU'RE NOT THE FIRST GIRL TO COME IN HERE AND GET *BLIND-SIDED* LIKE THIS. IS THERE A *FATHER* ON THE SCENE?

KIND OF.

IS IT *COMPLICATED?*

VERY.

LONG BEACH:

Kebabe

the **BLARNEY** inn
céad míle fáilte

TO LET

WELL, WELL, WELL. IF IT ISN'T MY OLD FRIEND *HUTCH.*

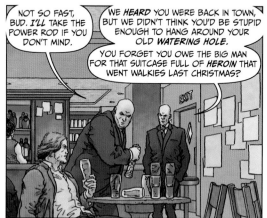

NOT SO FAST, BUD. *I'LL* TAKE THE POWER ROD IF YOU DON'T MIND.

WE *HEARD* YOU WERE BACK IN TOWN, BUT WE DIDN'T THINK YOU'D BE STUPID ENOUGH TO HANG AROUND YOUR OLD *WATERING HOLE.*

YOU FORGET YOU OWE THE BIG MAN FOR THAT SUITCASE FULL OF *HEROIN* THAT WENT WALKIES LAST CHRISTMAS?

'COURSE I DIDN'T FORGET. HOW DO YOU THINK I PAID FOR ALL THIS BOOZE.

THE BIG MAN PUT A HUNDRED *"G"S* ON THAT SMART MOUTH, HUTCH. THAT'S FIFTY GRAND EACH FOR ME AND MY BROTHER IF WE HAUL YOUR ASS DOWN TO *THE CLUB.*

NOW DON'T TRY ANYTHING *FOOLISH.* YOU'RE ONLY GONNA MAKE IT WORSE. WE'VE GOT *STRENGTH, SPEED, SONIC SCREAMS* AND *OPTIC BLASTS...*

...NOT TO MENTION THIS LITTLE *POWER ROD* YOU'RE ALWAYS WAVING AROUND. WHAT YOU GOTTA SAY TO *THAT?*

SHARK-INFESTED WATERS.

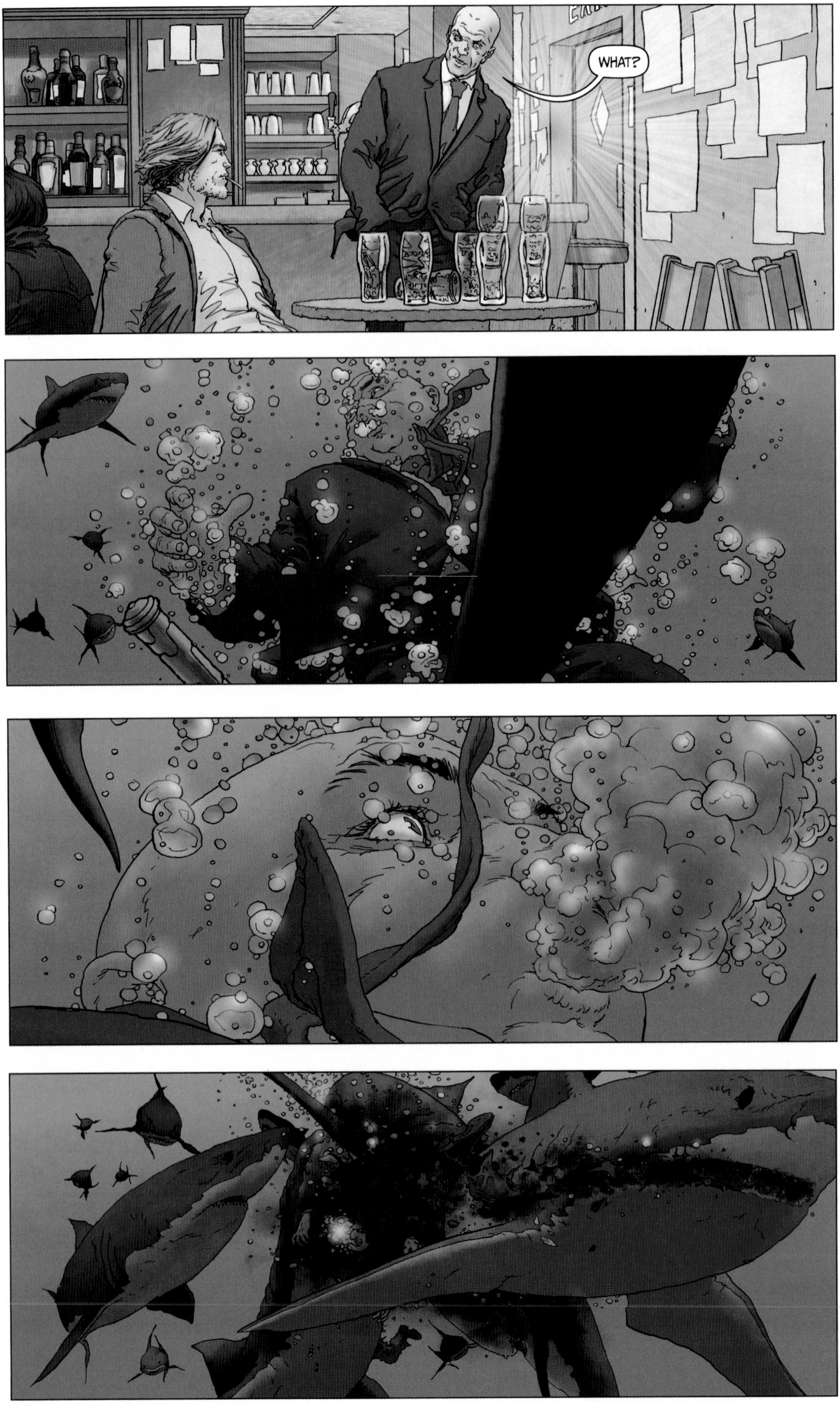
WHAT?

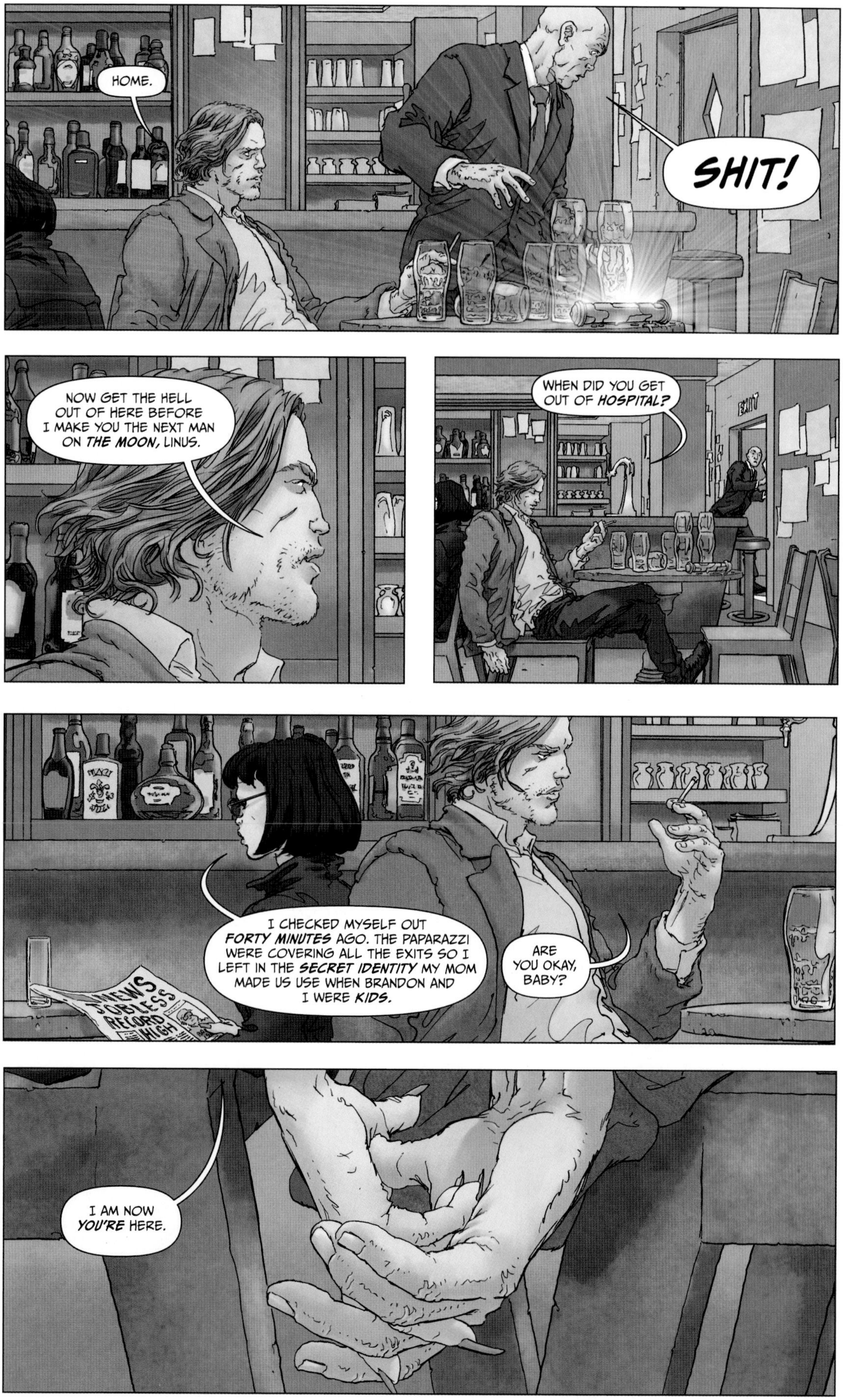
HOME.
SHIT!
NOW GET THE HELL OUT OF HERE BEFORE I MAKE YOU THE NEXT MAN ON THE MOON, LINUS.
WHEN DID YOU GET OUT OF HOSPITAL?
EXIT
ARE YOU OKAY, BABY?
I CHECKED MYSELF OUT FORTY MINUTES AGO. THE PAPARAZZI WERE COVERING ALL THE EXITS SO I LEFT IN THE SECRET IDENTITY MY MOM MADE US USE WHEN BRANDON AND I WERE KIDS.
NEWS
JOBLESS RECORD HIGH
I AM NOW YOU'RE HERE.

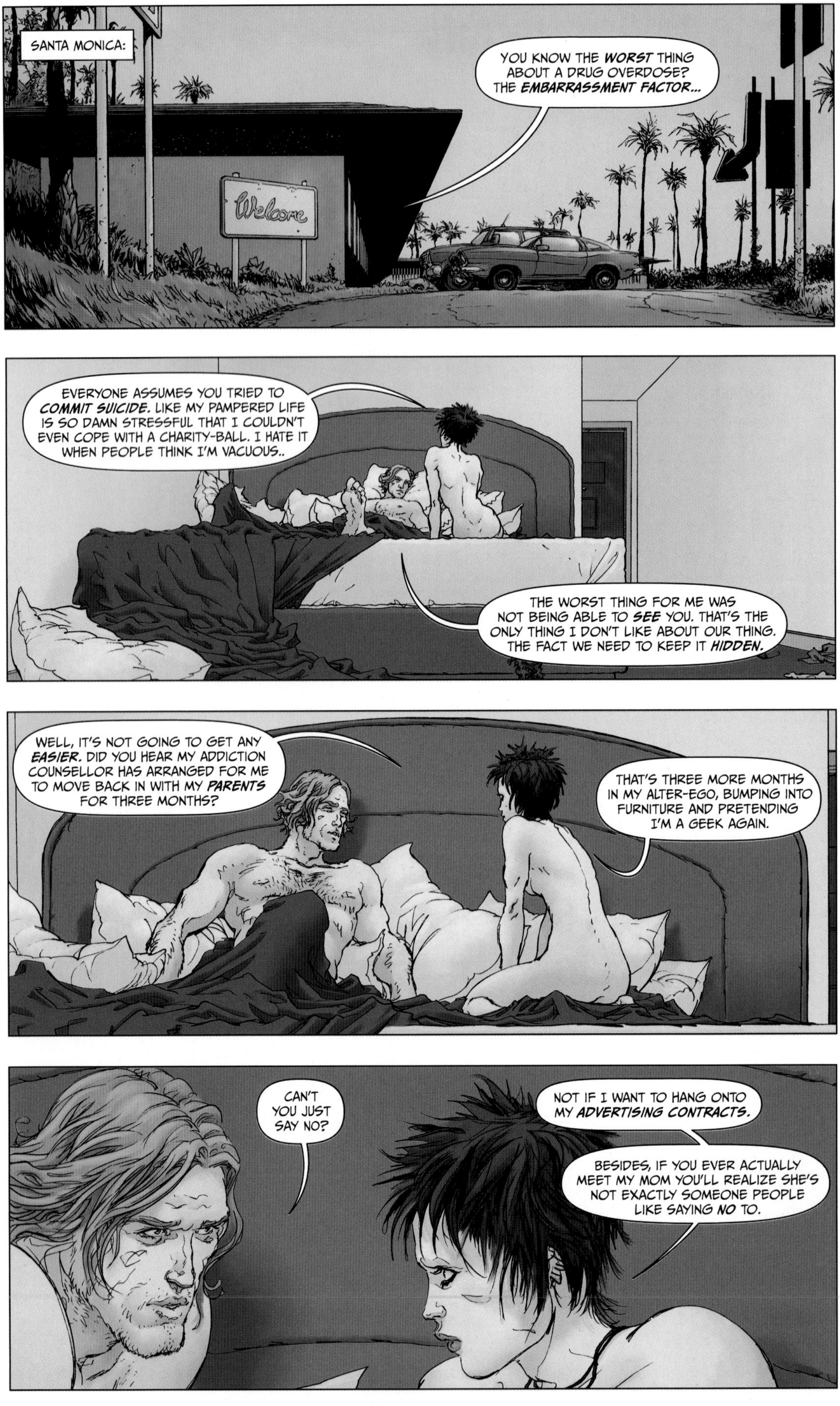
SANTA MONICA:
YOU KNOW THE WORST THING ABOUT A DRUG OVERDOSE? THE EMBARRASSMENT FACTOR...
Welcome
EVERYONE ASSUMES YOU TRIED TO COMMIT SUICIDE. LIKE MY PAMPERED LIFE IS SO DAMN STRESSFUL THAT I COULDN'T EVEN COPE WITH A CHARITY-BALL. I HATE IT WHEN PEOPLE THINK I'M VACUOUS..
THE WORST THING FOR ME WAS NOT BEING ABLE TO SEE YOU. THAT'S THE ONLY THING I DON'T LIKE ABOUT OUR THING. THE FACT WE NEED TO KEEP IT HIDDEN.
WELL, IT'S NOT GOING TO GET ANY EASIER. DID YOU HEAR MY ADDICTION COUNSELLOR HAS ARRANGED FOR ME TO MOVE BACK IN WITH MY PARENTS FOR THREE MONTHS?
THAT'S THREE MORE MONTHS IN MY ALTER-EGO, BUMPING INTO FURNITURE AND PRETENDING I'M A GEEK AGAIN.
CAN'T YOU JUST SAY NO?
NOT IF I WANT TO HANG ONTO MY ADVERTISING CONTRACTS.
BESIDES, IF YOU EVER ACTUALLY MEET MY MOM YOU'LL REALIZE SHE'S NOT EXACTLY SOMEONE PEOPLE LIKE SAYING NO TO.

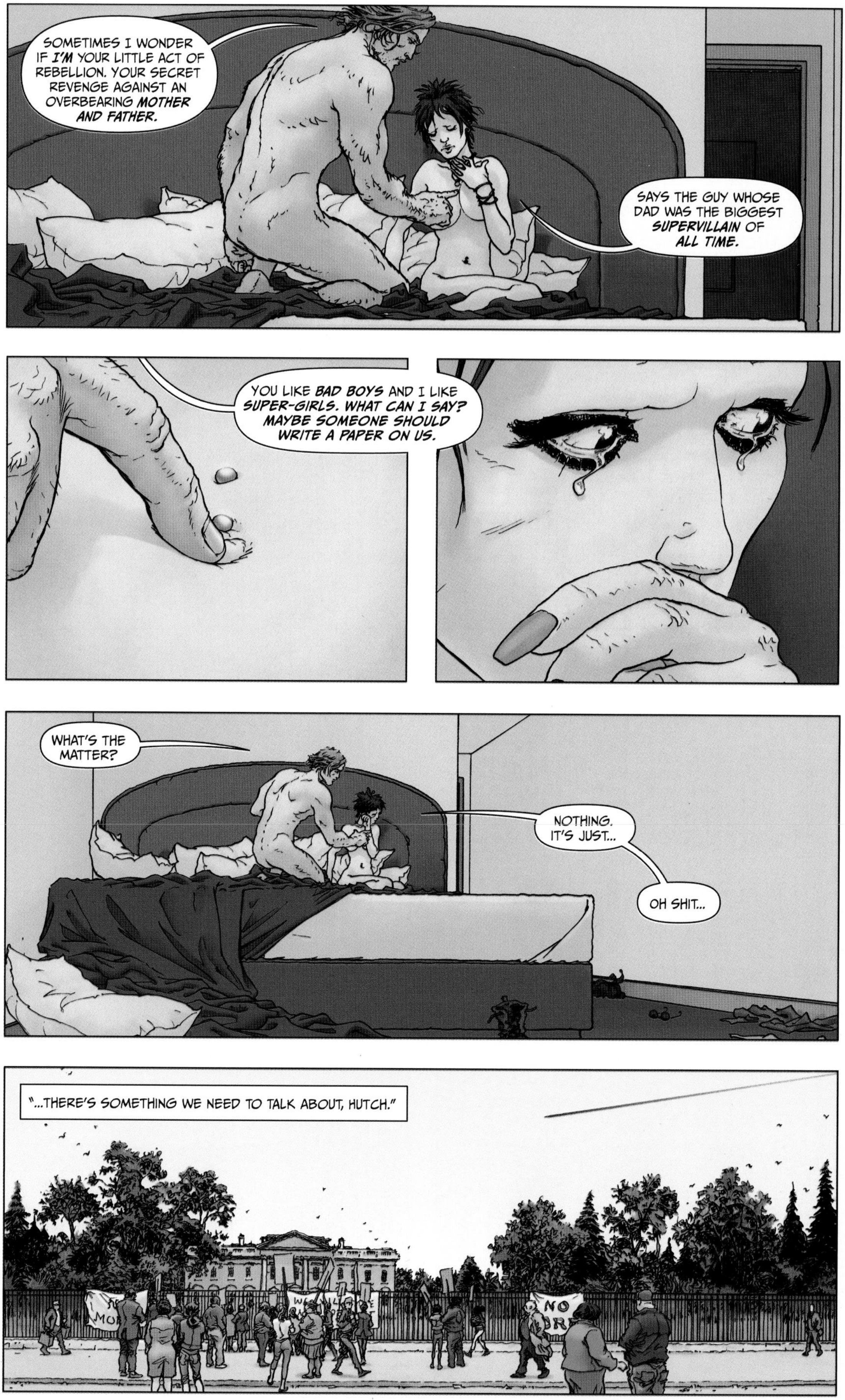
SOMETIMES I WONDER IF *I'M* YOUR LITTLE ACT OF REBELLION. YOUR SECRET REVENGE AGAINST AN OVERBEARING ***MOTHER AND FATHER.***
SAYS THE GUY WHOSE DAD WAS THE BIGGEST ***SUPERVILLAIN*** OF ***ALL TIME.***
YOU LIKE ***BAD BOYS*** AND I LIKE ***SUPER-GIRLS. WHAT CAN I SAY? MAYBE SOMEONE SHOULD WRITE A PAPER ON US.***
WHAT'S THE MATTER?
NOTHING. IT'S JUST...
OH SHIT...
"...THERE'S SOMETHING WE NEED TO TALK ABOUT, HUTCH."

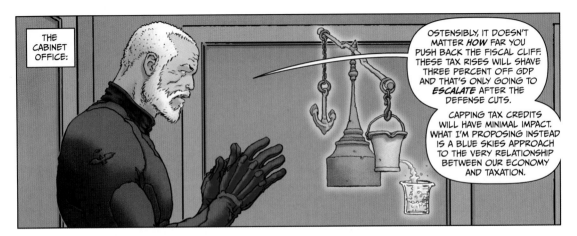

THE CABINET OFFICE:

OSTENSIBLY, IT DOESN'T MATTER *HOW* FAR YOU PUSH BACK THE FISCAL CLIFF. THESE TAX RISES WILL SHAVE THREE PERCENT OFF GDP AND THAT'S ONLY GOING TO *ESCALATE* AFTER THE DEFENSE CUTS.

CAPPING TAX CREDITS WILL HAVE MINIMAL IMPACT. WHAT I'M PROPOSING INSTEAD IS A BLUE SKIES APPROACH TO THE VERY RELATIONSHIP BETWEEN OUR ECONOMY AND TAXATION.

AT EASE, GENTLEMEN.

WALTER, I'D LIKE A *WORD.*

NOT NOW, UTOPIAN. I'M IN THE MIDDLE OF A *MEETING.*

I SAID A *WORD,* PLEASE, WALTER.

FORGIVE ME, LADIES AND GENTLEMEN, BUT I'M AFRAID THIS IS THE ONE PERSON MY PSYCHIC POWERS *DON'T WORK* ON.

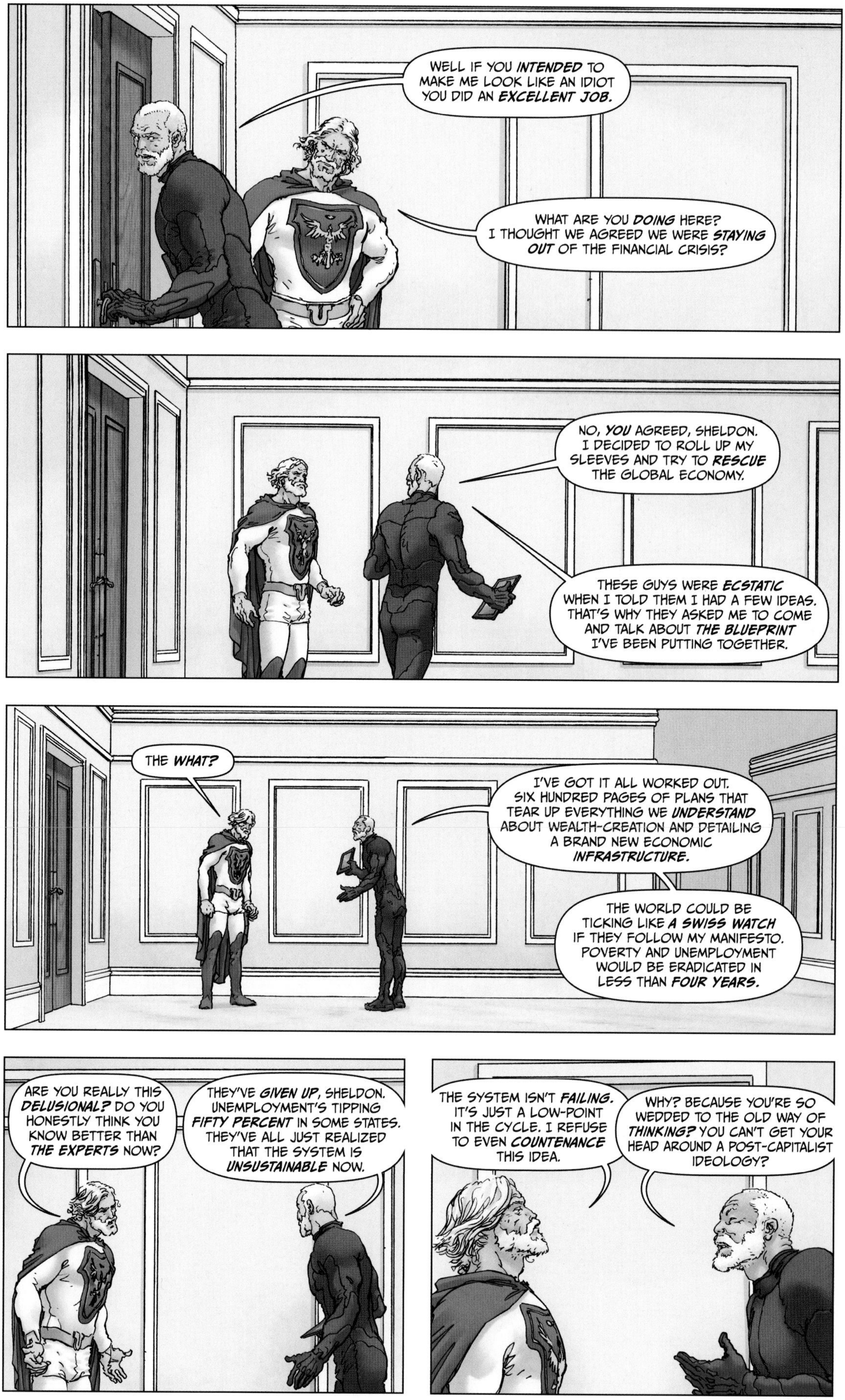
WELL IF YOU INTENDED TO MAKE ME LOOK LIKE AN IDIOT YOU DID AN EXCELLENT JOB.
WHAT ARE YOU DOING HERE? I THOUGHT WE AGREED WE WERE STAYING OUT OF THE FINANCIAL CRISIS?
NO, YOU AGREED, SHELDON. I DECIDED TO ROLL UP MY SLEEVES AND TRY TO RESCUE THE GLOBAL ECONOMY.
THESE GUYS WERE ECSTATIC WHEN I TOLD THEM I HAD A FEW IDEAS. THAT'S WHY THEY ASKED ME TO COME AND TALK ABOUT THE BLUEPRINT I'VE BEEN PUTTING TOGETHER.
THE WHAT?
I'VE GOT IT ALL WORKED OUT. SIX HUNDRED PAGES OF PLANS THAT TEAR UP EVERYTHING WE UNDERSTAND ABOUT WEALTH-CREATION AND DETAILING A BRAND NEW ECONOMIC INFRASTRUCTURE.
THE WORLD COULD BE TICKING LIKE A SWISS WATCH IF THEY FOLLOW MY MANIFESTO. POVERTY AND UNEMPLOYMENT WOULD BE ERADICATED IN LESS THAN FOUR YEARS.
ARE YOU REALLY THIS DELUSIONAL? DO YOU HONESTLY THINK YOU KNOW BETTER THAN THE EXPERTS NOW?
THEY'VE GIVEN UP, SHELDON. UNEMPLOYMENT'S TIPPING FIFTY PERCENT IN SOME STATES. THEY'VE ALL JUST REALIZED THAT THE SYSTEM IS UNSUSTAINABLE NOW.
THE SYSTEM ISN'T FAILING. IT'S JUST A LOW-POINT IN THE CYCLE. I REFUSE TO EVEN COUNTENANCE THIS IDEA.
WHY? BECAUSE YOU'RE SO WEDDED TO THE OLD WAY OF THINKING? YOU CAN'T GET YOUR HEAD AROUND A POST-CAPITALIST IDEOLOGY?

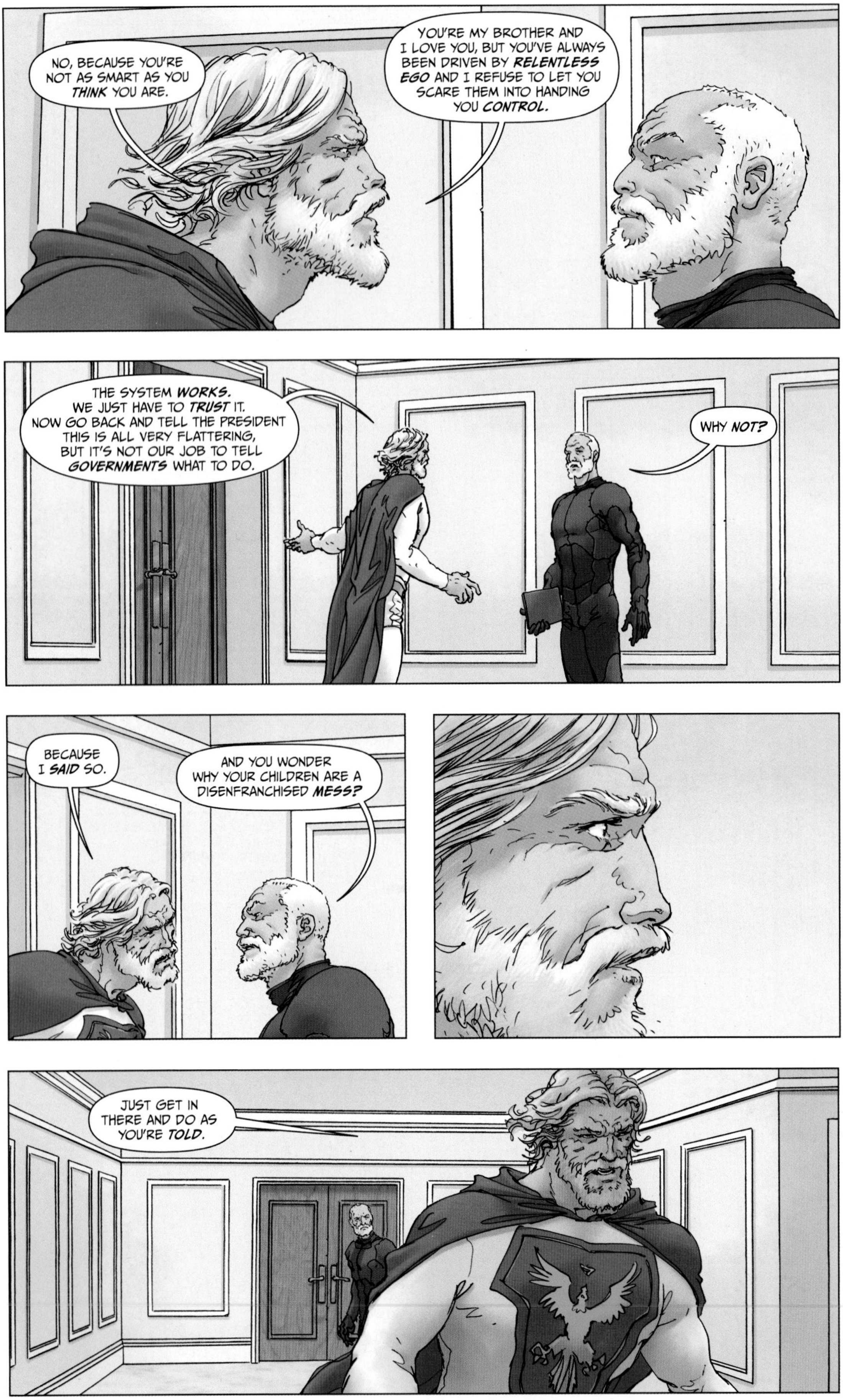
NO, BECAUSE YOU'RE NOT AS SMART AS YOU THINK YOU ARE.
YOU'RE MY BROTHER AND I LOVE YOU, BUT YOU'VE ALWAYS BEEN DRIVEN BY RELENTLESS EGO AND I REFUSE TO LET YOU SCARE THEM INTO HANDING YOU CONTROL.
THE SYSTEM WORKS. WE JUST HAVE TO TRUST IT. NOW GO BACK AND TELL THE PRESIDENT THIS IS ALL VERY FLATTERING, BUT IT'S NOT OUR JOB TO TELL GOVERNMENTS WHAT TO DO.
WHY NOT?
BECAUSE I SAID SO.
AND YOU WONDER WHY YOUR CHILDREN ARE A DISENFRANCHISED MESS?
JUST GET IN THERE AND DO AS YOU'RE TOLD.

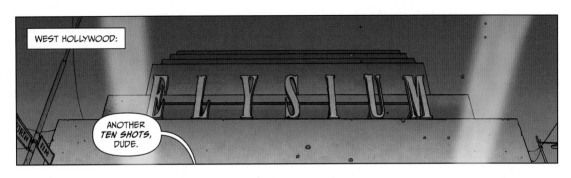

WEST HOLLYWOOD:

ANOTHER *TEN SHOTS,* DUDE.

IN FACT, MAKE IT ANOTHER *TWENTY.* IT'LL SAVE ME *CATCHING YOUR EYE* AGAIN IN FIVE MINUTES.

I HEARD ABOUT WHAT HAPPENED, BRANDON. THE BOYS WERE SAYING HE *HUMILIATED* YOU AGAIN AND I JUST WANTED TO CHECK YOU WERE DOING *OKAY.*

YEAH, WELL. LET'S JUST SAY I'M *GETTING USED* TO IT, UNCLE WALTER.

I JUST WISH HE'D STOP *COMPARING* US. IT'S SO *UNFAIR.* I *KNOW* I'M NOT AS SMART AS HE IS. I *KNOW* I'LL NEVER BE THE SAME *PERFECT EXAMPLE* OF *AMERICAN MASCULINITY.*

OH, YOUR FATHER ISN'T *PERFECT,* BRANDON. BELIEVE ME. YOU HAVE TO REMEMBER I WAS *THERE* BACK IN THE OLD DAYS

IT'S *ONLY HUMAN* TO IDEALIZE OUR PARENTS, BUT THE OLD HAVE REALLY NO MORE WISDOM THAN *THE YOUNG.* WE'RE JUST UGLY ENOUGH TO *LOOK* WISE AND NOT SO DRIVEN BY OUR *GENITALIA.*

I *HATE* HIM, MAN. I TOTALLY *HATE* HIM. I KNOW HE'S MY DAD AND I'M SUPPOSED TO LOVE HIM, BUT I REALLY WANT TO *STRANGLE* HIM WHEN HE MAKES ME FEEL THIS LOW.

SO DO SOMETHING *ABOUT* IT.

WHAT?

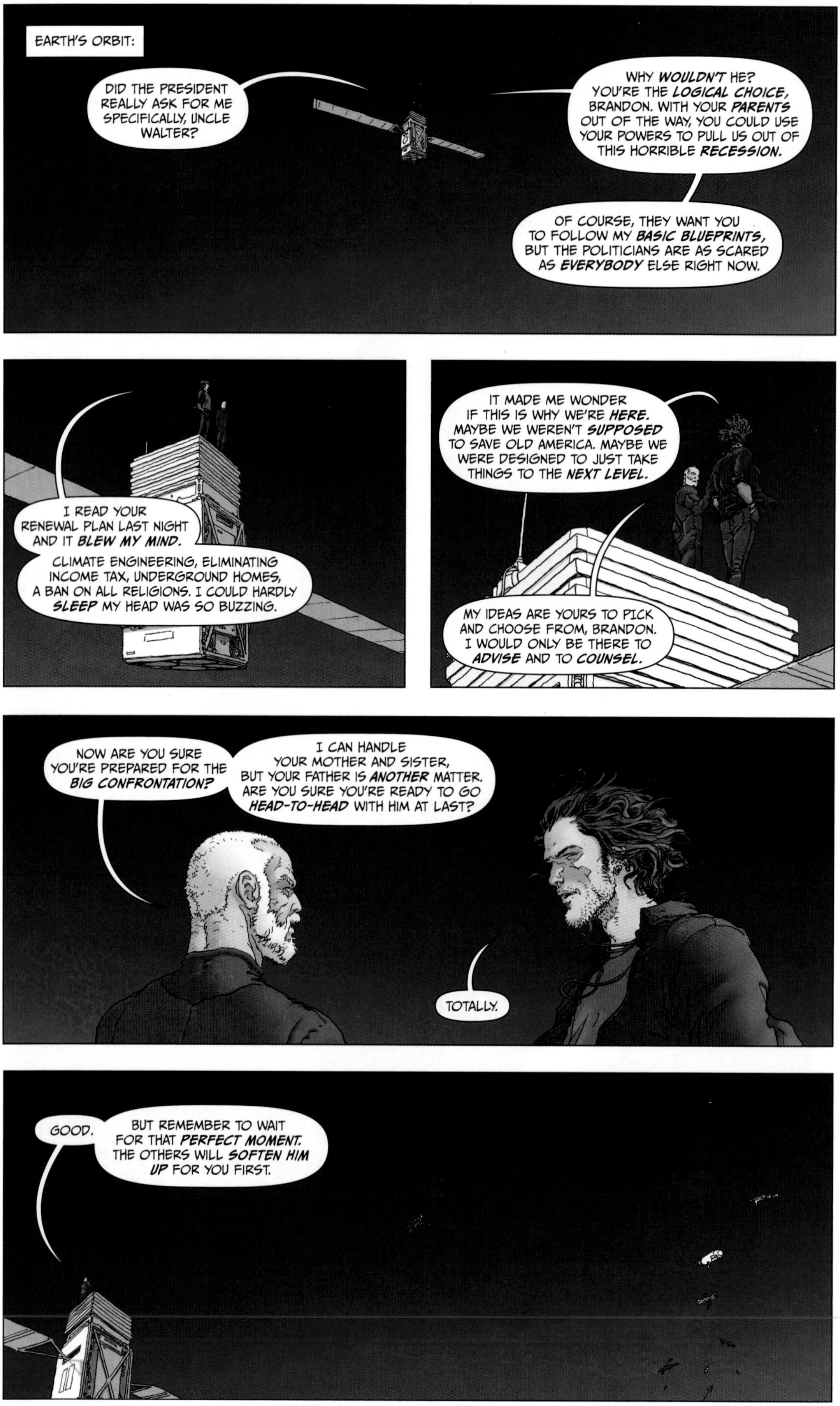
EARTH'S ORBIT:
DID THE PRESIDENT REALLY ASK FOR ME SPECIFICALLY, UNCLE WALTER?
WHY *WOULDN'T* HE? YOU'RE THE *LOGICAL CHOICE,* BRANDON. WITH YOUR *PARENTS* OUT OF THE WAY, YOU COULD USE YOUR POWERS TO PULL US OUT OF THIS HORRIBLE *RECESSION.*
OF COURSE, THEY WANT YOU TO FOLLOW MY *BASIC BLUEPRINTS,* BUT THE POLITICIANS ARE AS SCARED AS *EVERYBODY* ELSE RIGHT NOW.
I READ YOUR RENEWAL PLAN LAST NIGHT AND IT *BLEW MY MIND.*
CLIMATE ENGINEERING, ELIMINATING INCOME TAX, UNDERGROUND HOMES, A BAN ON ALL RELIGIONS. I COULD HARDLY *SLEEP* MY HEAD WAS SO BUZZING.
IT MADE ME WONDER IF THIS IS WHY WE'RE *HERE.* MAYBE WE WEREN'T *SUPPOSED* TO SAVE OLD AMERICA. MAYBE WE WERE DESIGNED TO JUST TAKE THINGS TO THE *NEXT LEVEL.*
MY IDEAS ARE YOURS TO PICK AND CHOOSE FROM, BRANDON. I WOULD ONLY BE THERE TO *ADVISE* AND TO *COUNSEL.*
NOW ARE YOU SURE YOU'RE PREPARED FOR THE *BIG CONFRONTATION?*
I CAN HANDLE YOUR MOTHER AND SISTER, BUT YOUR FATHER IS *ANOTHER* MATTER. ARE YOU SURE YOU'RE READY TO GO *HEAD-TO-HEAD* WITH HIM AT LAST?
TOTALLY.
GOOD.
BUT REMEMBER TO WAIT FOR THAT *PERFECT MOMENT.* THE OTHERS WILL *SOFTEN HIM UP* FOR YOU FIRST.

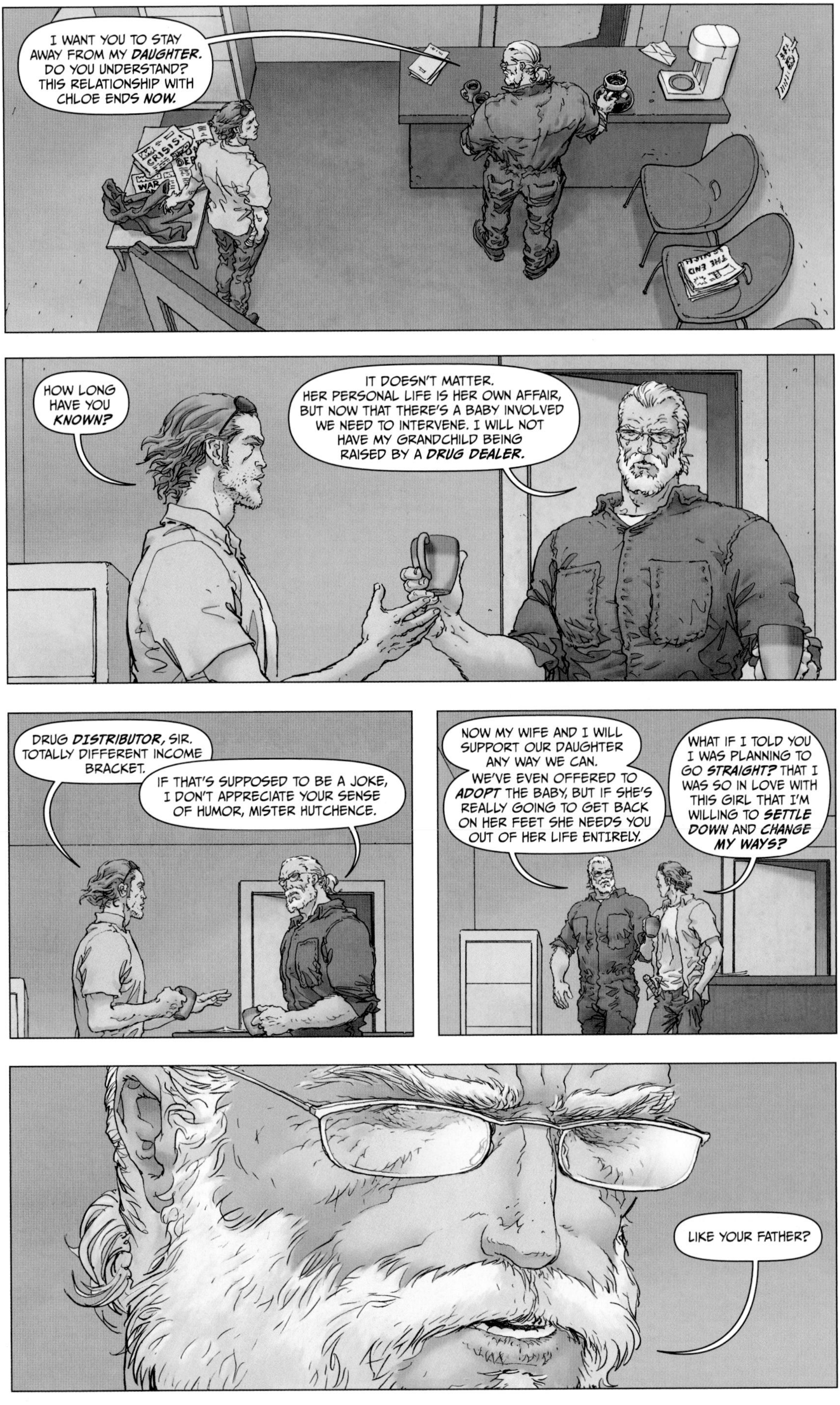
I WANT YOU TO STAY AWAY FROM MY DAUGHTER. DO YOU UNDERSTAND? THIS RELATIONSHIP WITH CHLOE ENDS NOW.
CRISIS!
WAR
THE END
HOW LONG HAVE YOU KNOWN?
IT DOESN'T MATTER. HER PERSONAL LIFE IS HER OWN AFFAIR, BUT NOW THAT THERE'S A BABY INVOLVED WE NEED TO INTERVENE. I WILL NOT HAVE MY GRANDCHILD BEING RAISED BY A DRUG DEALER.
DRUG DISTRIBUTOR, SIR. TOTALLY DIFFERENT INCOME BRACKET.
IF THAT'S SUPPOSED TO BE A JOKE, I DON'T APPRECIATE YOUR SENSE OF HUMOR, MISTER HUTCHENCE.
NOW MY WIFE AND I WILL SUPPORT OUR DAUGHTER ANY WAY WE CAN.
WE'VE EVEN OFFERED TO ADOPT THE BABY, BUT IF SHE'S REALLY GOING TO GET BACK ON HER FEET SHE NEEDS YOU OUT OF HER LIFE ENTIRELY.
WHAT IF I TOLD YOU I WAS PLANNING TO GO STRAIGHT? THAT I WAS SO IN LOVE WITH THIS GIRL THAT I'M WILLING TO SETTLE DOWN AND CHANGE MY WAYS?
LIKE YOUR FATHER?

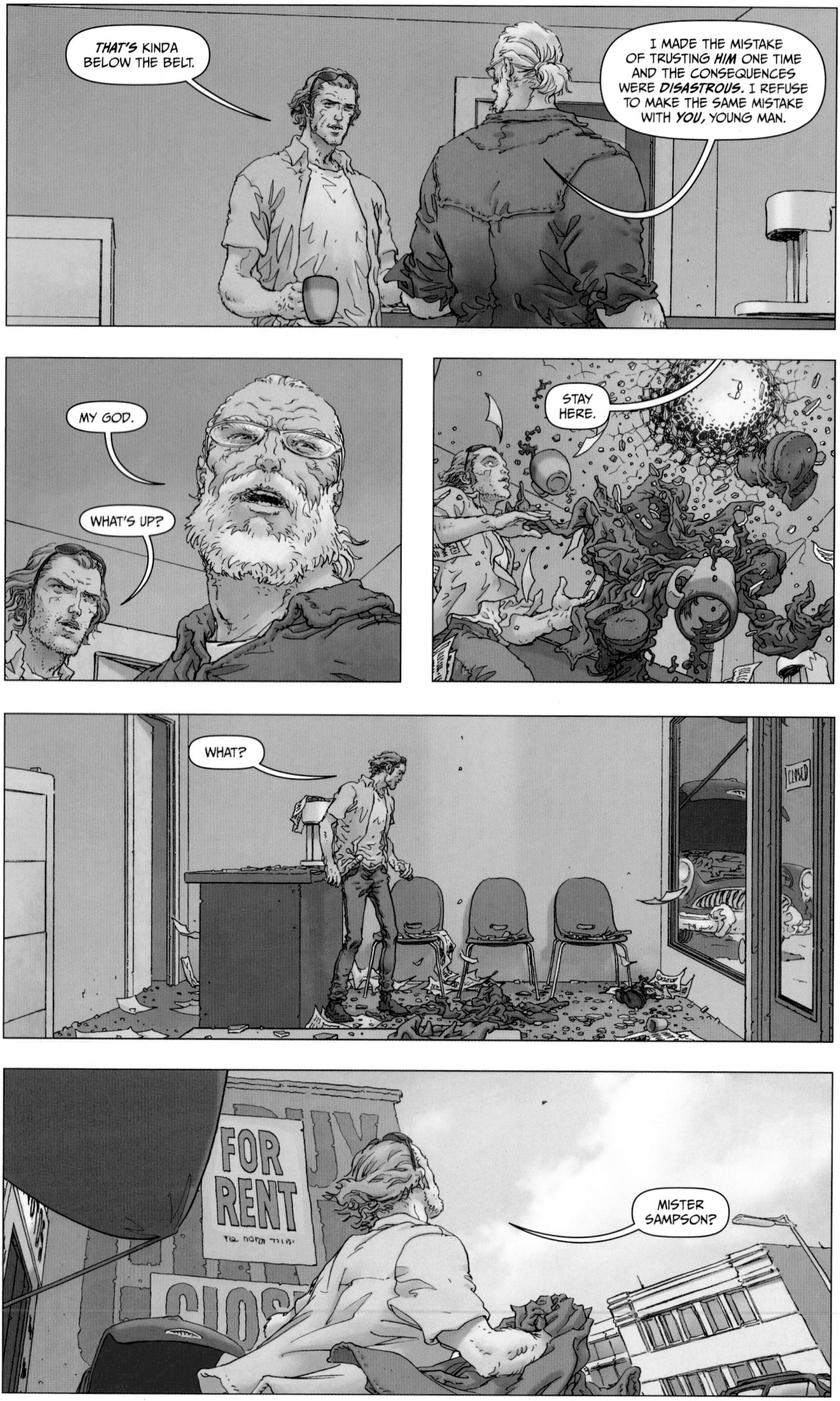
THAT'S KINDA BELOW THE BELT.
I MADE THE MISTAKE OF TRUSTING HIM ONE TIME AND THE CONSEQUENCES WERE DISASTROUS. I REFUSE TO MAKE THE SAME MISTAKE WITH YOU, YOUNG MAN.
MY GOD.
WHAT'S UP?
STAY HERE.
WHAT?
FOR RENT
MISTER SAMPSON?

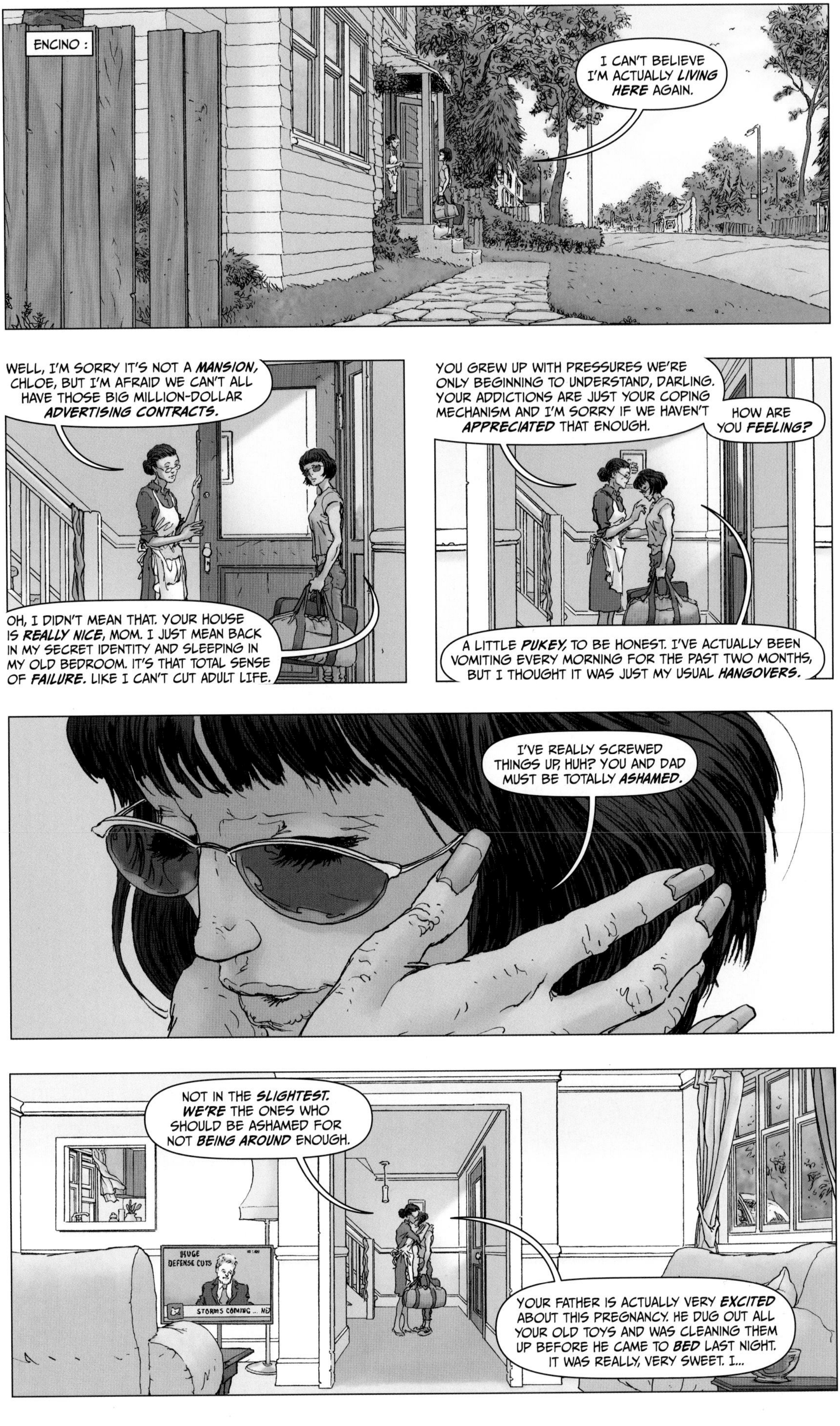
ENCINO :
I CAN'T BELIEVE I'M ACTUALLY LIVING HERE AGAIN.
WELL, I'M SORRY IT'S NOT A MANSION, CHLOE, BUT I'M AFRAID WE CAN'T ALL HAVE THOSE BIG MILLION-DOLLAR ADVERTISING CONTRACTS.
OH, I DIDN'T MEAN THAT. YOUR HOUSE IS REALLY NICE, MOM. I JUST MEAN BACK IN MY SECRET IDENTITY AND SLEEPING IN MY OLD BEDROOM. IT'S THAT TOTAL SENSE OF FAILURE. LIKE I CAN'T CUT ADULT LIFE.
YOU GREW UP WITH PRESSURES WE'RE ONLY BEGINNING TO UNDERSTAND, DARLING. YOUR ADDICTIONS ARE JUST YOUR COPING MECHANISM AND I'M SORRY IF WE HAVEN'T APPRECIATED THAT ENOUGH.
HOW ARE YOU FEELING?
A LITTLE PUKEY, TO BE HONEST. I'VE ACTUALLY BEEN VOMITING EVERY MORNING FOR THE PAST TWO MONTHS, BUT I THOUGHT IT WAS JUST MY USUAL HANGOVERS.
I'VE REALLY SCREWED THINGS UP, HUH? YOU AND DAD MUST BE TOTALLY ASHAMED.
NOT IN THE SLIGHTEST. WE'RE THE ONES WHO SHOULD BE ASHAMED FOR NOT BEING AROUND ENOUGH.
HUGE DEFENSE CUTS
STORMS COMING ... NE
YOUR FATHER IS ACTUALLY VERY EXCITED ABOUT THIS PREGNANCY. HE DUG OUT ALL YOUR OLD TOYS AND WAS CLEANING THEM UP BEFORE HE CAME TO BED LAST NIGHT. IT WAS REALLY, VERY SWEET. I...

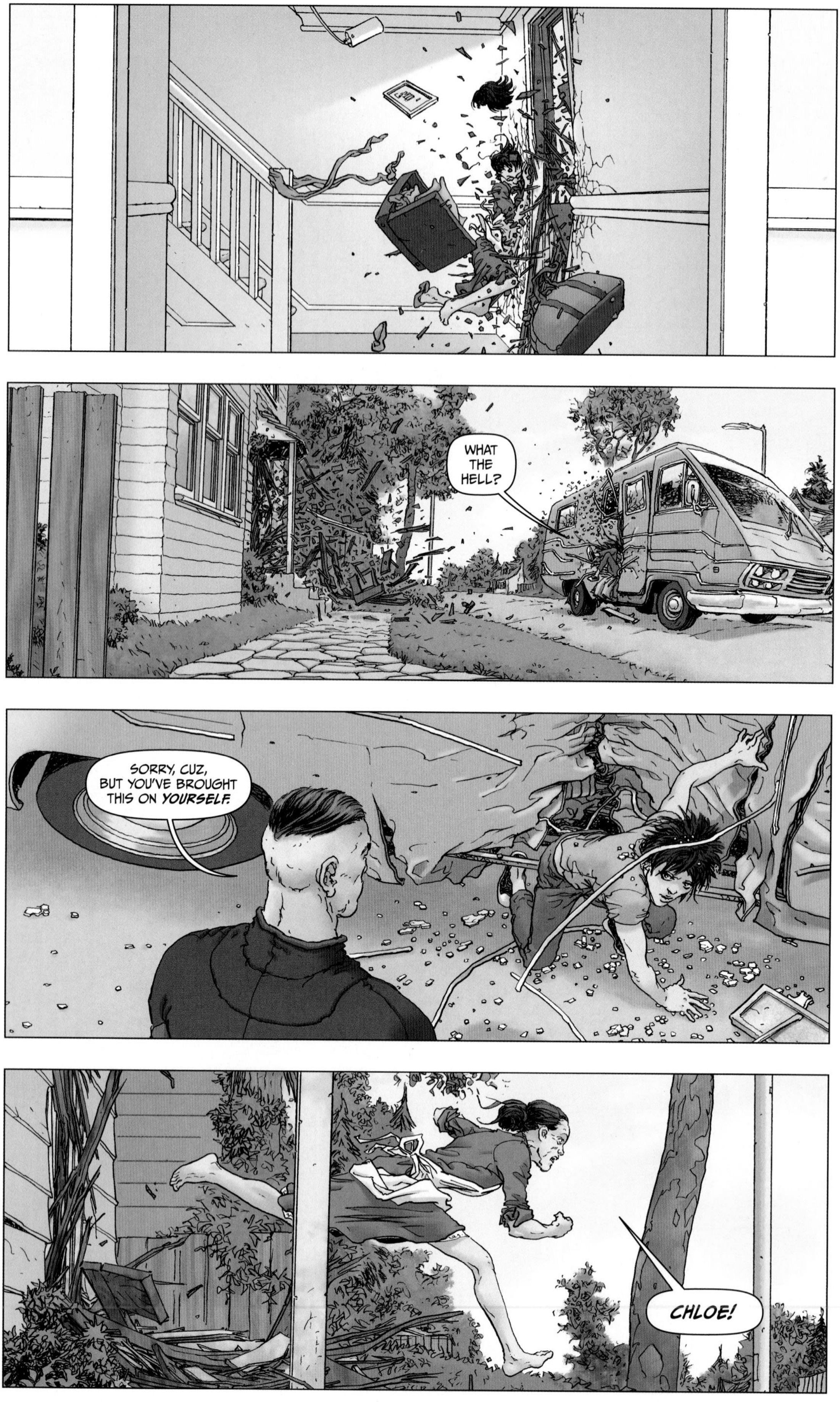
WHAT THE HELL?
SORRY, CUZ, BUT YOU'VE BROUGHT THIS ON *YOURSELF.*
CHLOE!

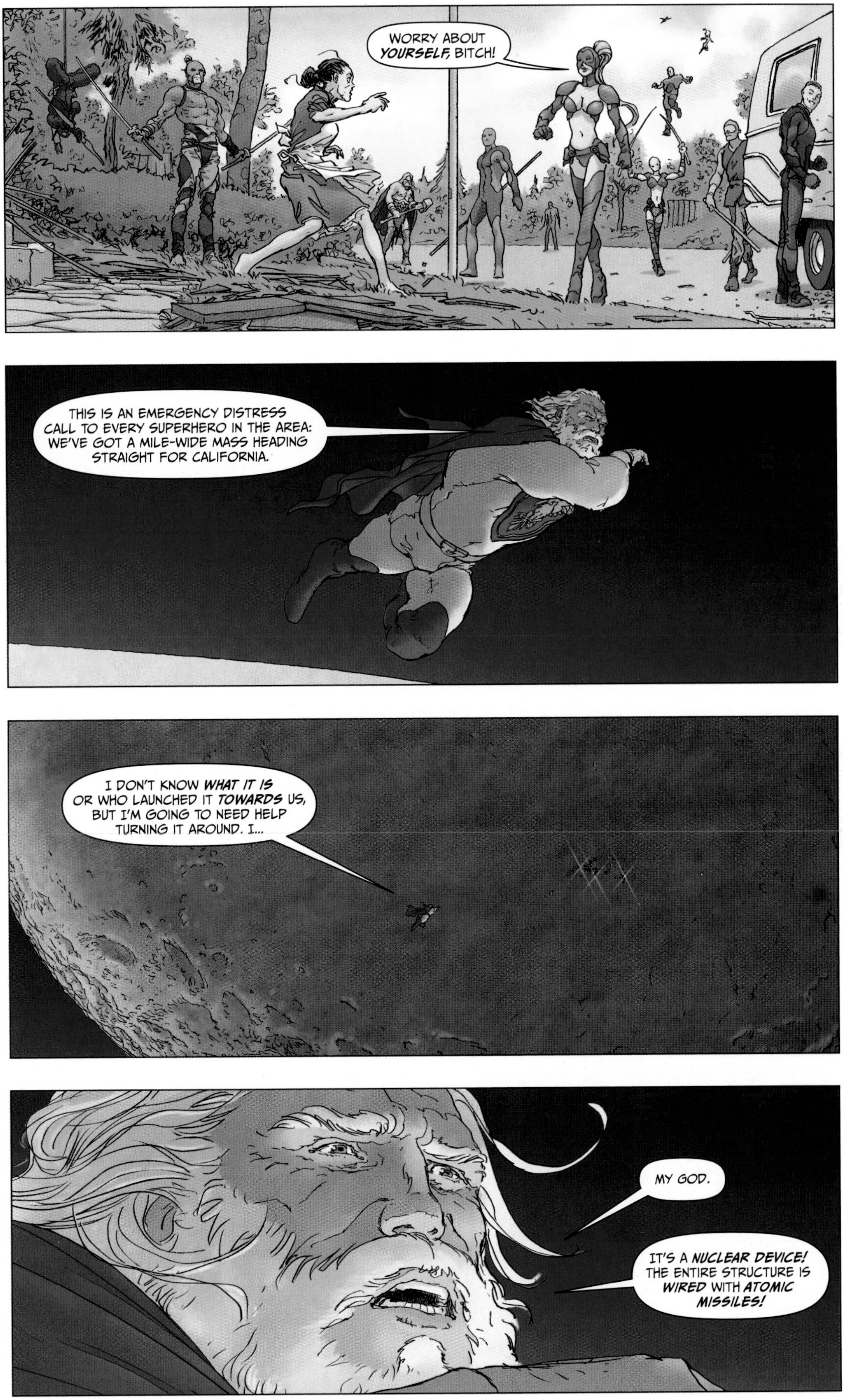
WORRY ABOUT *YOURSELF*, BITCH!
THIS IS AN EMERGENCY DISTRESS CALL TO EVERY SUPERHERO IN THE AREA: WE'VE GOT A MILE-WIDE MASS HEADING STRAIGHT FOR CALIFORNIA.
I DON'T KNOW *WHAT IT IS* OR WHO LAUNCHED IT *TOWARDS* US, BUT I'M GOING TO NEED HELP TURNING IT AROUND. I...
MY GOD.
IT'S A *NUCLEAR DEVICE!* THE ENTIRE STRUCTURE IS *WIRED* WITH *ATOMIC MISSILES!*

WE CAN'T LET IT *NEAR* THE POPULATION! SOMEBODY HELP ME *PUSH THIS THING BACK!*

NOW.

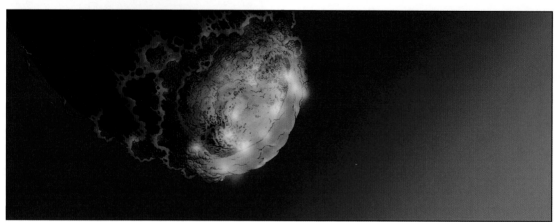

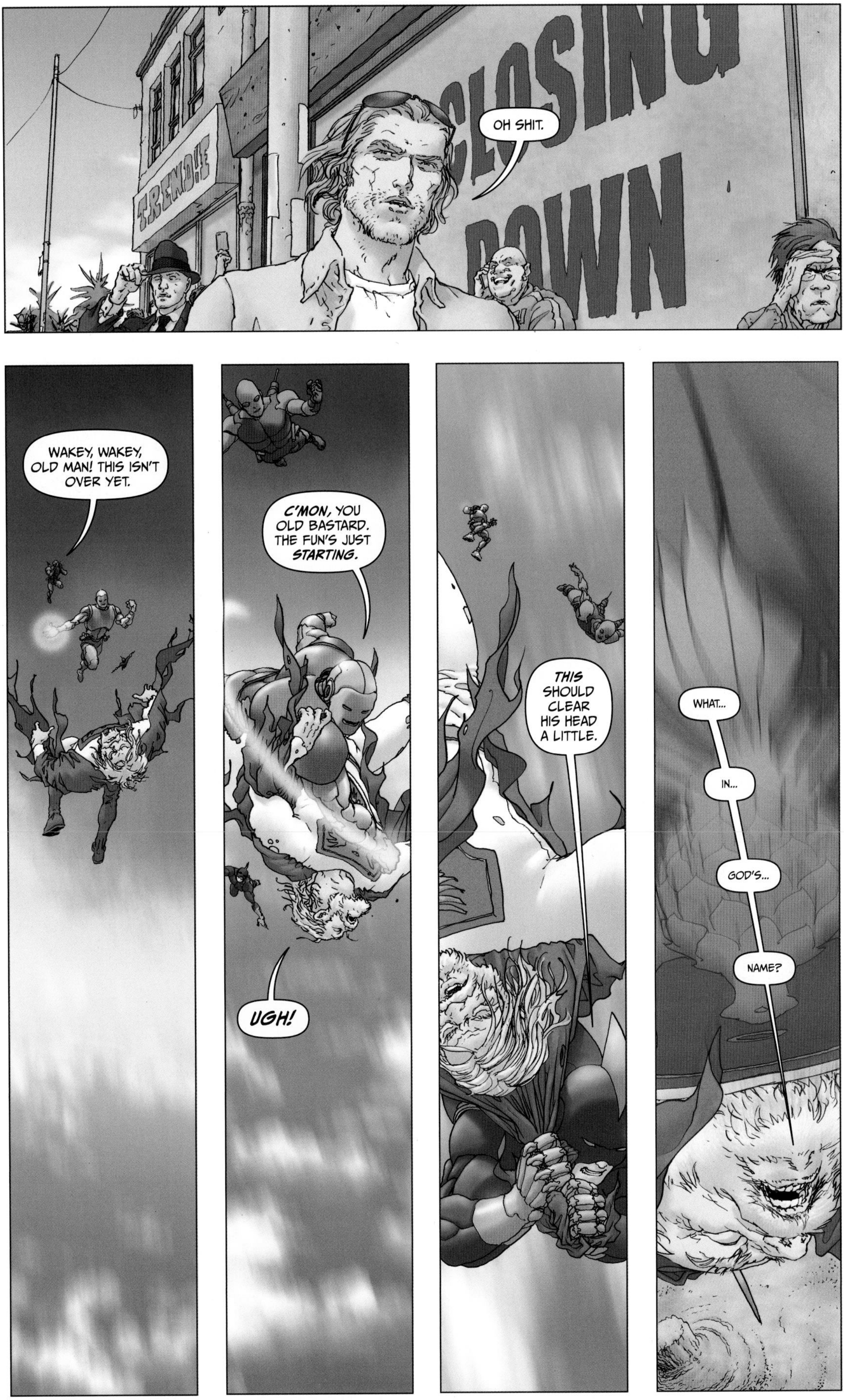
CLOSING DOWN
OH SHIT.
WAKEY, WAKEY, OLD MAN! THIS ISN'T OVER YET.
C'MON, YOU OLD BASTARD. THE FUN'S JUST *STARTING.*
UGH!
THIS SHOULD CLEAR HIS HEAD A LITTLE.
WHAT...
IN...
GOD'S...
NAME?

TH-THIS IS THE UTOPIAN. WHERE IS EVERYBODY? WHOEVER'S BEHIND THIS IS IMPERSONATING OUR *TEAMMATES.* I NEED *BACKUP!*

AW, HELL. WOULD YOU *LISTEN* TO HIM? IS HE REALLY SUCH A *DUMB-ASS?*

NOBODY'S IMPERSONATING *ANYONE,* GRAMPS. *WE'RE* YOUR TEAMMATES. DON'T YOU *GET* IT?

WE'RE JUST SICK AND TIRED OF ALL YOUR *BULLSHIT,* MAN... ALWAYS TELLING US WHAT TO DO. ALWAYS *BITCHING* ABOUT US NOT BEING *GOOD ENOUGH.*

I BET YOU WISH YOU'D BEEN *NICER* TO US NOW, HUH?

UGH!

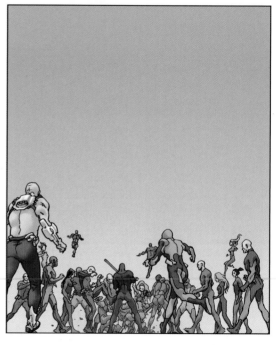

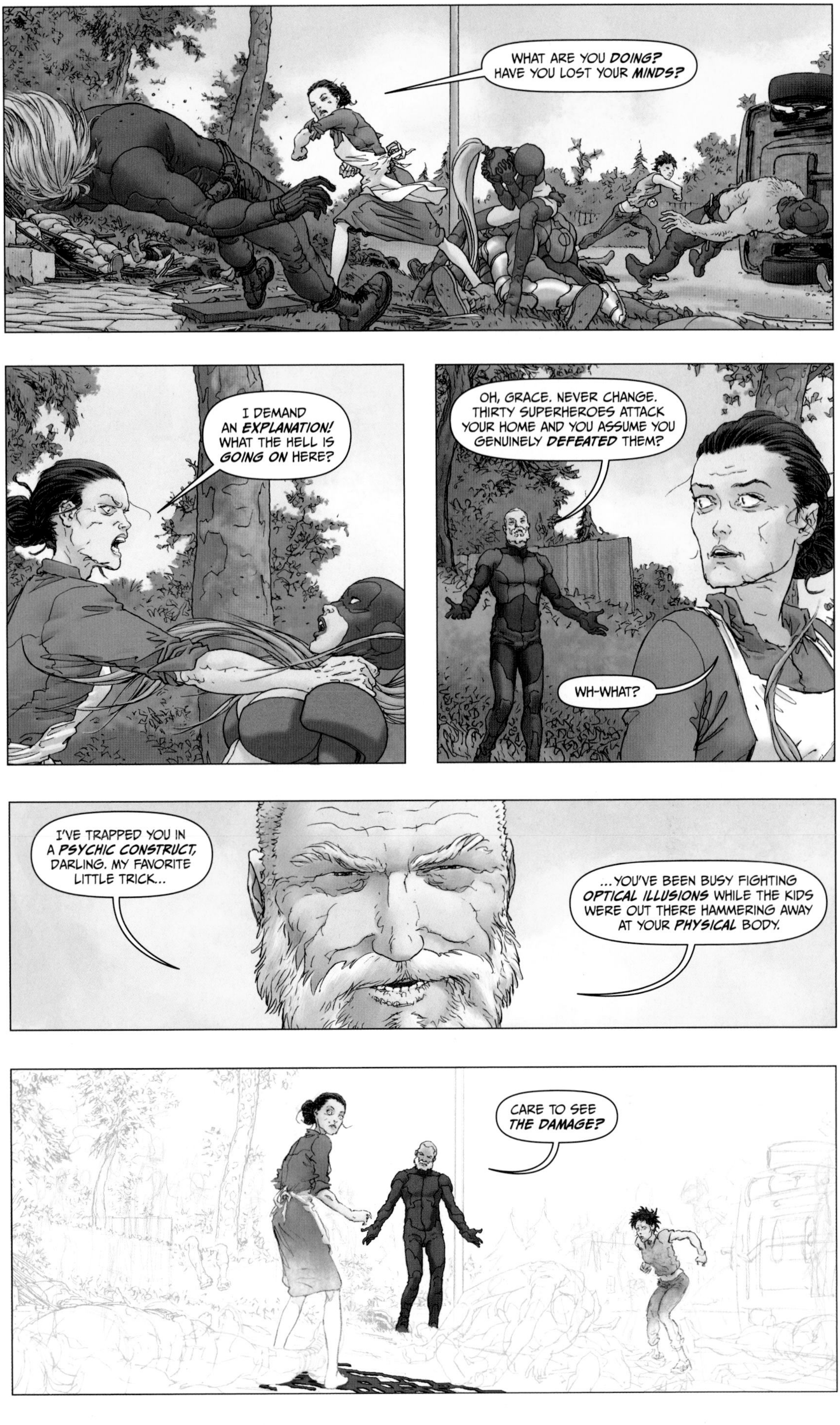
WHAT ARE YOU DOING? HAVE YOU LOST YOUR MINDS?
I DEMAND AN EXPLANATION! WHAT THE HELL IS GOING ON HERE?
OH, GRACE. NEVER CHANGE. THIRTY SUPERHEROES ATTACK YOUR HOME AND YOU ASSUME YOU GENUINELY DEFEATED THEM?
WH-WHAT?
I'VE TRAPPED YOU IN A PSYCHIC CONSTRUCT, DARLING. MY FAVORITE LITTLE TRICK...
...YOU'VE BEEN BUSY FIGHTING OPTICAL ILLUSIONS WHILE THE KIDS WERE OUT THERE HAMMERING AWAY AT YOUR PHYSICAL BODY.
CARE TO SEE THE DAMAGE?

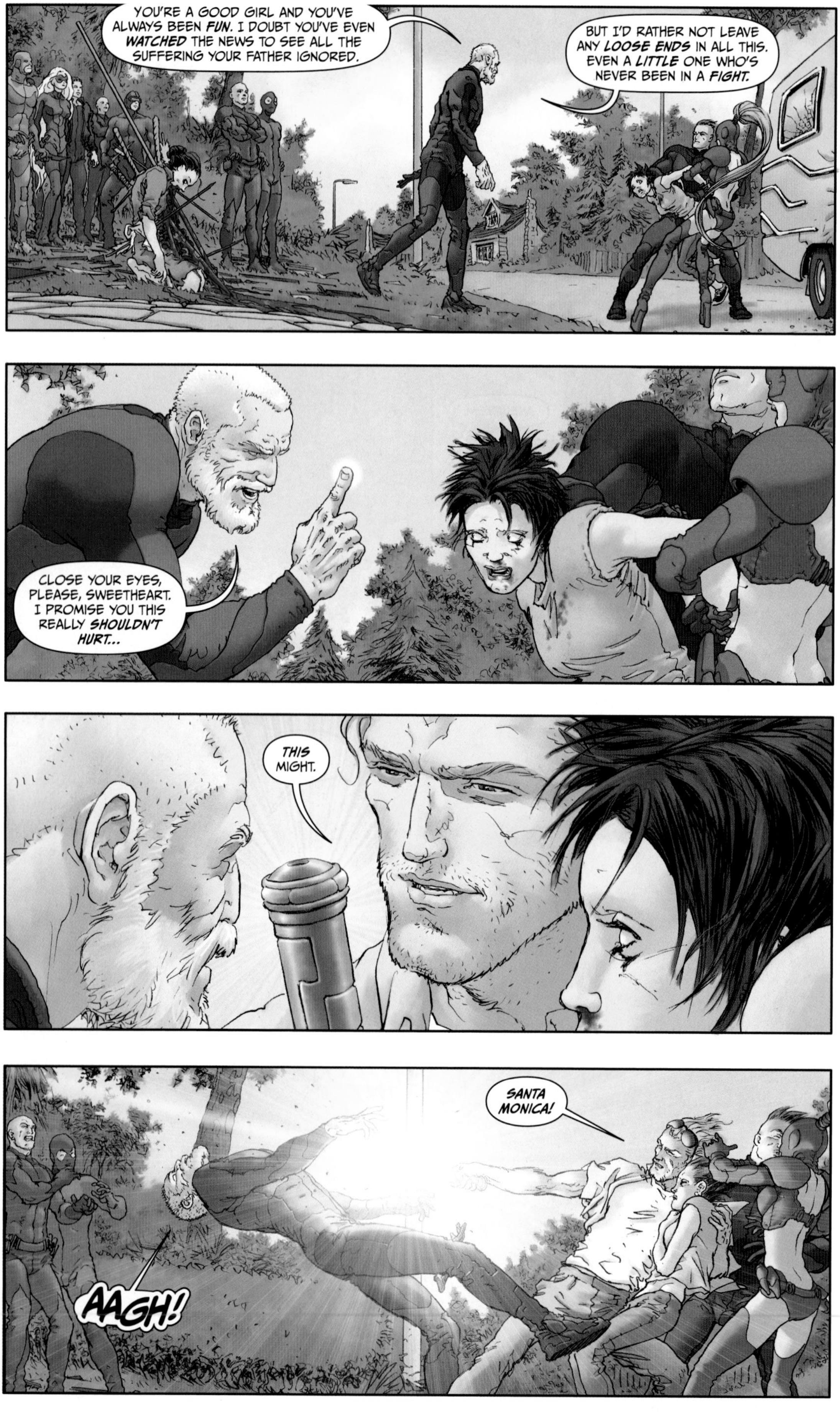

YOU'RE A GOOD GIRL AND YOU'VE ALWAYS BEEN FUN. I DOUBT YOU'VE EVEN WATCHED THE NEWS TO SEE ALL THE SUFFERING YOUR FATHER IGNORED.
BUT I'D RATHER NOT LEAVE ANY LOOSE ENDS IN ALL THIS. EVEN A LITTLE ONE WHO'S NEVER BEEN IN A FIGHT.
CLOSE YOUR EYES, PLEASE, SWEETHEART. I PROMISE YOU THIS REALLY SHOULDN'T HURT...
THIS MIGHT.
SANTA MONICA!
AAGH!

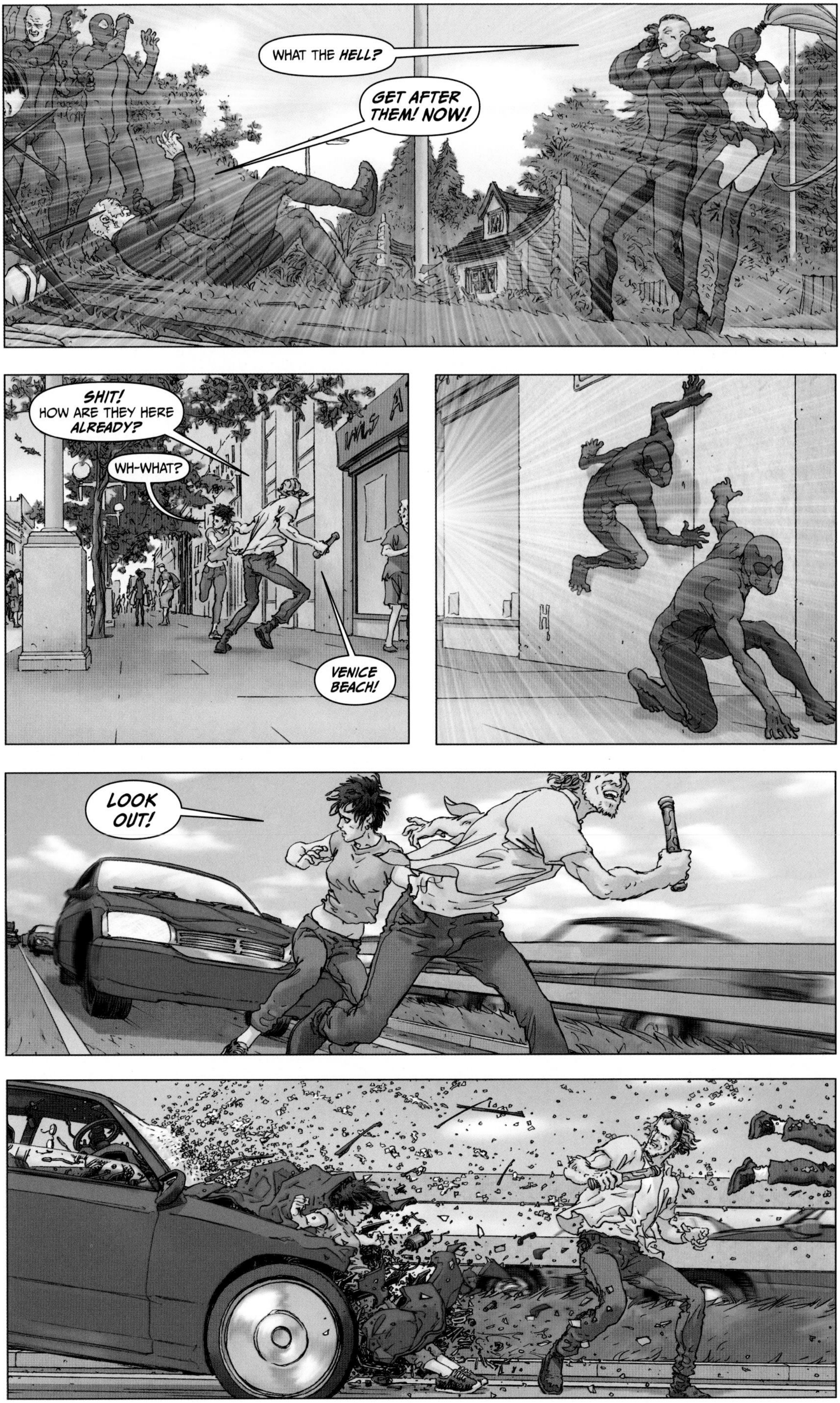
WHAT THE HELL?
GET AFTER THEM! NOW!
SHIT! HOW ARE THEY HERE ALREADY?
WH-WHAT?
VENICE BEACH!
LOOK OUT!

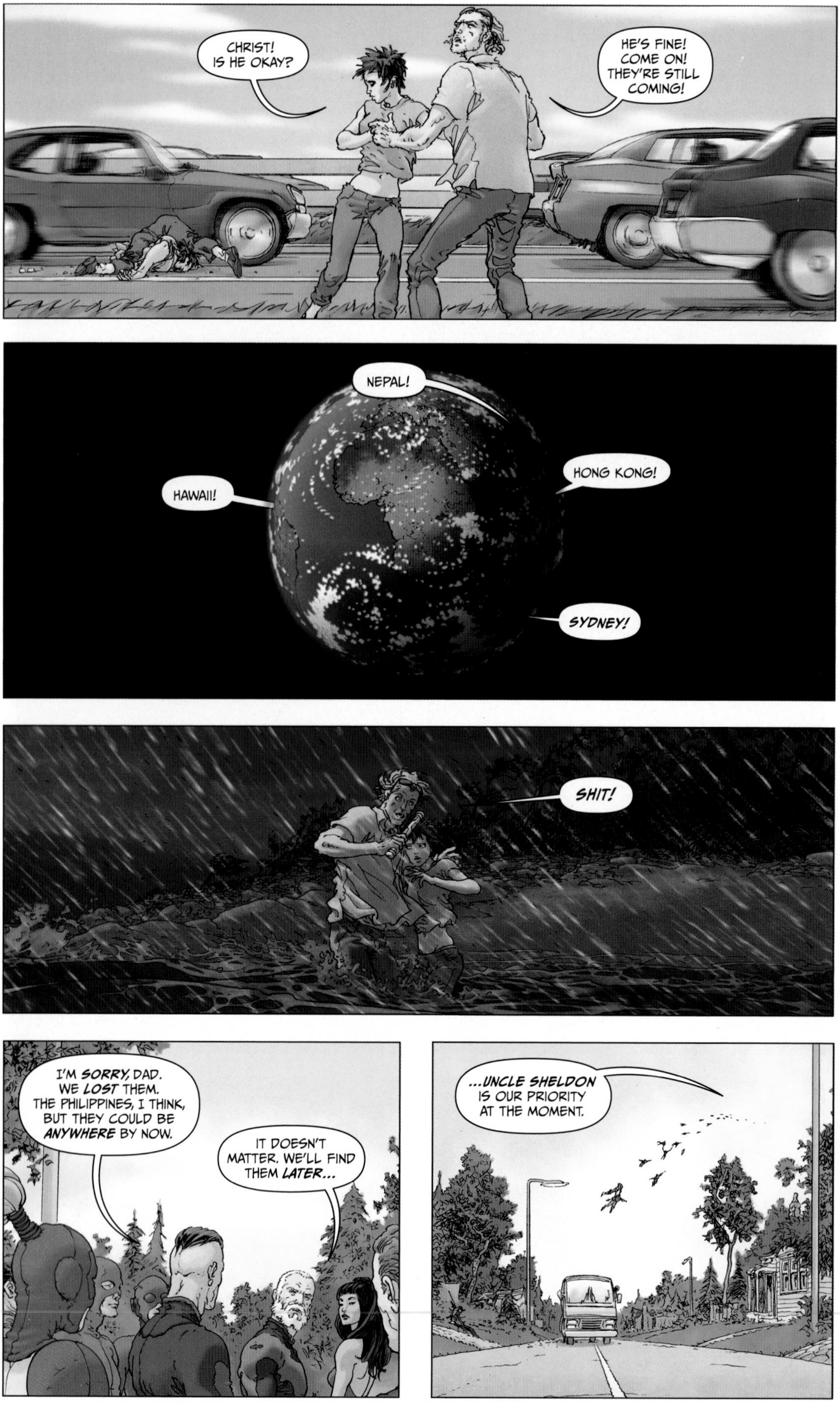
CHRIST! IS HE OKAY?
HE'S FINE! COME ON! THEY'RE STILL COMING!
NEPAL!
HAWAII!
HONG KONG!
SYDNEY!
SHIT!
I'M SORRY, DAD. WE LOST THEM. THE PHILIPPINES, I THINK, BUT THEY COULD BE ANYWHERE BY NOW.
IT DOESN'T MATTER. WE'LL FIND THEM LATER...
...UNCLE SHELDON IS OUR PRIORITY AT THE MOMENT.

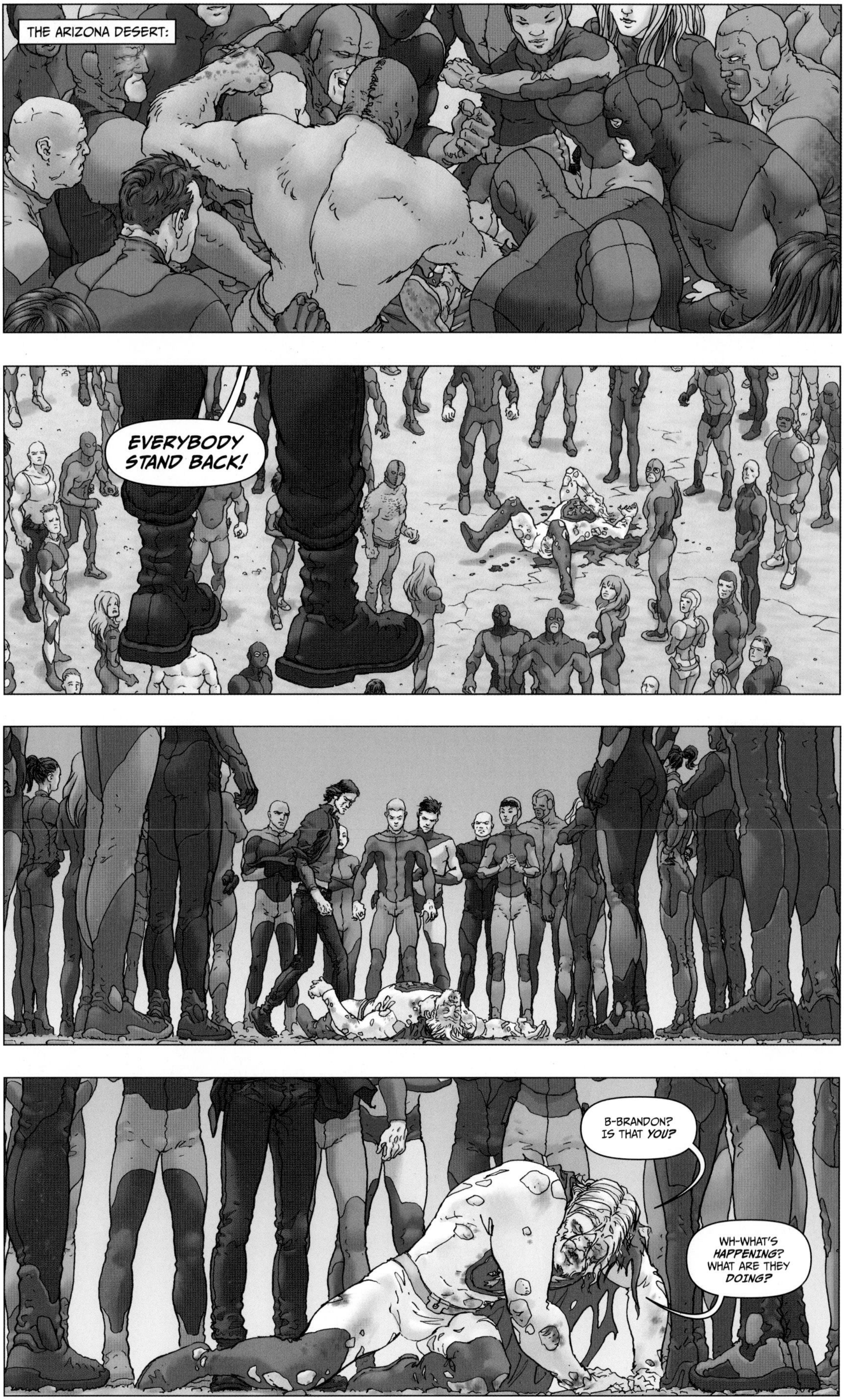
THE ARIZONA DESERT:
EVERYBODY STAND BACK!
B-BRANDON? IS THAT YOU?
WH-WHAT'S HAPPENING? WHAT ARE THEY DOING?

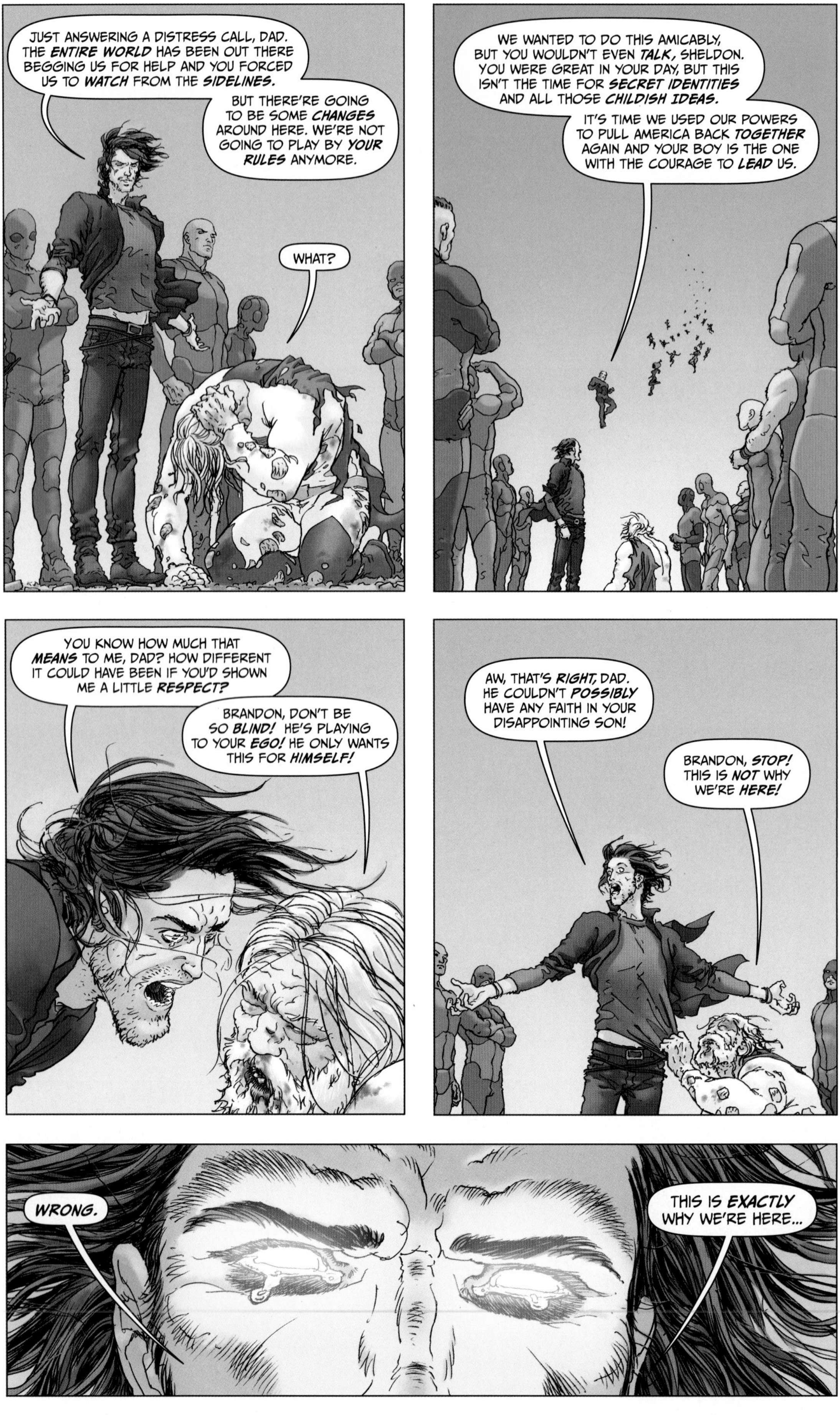
JUST ANSWERING A DISTRESS CALL, DAD. THE ENTIRE WORLD HAS BEEN OUT THERE BEGGING US FOR HELP AND YOU FORCED US TO WATCH FROM THE SIDELINES.
BUT THERE'RE GOING TO BE SOME CHANGES AROUND HERE. WE'RE NOT GOING TO PLAY BY YOUR RULES ANYMORE.
WHAT?
WE WANTED TO DO THIS AMICABLY, BUT YOU WOULDN'T EVEN TALK, SHELDON. YOU WERE GREAT IN YOUR DAY, BUT THIS ISN'T THE TIME FOR SECRET IDENTITIES AND ALL THOSE CHILDISH IDEAS.
IT'S TIME WE USED OUR POWERS TO PULL AMERICA BACK TOGETHER AGAIN AND YOUR BOY IS THE ONE WITH THE COURAGE TO LEAD US.
YOU KNOW HOW MUCH THAT MEANS TO ME, DAD? HOW DIFFERENT IT COULD HAVE BEEN IF YOU'D SHOWN ME A LITTLE RESPECT?
BRANDON, DON'T BE SO BLIND! HE'S PLAYING TO YOUR EGO! HE ONLY WANTS THIS FOR HIMSELF!
AW, THAT'S RIGHT, DAD. HE COULDN'T POSSIBLY HAVE ANY FAITH IN YOUR DISAPPOINTING SON!
BRANDON, STOP! THIS IS NOT WHY WE'RE HERE!
WRONG.
THIS IS EXACTLY WHY WE'RE HERE...

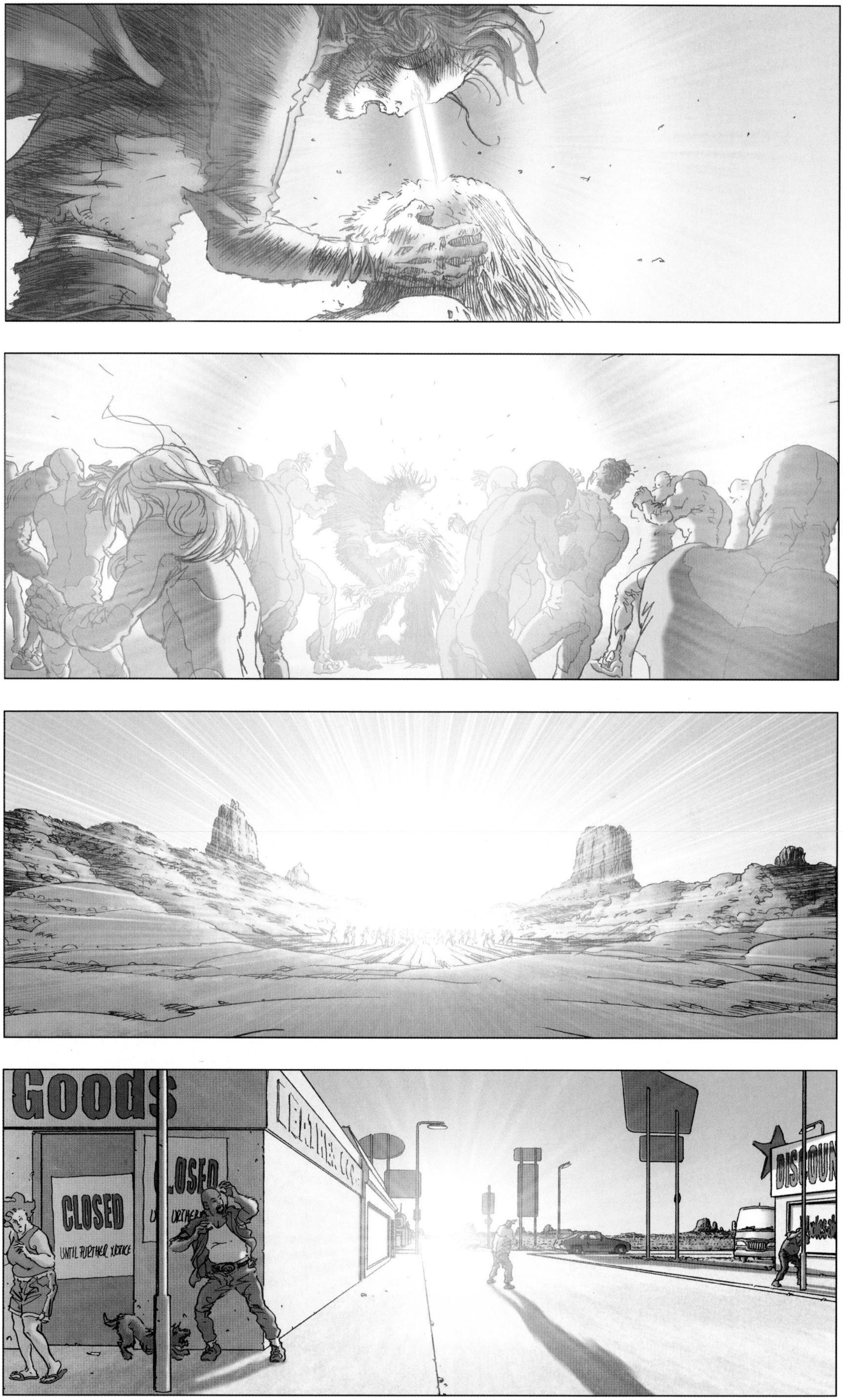
Goods
CLOSED
UNTIL FURTHER NOTICE

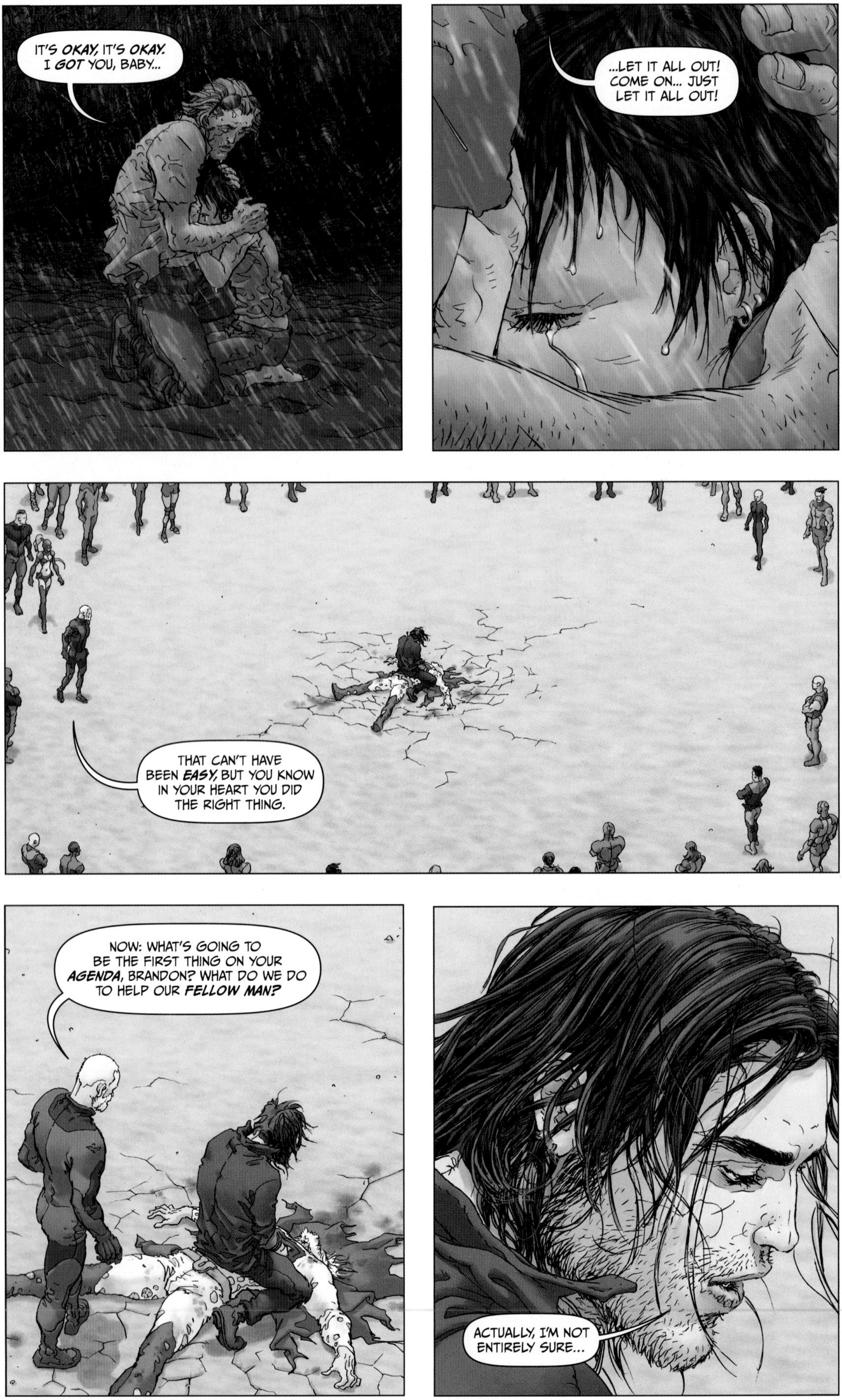
IT'S *OKAY,* IT'S *OKAY.* I *GOT* YOU, BABY...
...LET IT ALL OUT! COME ON... JUST LET IT ALL OUT!
THAT CAN'T HAVE BEEN *EASY,* BUT YOU KNOW IN YOUR HEART YOU DID THE RIGHT THING.
NOW: WHAT'S GOING TO BE THE FIRST THING ON YOUR *AGENDA,* BRANDON? WHAT DO WE DO TO HELP OUR *FELLOW MAN?*
ACTUALLY, I'M NOT ENTIRELY SURE...

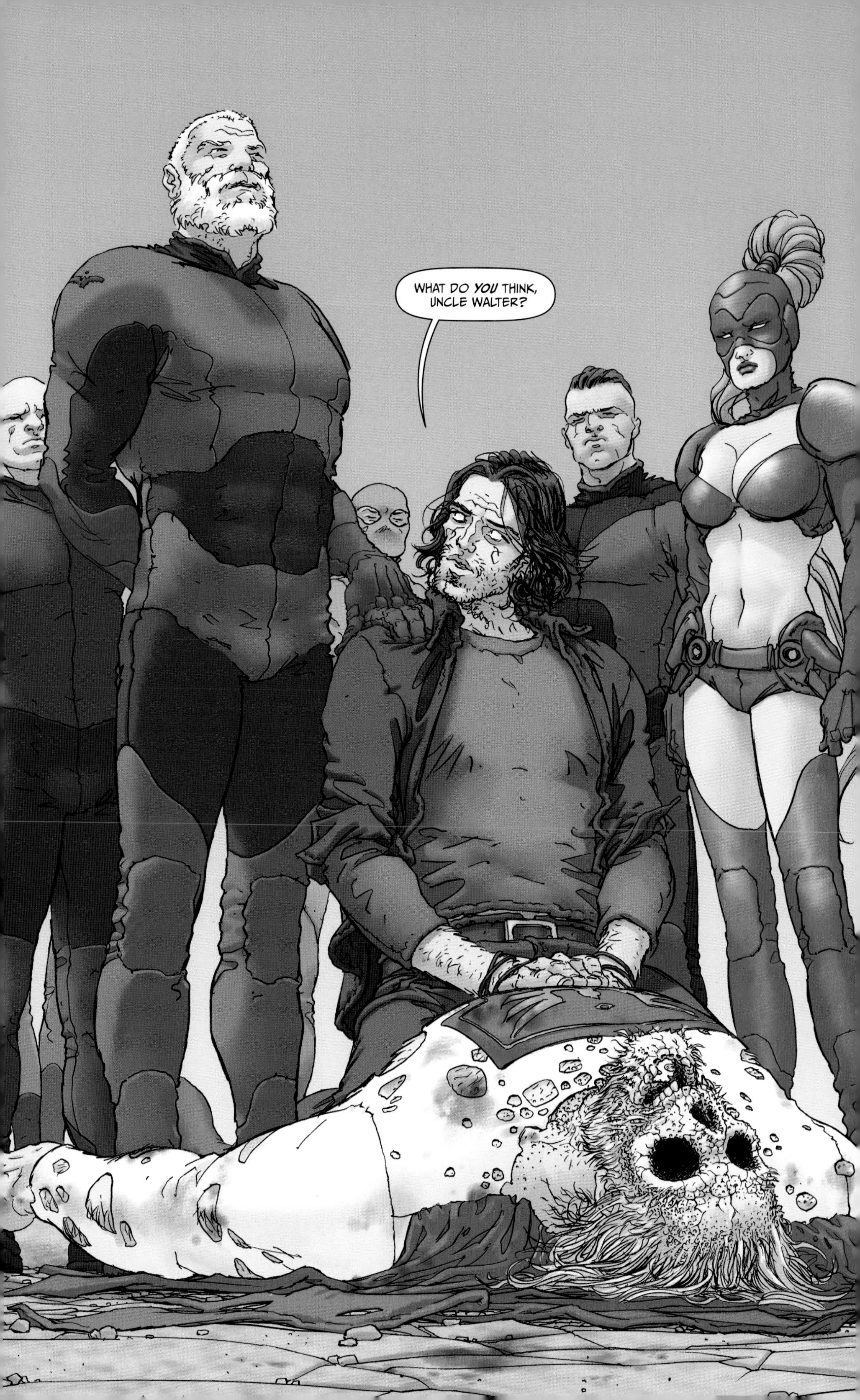
WHAT DO YOU THINK, UNCLE WALTER?

CHAPTER 4

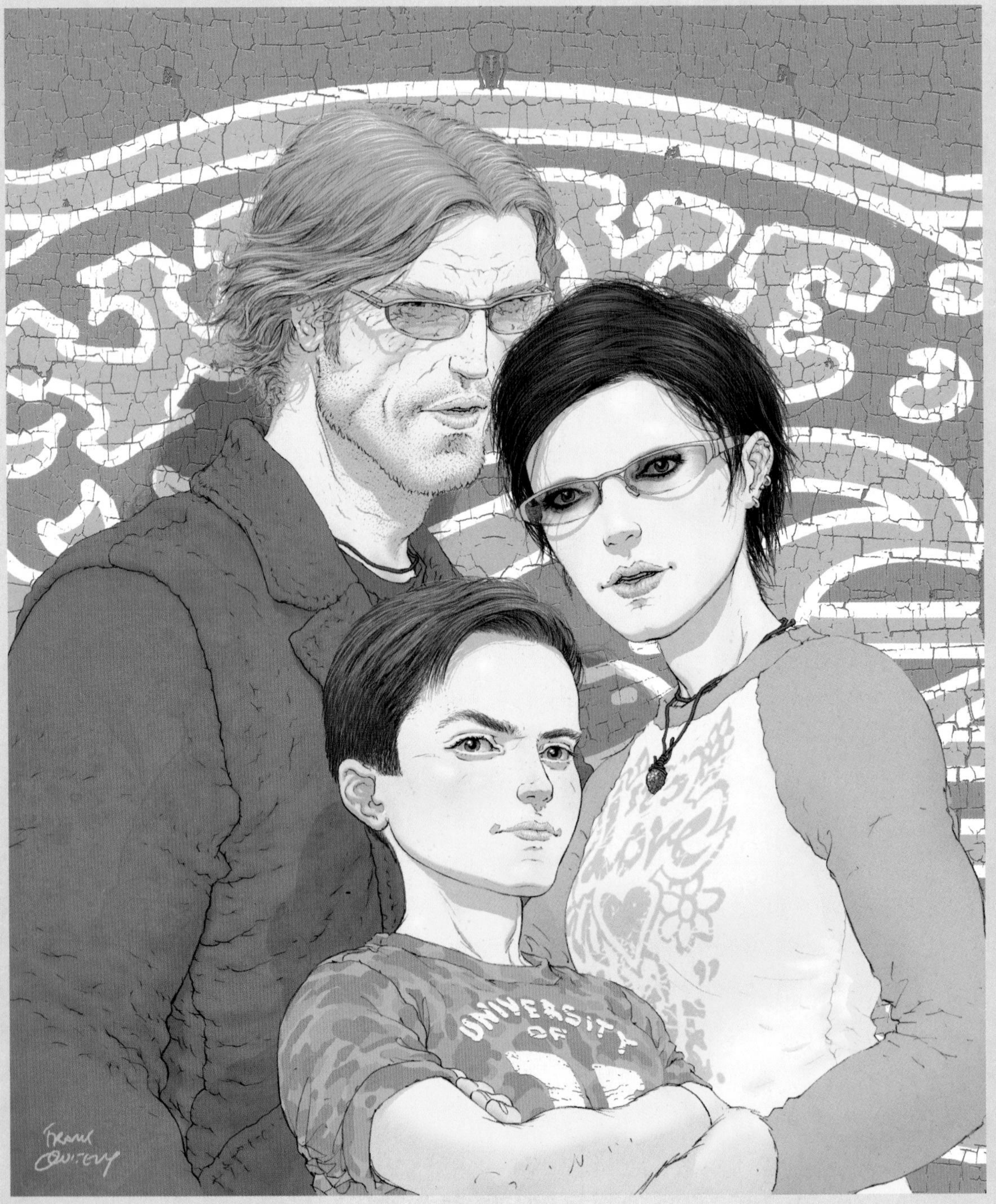

UNIVERSITY
OF

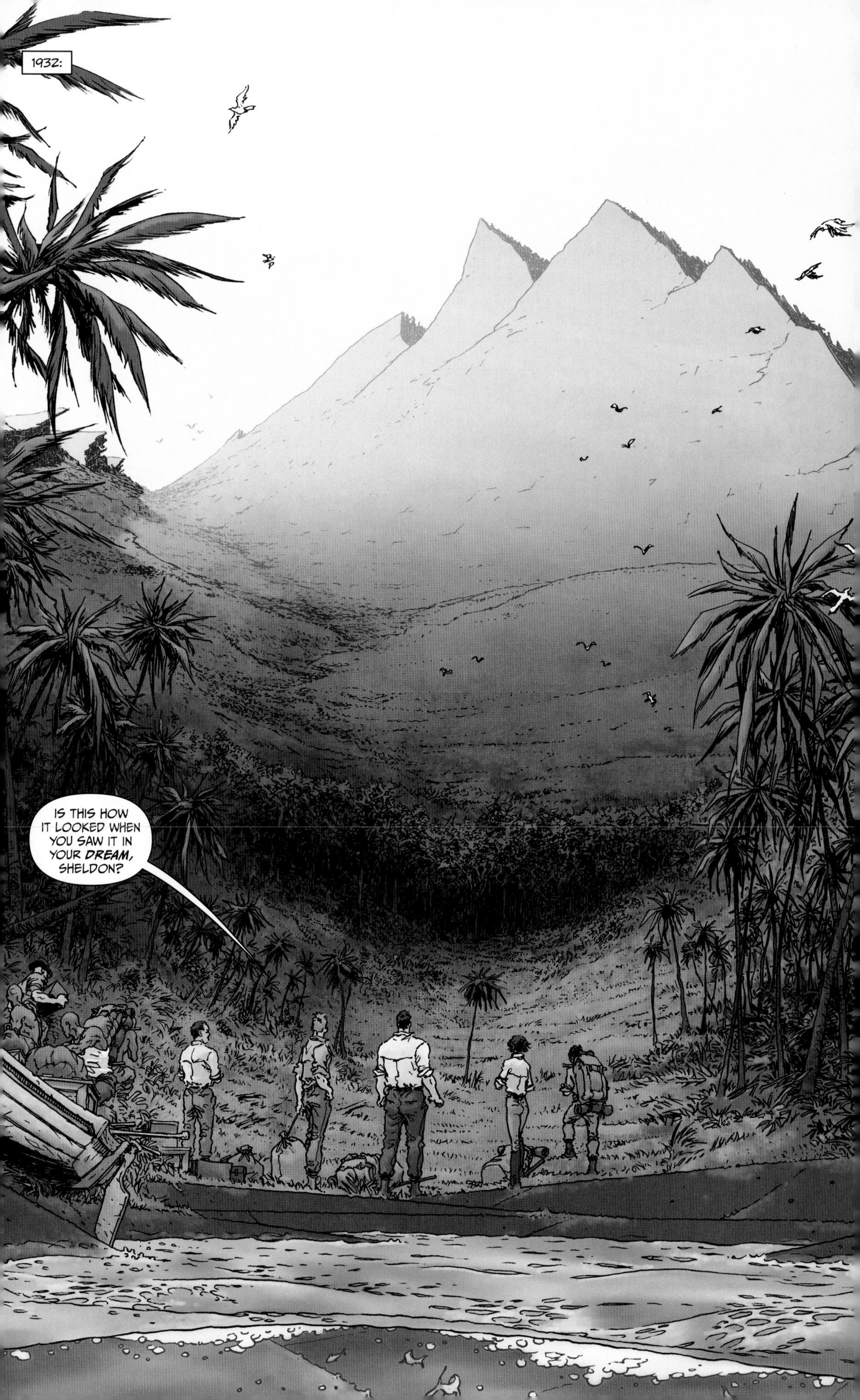
1932:
IS THIS HOW IT LOOKED WHEN YOU SAW IT IN YOUR DREAM, SHELDON?

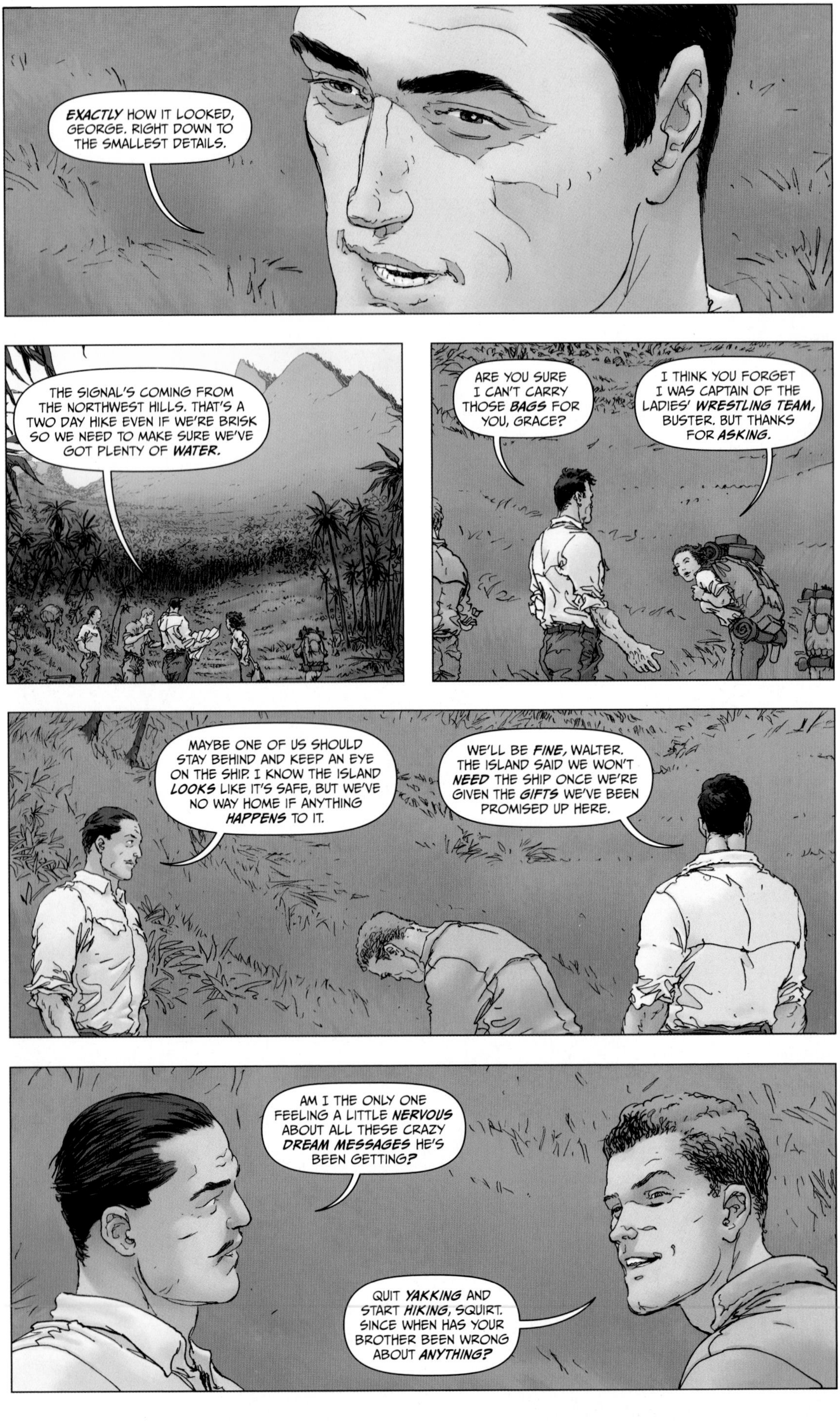
EXACTLY HOW IT LOOKED, GEORGE. RIGHT DOWN TO THE SMALLEST DETAILS.
THE SIGNAL'S COMING FROM THE NORTHWEST HILLS. THAT'S A TWO DAY HIKE EVEN IF WE'RE BRISK SO WE NEED TO MAKE SURE WE'VE GOT PLENTY OF WATER.
ARE YOU SURE I CAN'T CARRY THOSE BAGS FOR YOU, GRACE?
I THINK YOU FORGET I WAS CAPTAIN OF THE LADIES' WRESTLING TEAM, BUSTER. BUT THANKS FOR ASKING.
MAYBE ONE OF US SHOULD STAY BEHIND AND KEEP AN EYE ON THE SHIP. I KNOW THE ISLAND LOOKS LIKE IT'S SAFE, BUT WE'VE NO WAY HOME IF ANYTHING HAPPENS TO IT.
WE'LL BE FINE, WALTER. THE ISLAND SAID WE WON'T NEED THE SHIP ONCE WE'RE GIVEN THE GIFTS WE'VE BEEN PROMISED UP HERE.
AM I THE ONLY ONE FEELING A LITTLE NERVOUS ABOUT ALL THESE CRAZY DREAM MESSAGES HE'S BEEN GETTING?
QUIT YAKKING AND START HIKING, SQUIRT. SINCE WHEN HAS YOUR BROTHER BEEN WRONG ABOUT ANYTHING?

"IT WASN'T UNTIL LATER THEY REALIZED WHAT THEY WERE HIKING ACROSS.

"WHAT SEEMED LIKE ROCK WAS *ALIEN HARDWARE.* WHAT LOOKED LIKE JUNGLE JUST CENTURIES OF *VEGETATION.*

"THE HILLS THEMSELVES WERE CRISS-CROSSED WITH A SPECIAL METAL THAT NOBODY HAD EVER *SEEN* BEFORE, AND AS THEY CLIMBED IT SOON BECAME OBVIOUS THE ISLAND WAS A *MACHINE.*

"IT HAD BEEN POSITIONED HERE FOR A VERY LONG TIME, WAITING FOR THE PERFECT CANDIDATES AND SHROUDED IN WHAT YOU AND I WOULD CALL A *CLOAKING DEVICE.*

"BUT MOM AND DAD HAD NO IDEA UNTIL THEY MADE THEIR WAY TO THE TOP OF THE TOWER AND GOT TO SEE WHAT DAD HAD BEEN *DREAMING* ABOUT..."

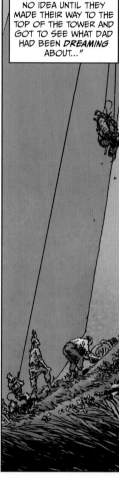

C'MON, MISS SAMPSON. GIVE ME THAT PRETTY HAND...

GET OFF MY BACK, GEORGE. I'M NOT GOING TO WARN YOU AGAIN ABOUT THESE STUPID CRACKS.

PIPE DOWN! BOTH OF YOU! WE'RE ALL GOING TO NEED OUR *WITS* ONCE WE'RE THROUGH TO THE OTHER SIDE...

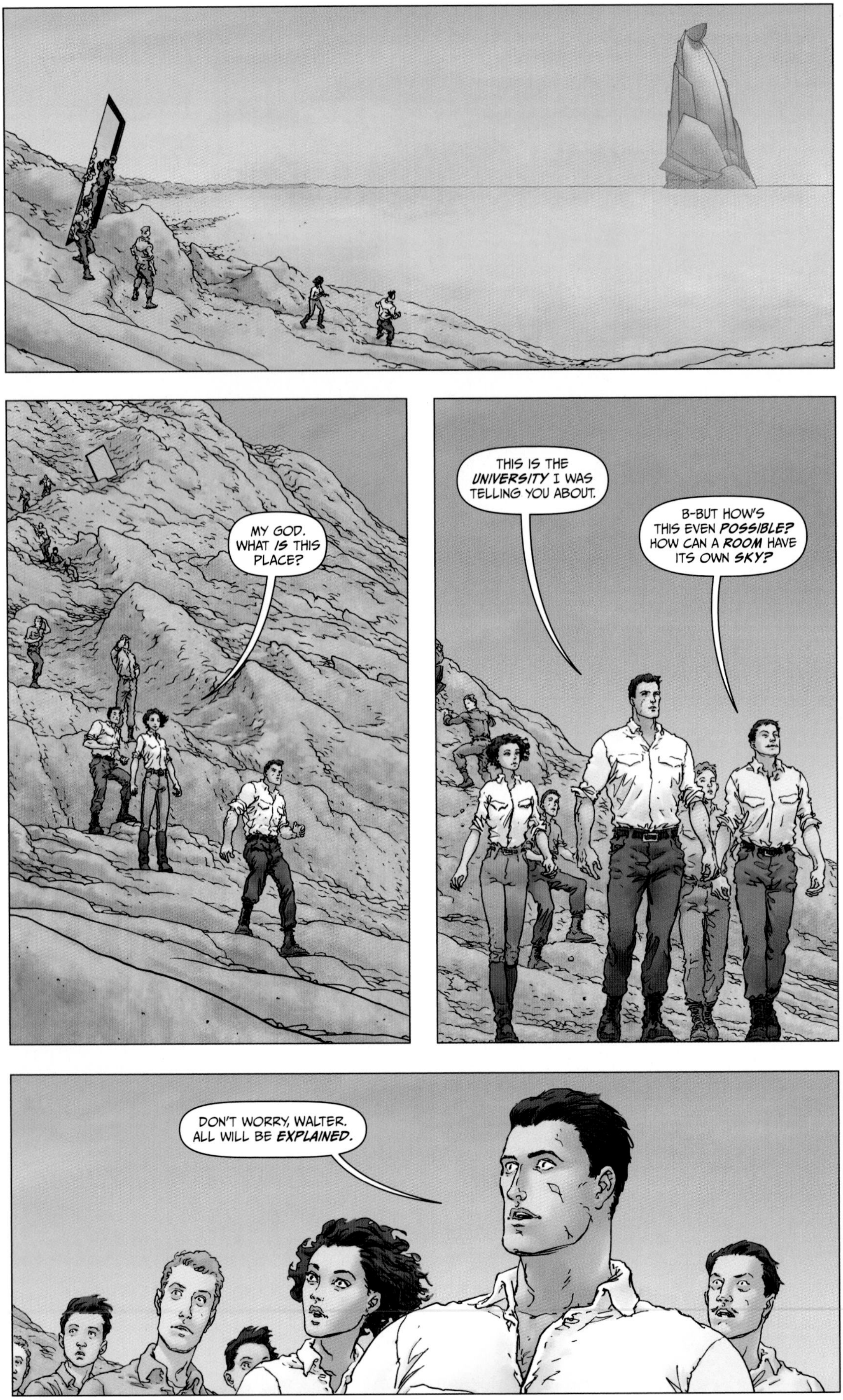
MY GOD. WHAT IS THIS PLACE?
THIS IS THE UNIVERSITY I WAS TELLING YOU ABOUT.
B-BUT HOW'S THIS EVEN POSSIBLE? HOW CAN A ROOM HAVE ITS OWN SKY?
DON'T WORRY, WALTER. ALL WILL BE EXPLAINED.

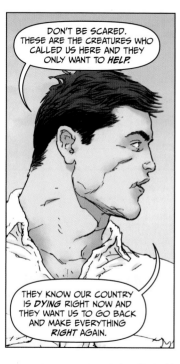

DON'T BE SCARED. THESE ARE THE CREATURES WHO CALLED US HERE AND THEY ONLY WANT TO *HELP.*

THEY KNOW OUR COUNTRY IS *DYING* RIGHT NOW AND THEY WANT US TO GO BACK AND MAKE EVERYTHING *RIGHT* AGAIN.

BUT *HOW?*

THEY'RE GOING TO GIVE US *POWERS,* GEORGE. THEY'RE GOING TO MAKE US BETTER THAN ANY OF US COULD EVER *DREAM.*

WE JUST HAVE TO *TRUST* THEM.

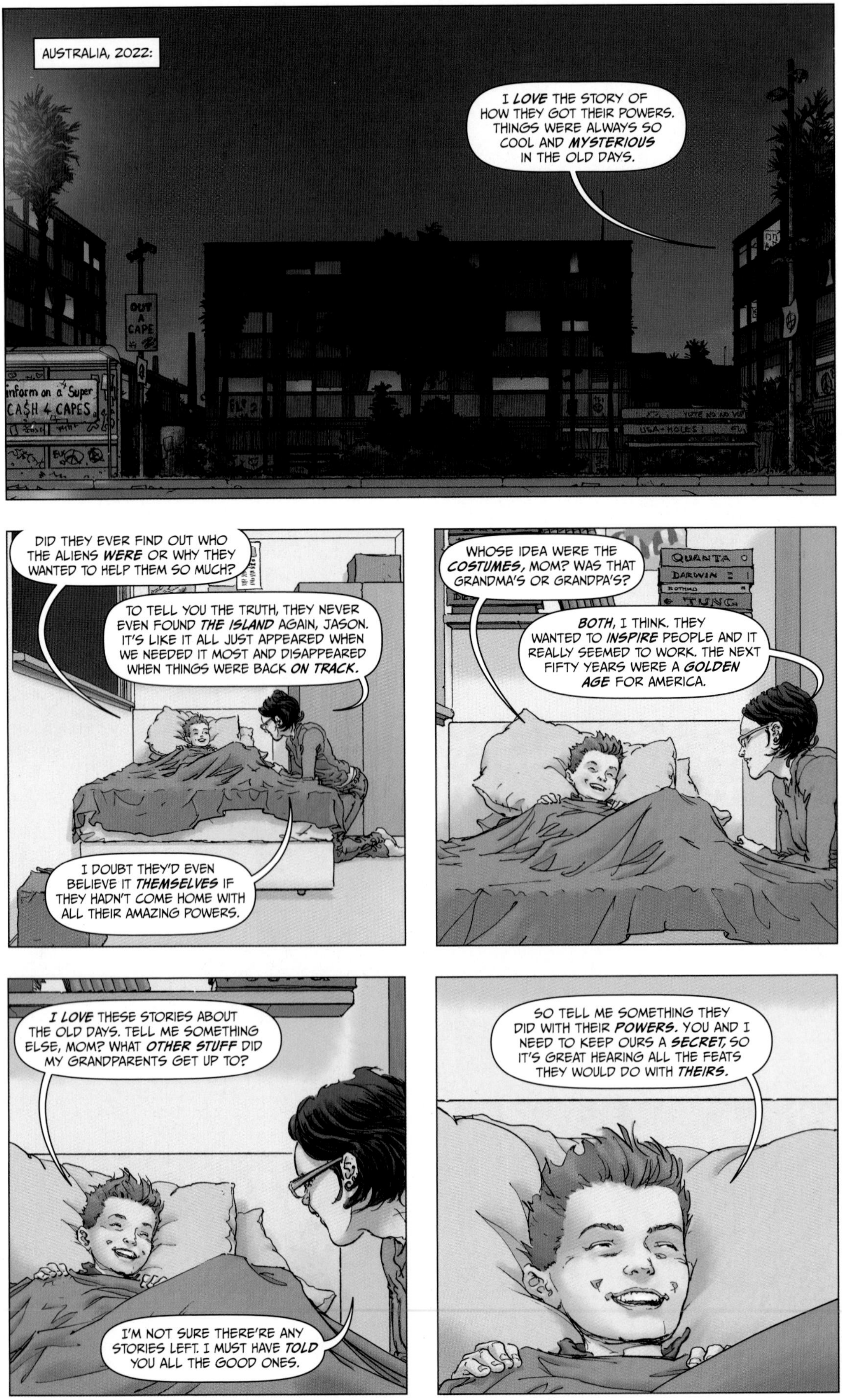
AUSTRALIA, 2022:
I LOVE THE STORY OF HOW THEY GOT THEIR POWERS. THINGS WERE ALWAYS SO COOL AND MYSTERIOUS IN THE OLD DAYS.
OUT A CAPE
inform on a Super
CA$H 4 CAPES
USA-HOLES!
DID THEY EVER FIND OUT WHO THE ALIENS WERE OR WHY THEY WANTED TO HELP THEM SO MUCH?
TO TELL YOU THE TRUTH, THEY NEVER EVEN FOUND THE ISLAND AGAIN, JASON. IT'S LIKE IT ALL JUST APPEARED WHEN WE NEEDED IT MOST AND DISAPPEARED WHEN THINGS WERE BACK ON TRACK.
I DOUBT THEY'D EVEN BELIEVE IT THEMSELVES IF THEY HADN'T COME HOME WITH ALL THEIR AMAZING POWERS.
WHOSE IDEA WERE THE COSTUMES, MOM? WAS THAT GRANDMA'S OR GRANDPA'S?
QUANTA
DARWIN
TUNG
BOTH, I THINK. THEY WANTED TO INSPIRE PEOPLE AND IT REALLY SEEMED TO WORK. THE NEXT FIFTY YEARS WERE A GOLDEN AGE FOR AMERICA.
I LOVE THESE STORIES ABOUT THE OLD DAYS. TELL ME SOMETHING ELSE, MOM? WHAT OTHER STUFF DID MY GRANDPARENTS GET UP TO?
I'M NOT SURE THERE'RE ANY STORIES LEFT. I MUST HAVE TOLD YOU ALL THE GOOD ONES.
SO TELL ME SOMETHING THEY DID WITH THEIR POWERS. YOU AND I NEED TO KEEP OURS A SECRET, SO IT'S GREAT HEARING ALL THE FEATS THEY WOULD DO WITH THEIRS.

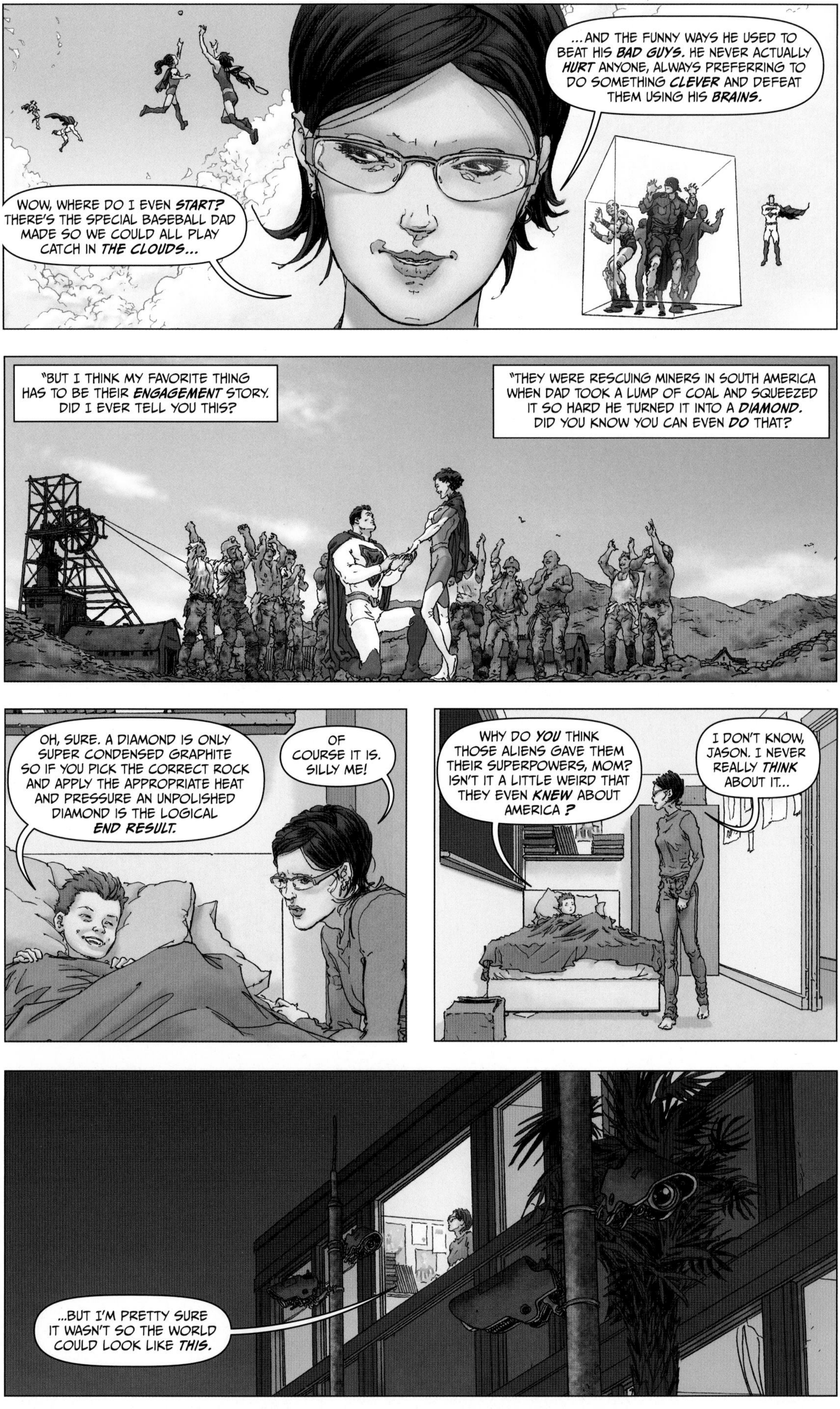
WOW, WHERE DO I EVEN START? THERE'S THE SPECIAL BASEBALL DAD MADE SO WE COULD ALL PLAY CATCH IN THE CLOUDS...
...AND THE FUNNY WAYS HE USED TO BEAT HIS BAD GUYS. HE NEVER ACTUALLY HURT ANYONE, ALWAYS PREFERRING TO DO SOMETHING CLEVER AND DEFEAT THEM USING HIS BRAINS.
"BUT I THINK MY FAVORITE THING HAS TO BE THEIR ENGAGEMENT STORY. DID I EVER TELL YOU THIS?
"THEY WERE RESCUING MINERS IN SOUTH AMERICA WHEN DAD TOOK A LUMP OF COAL AND SQUEEZED IT SO HARD HE TURNED IT INTO A DIAMOND. DID YOU KNOW YOU CAN EVEN DO THAT?
OH, SURE. A DIAMOND IS ONLY SUPER CONDENSED GRAPHITE SO IF YOU PICK THE CORRECT ROCK AND APPLY THE APPROPRIATE HEAT AND PRESSURE AN UNPOLISHED DIAMOND IS THE LOGICAL END RESULT.
OF COURSE IT IS. SILLY ME!
WHY DO YOU THINK THOSE ALIENS GAVE THEM THEIR SUPERPOWERS, MOM? ISN'T IT A LITTLE WEIRD THAT THEY EVEN KNEW ABOUT AMERICA ?
I DON'T KNOW, JASON. I NEVER REALLY THINK ABOUT IT...
...BUT I'M PRETTY SURE IT WASN'T SO THE WORLD COULD LOOK LIKE THIS.

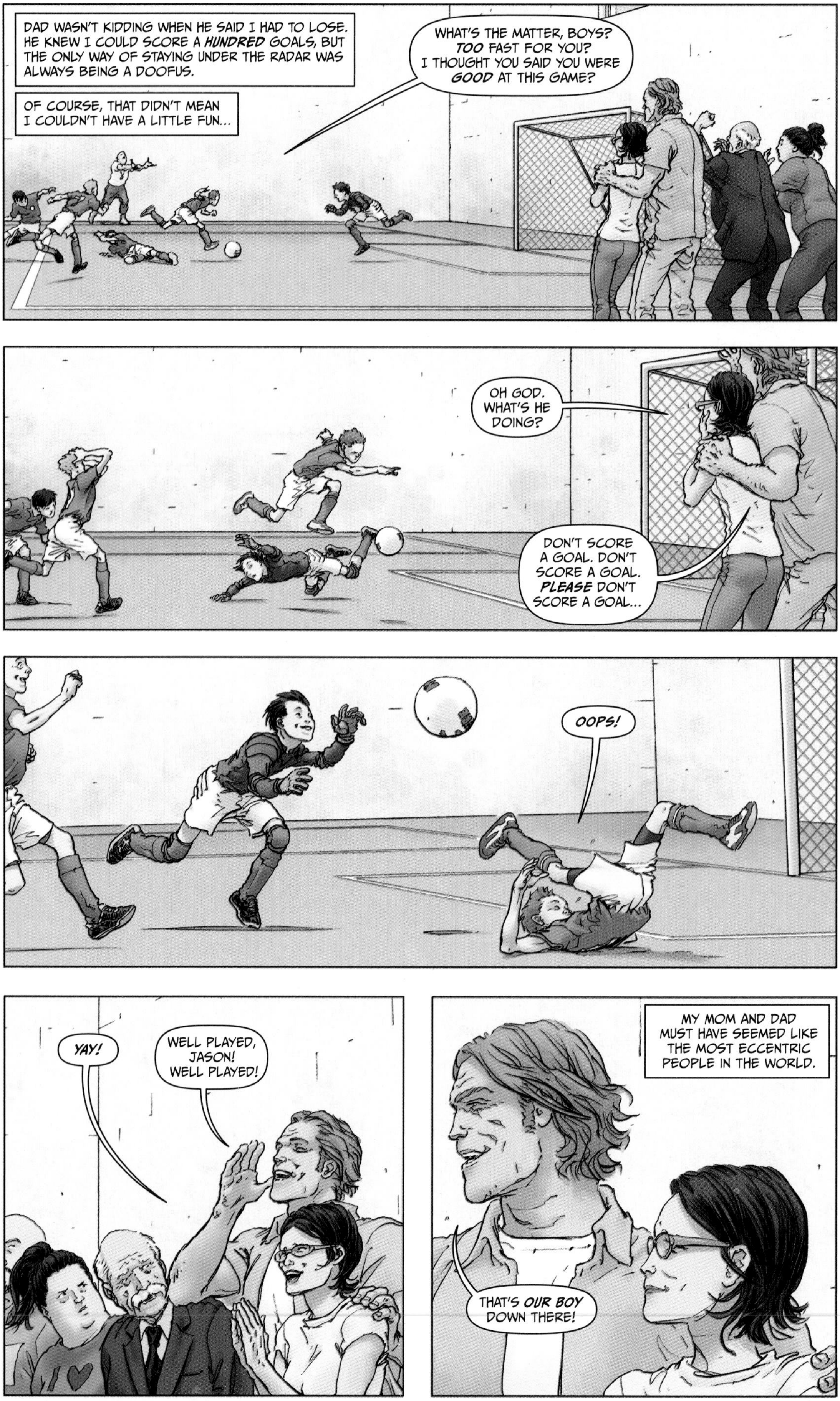
DAD WASN'T KIDDING WHEN HE SAID I HAD TO LOSE. HE KNEW I COULD SCORE A *HUNDRED* GOALS, BUT THE ONLY WAY OF STAYING UNDER THE RADAR WAS ALWAYS BEING A DOOFUS.
OF COURSE, THAT DIDN'T MEAN I COULDN'T HAVE A LITTLE FUN...
WHAT'S THE MATTER, BOYS? *TOO* FAST FOR YOU? I THOUGHT YOU SAID YOU WERE *GOOD* AT THIS GAME?
OH GOD. WHAT'S HE DOING?
DON'T SCORE A GOAL. DON'T SCORE A GOAL. *PLEASE* DON'T SCORE A GOAL...
OOPS!
YAY!
WELL PLAYED, JASON! WELL PLAYED!
MY MOM AND DAD MUST HAVE SEEMED LIKE THE MOST ECCENTRIC PEOPLE IN THE WORLD.
THAT'S *OUR BOY* DOWN THERE!

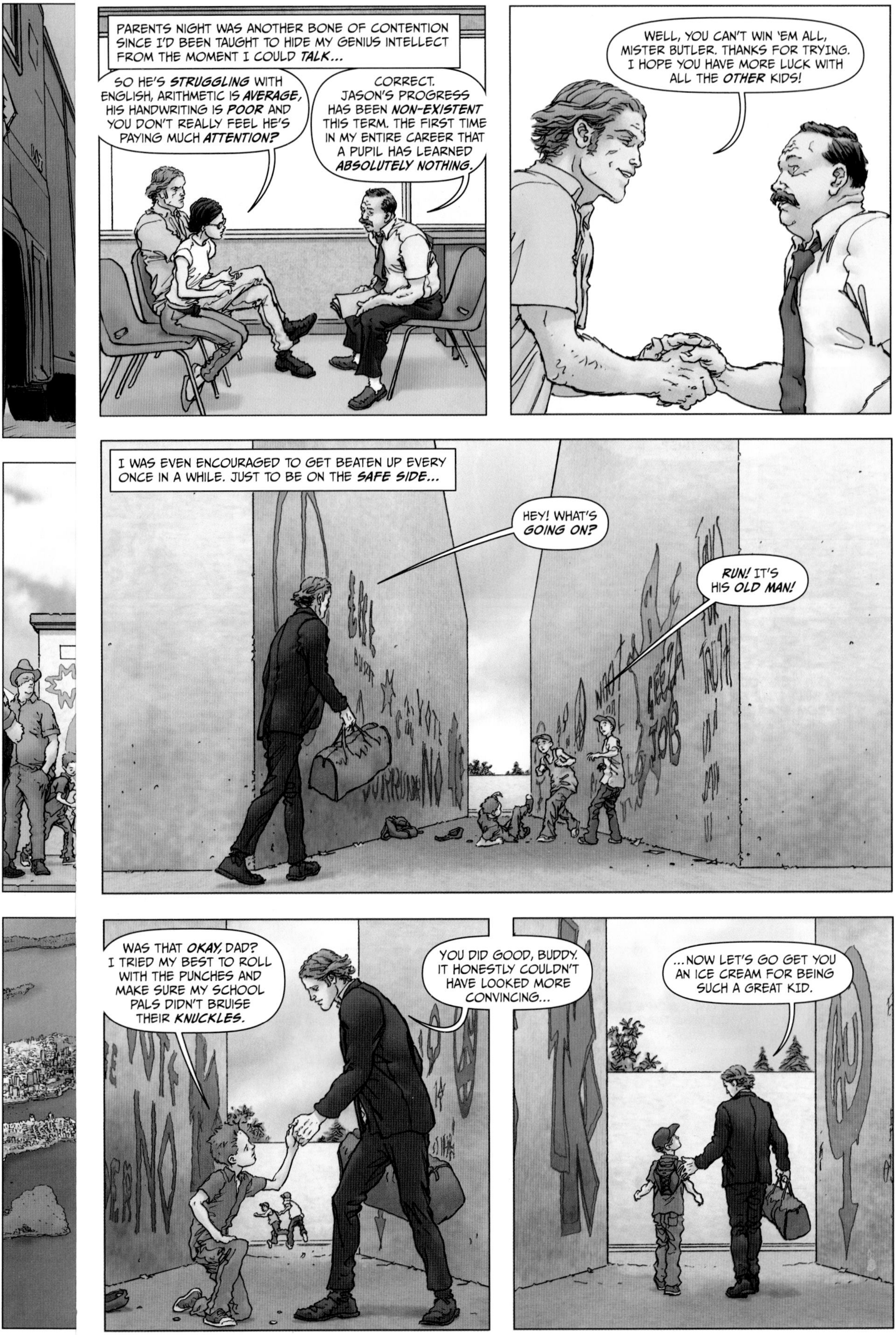

PARENTS NIGHT WAS ANOTHER BONE OF CONTENTION SINCE I'D BEEN TAUGHT TO HIDE MY GENIUS INTELLECT FROM THE MOMENT I COULD TALK...
SO HE'S STRUGGLING WITH ENGLISH, ARITHMETIC IS AVERAGE, HIS HANDWRITING IS POOR AND YOU DON'T REALLY FEEL HE'S PAYING MUCH ATTENTION?
CORRECT. JASON'S PROGRESS HAS BEEN NON-EXISTENT THIS TERM. THE FIRST TIME IN MY ENTIRE CAREER THAT A PUPIL HAS LEARNED ABSOLUTELY NOTHING.
WELL, YOU CAN'T WIN 'EM ALL, MISTER BUTLER. THANKS FOR TRYING. I HOPE YOU HAVE MORE LUCK WITH ALL THE OTHER KIDS!
I WAS EVEN ENCOURAGED TO GET BEATEN UP EVERY ONCE IN A WHILE. JUST TO BE ON THE SAFE SIDE...
HEY! WHAT'S GOING ON?
RUN! IT'S HIS OLD MAN!
WAS THAT OKAY, DAD? I TRIED MY BEST TO ROLL WITH THE PUNCHES AND MAKE SURE MY SCHOOL PALS DIDN'T BRUISE THEIR KNUCKLES.
YOU DID GOOD, BUDDY. IT HONESTLY COULDN'T HAVE LOOKED MORE CONVINCING...
...NOW LET'S GO GET YOU AN ICE CREAM FOR BEING SUCH A GREAT KID.

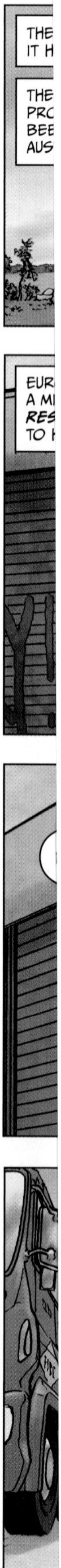

THE
IT H

THE
PRO
BEE
AUS

EUR
A M
RES
TO H

MAN, THAT'S THE WEIRDEST THING I EVER SAW IN MY LIFE. YOU SEE THE WAY THAT THUNDERCLOUD JUST CAME OUT OF *NOWHERE?*

FREAKY.

SEE, THAT'S WHAT I'M ALWAYS TELLING YOUR *MOM.* SUPERHEROES *THINK* THEY NEED TO STICK THEIR NOSES INTO THINGS, BUT LIFE HAS A WAY OF WORKING *ITSELF* OUT.

I COULDN'T AGREE *MORE,* DAD.

NOW LET'S GO HOME SO YOU CAN FAKE FLUNKING YOUR *HOMEWORK.*

SAY NO

35

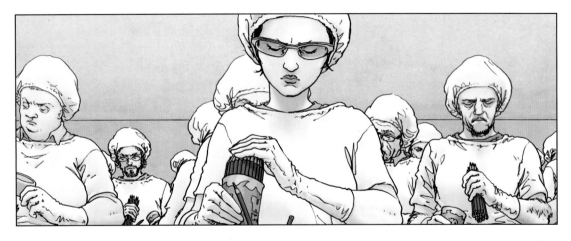

WASHINGTON D.C. :

BRANDON, COME AWAY FROM THE WINDOW AND *IGNORE* THOSE IDIOTS. YOU'RE SUPPOSED TO BE CELEBRATING *NINE YEARS* IN *POWER*.

FOOD BANKS? RIOTS IN THE STREETS? I'M NOT REALLY SURE THERE'S ANYTHING TO *CELEBRATE*, UNCLE WALTER.

THIS ISN'T HOW THINGS WERE SUPPOSED TO *TURN OUT*, MAN. THE PLAN WAS TO MAKE THINGS *BETTER* FOR EVERYONE, BUT IT'S ALL JUST BEEN CONSTANT *GRIEF*.

OH, COME ON. WHERE WAS AMERICA GOING BEFORE *WE* TOOK OVER?

YES, THERE'VE BEEN SETBACKS WITH JOBS AND HOMES, BUT WE'RE OVERTURNING AN *ENTIRE CONSTITUTION* HERE. IT'S ONLY NATURAL THERE ARE GOING TO BE A FEW BUMPS ON *THE ROAD*.

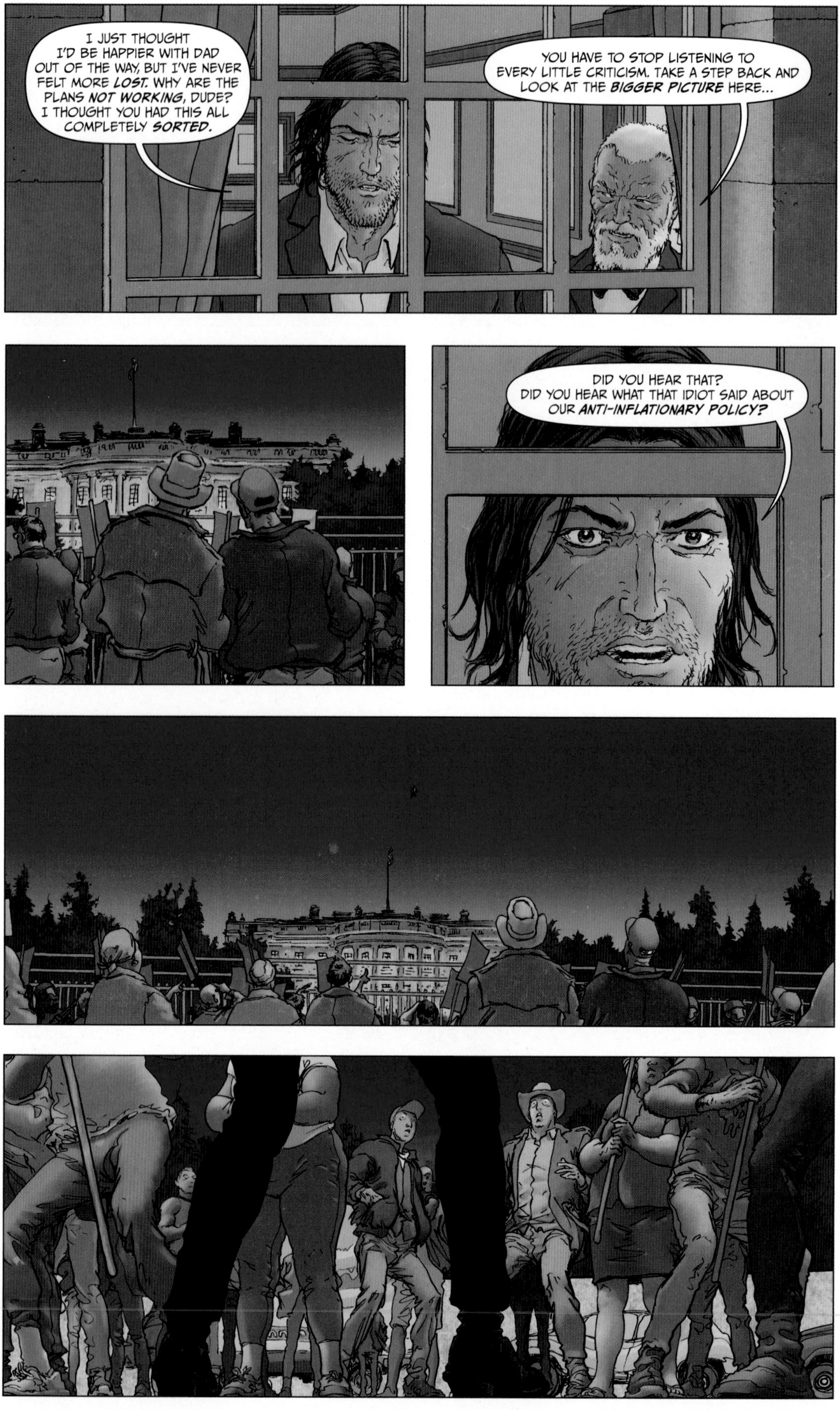
I JUST THOUGHT I'D BE HAPPIER WITH DAD OUT OF THE WAY, BUT I'VE NEVER FELT MORE LOST. WHY ARE THE PLANS NOT WORKING, DUDE? I THOUGHT YOU HAD THIS ALL COMPLETELY SORTED.
YOU HAVE TO STOP LISTENING TO EVERY LITTLE CRITICISM. TAKE A STEP BACK AND LOOK AT THE BIGGER PICTURE HERE...
DID YOU HEAR THAT? DID YOU HEAR WHAT THAT IDIOT SAID ABOUT OUR ANTI-INFLATIONARY POLICY?

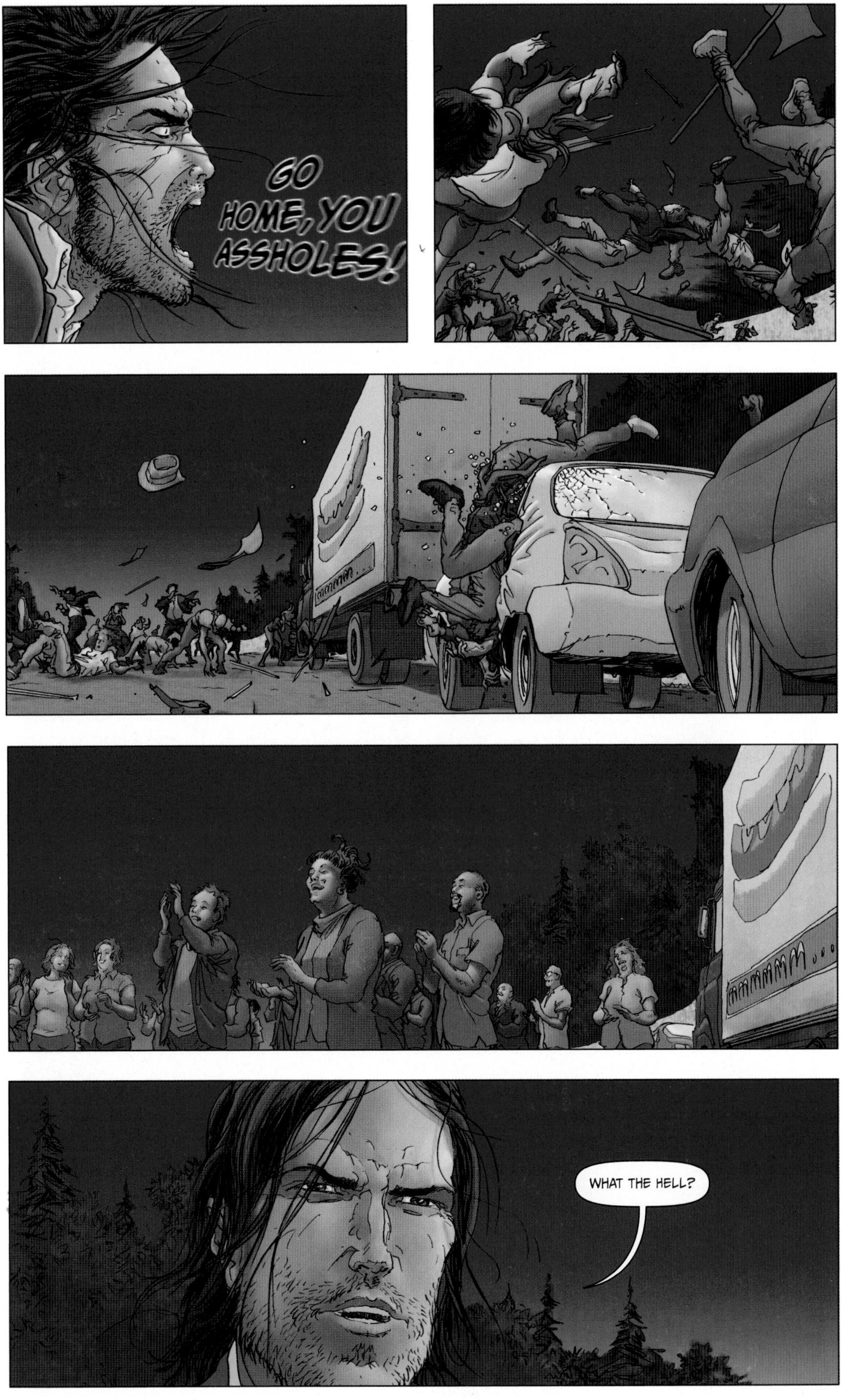
GO HOME, YOU ASSHOLES!
WHAT THE HELL?

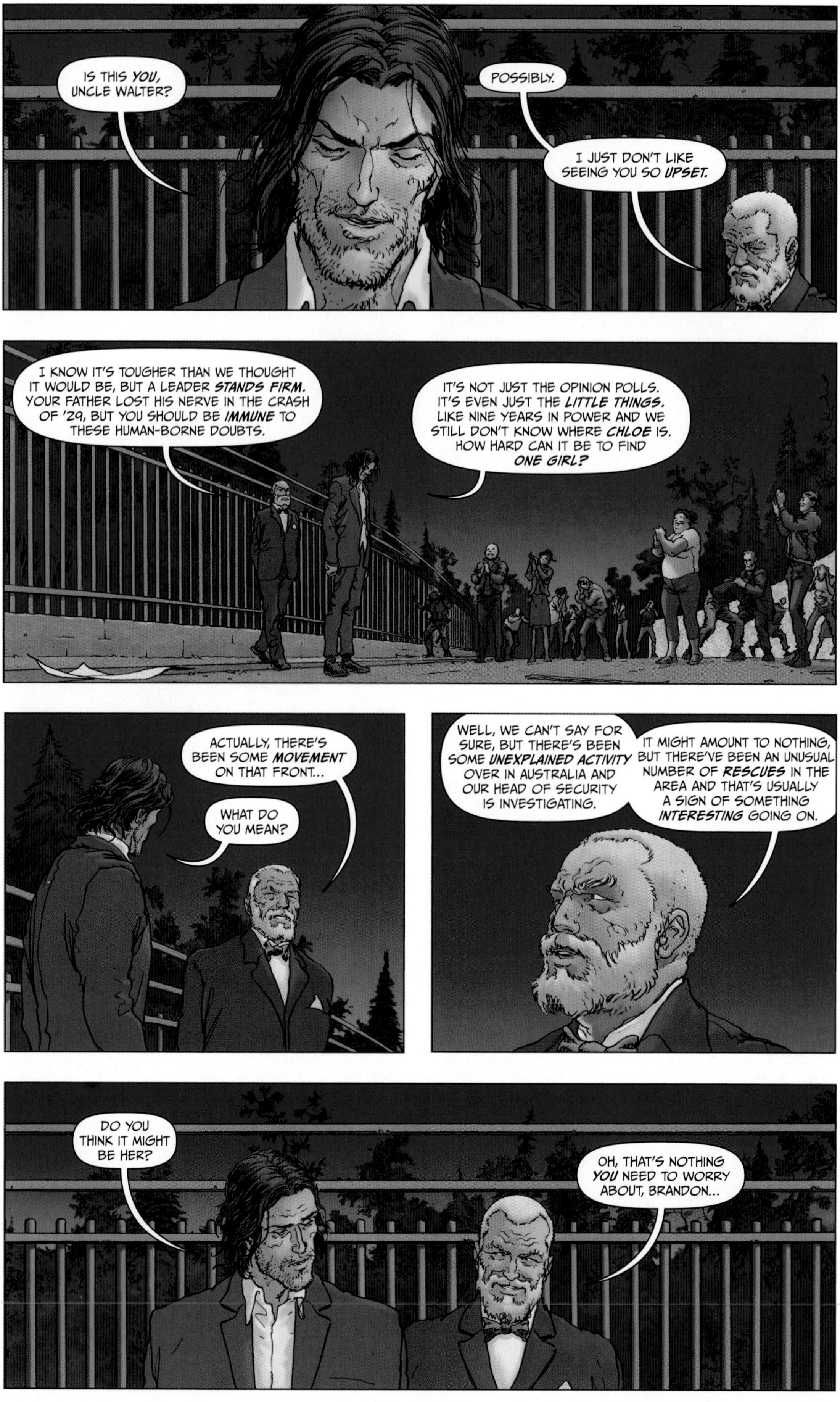
IS THIS YOU, UNCLE WALTER?
POSSIBLY.
I JUST DON'T LIKE SEEING YOU SO UPSET.
I KNOW IT'S TOUGHER THAN WE THOUGHT IT WOULD BE, BUT A LEADER STANDS FIRM. YOUR FATHER LOST HIS NERVE IN THE CRASH OF '29, BUT YOU SHOULD BE IMMUNE TO THESE HUMAN-BORNE DOUBTS.
IT'S NOT JUST THE OPINION POLLS. IT'S EVEN JUST THE LITTLE THINGS. LIKE NINE YEARS IN POWER AND WE STILL DON'T KNOW WHERE CHLOE IS. HOW HARD CAN IT BE TO FIND ONE GIRL?
ACTUALLY, THERE'S BEEN SOME MOVEMENT ON THAT FRONT...
WHAT DO YOU MEAN?
WELL, WE CAN'T SAY FOR SURE, BUT THERE'S BEEN SOME UNEXPLAINED ACTIVITY OVER IN AUSTRALIA AND OUR HEAD OF SECURITY IS INVESTIGATING.
IT MIGHT AMOUNT TO NOTHING, BUT THERE'VE BEEN AN UNUSUAL NUMBER OF RESCUES IN THE AREA AND THAT'S USUALLY A SIGN OF SOMETHING INTERESTING GOING ON.
DO YOU THINK IT MIGHT BE HER?
OH, THAT'S NOTHING YOU NEED TO WORRY ABOUT, BRANDON...

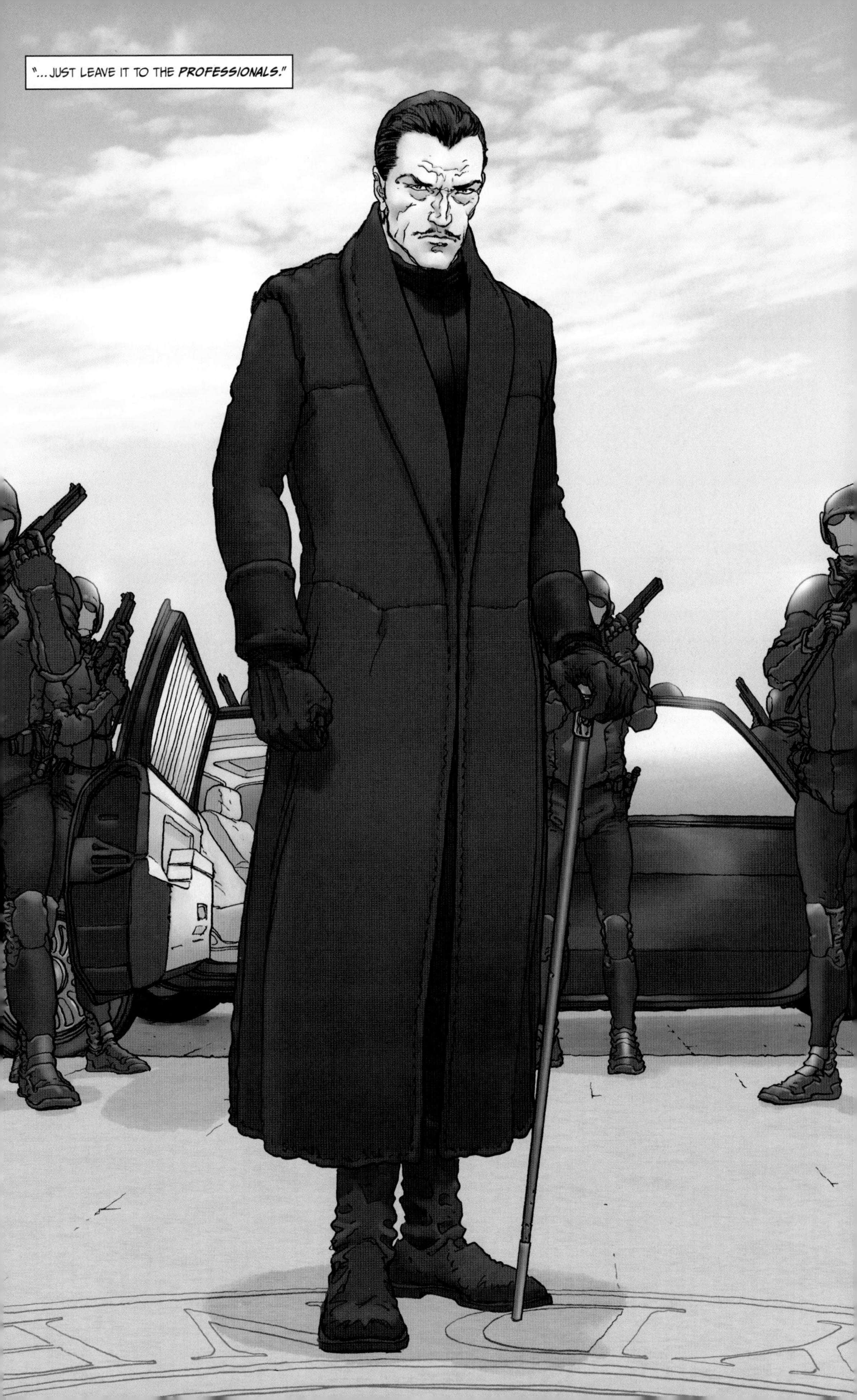
"...JUST LEAVE IT TO THE *PROFESSIONALS.*"

CHAPTER 5

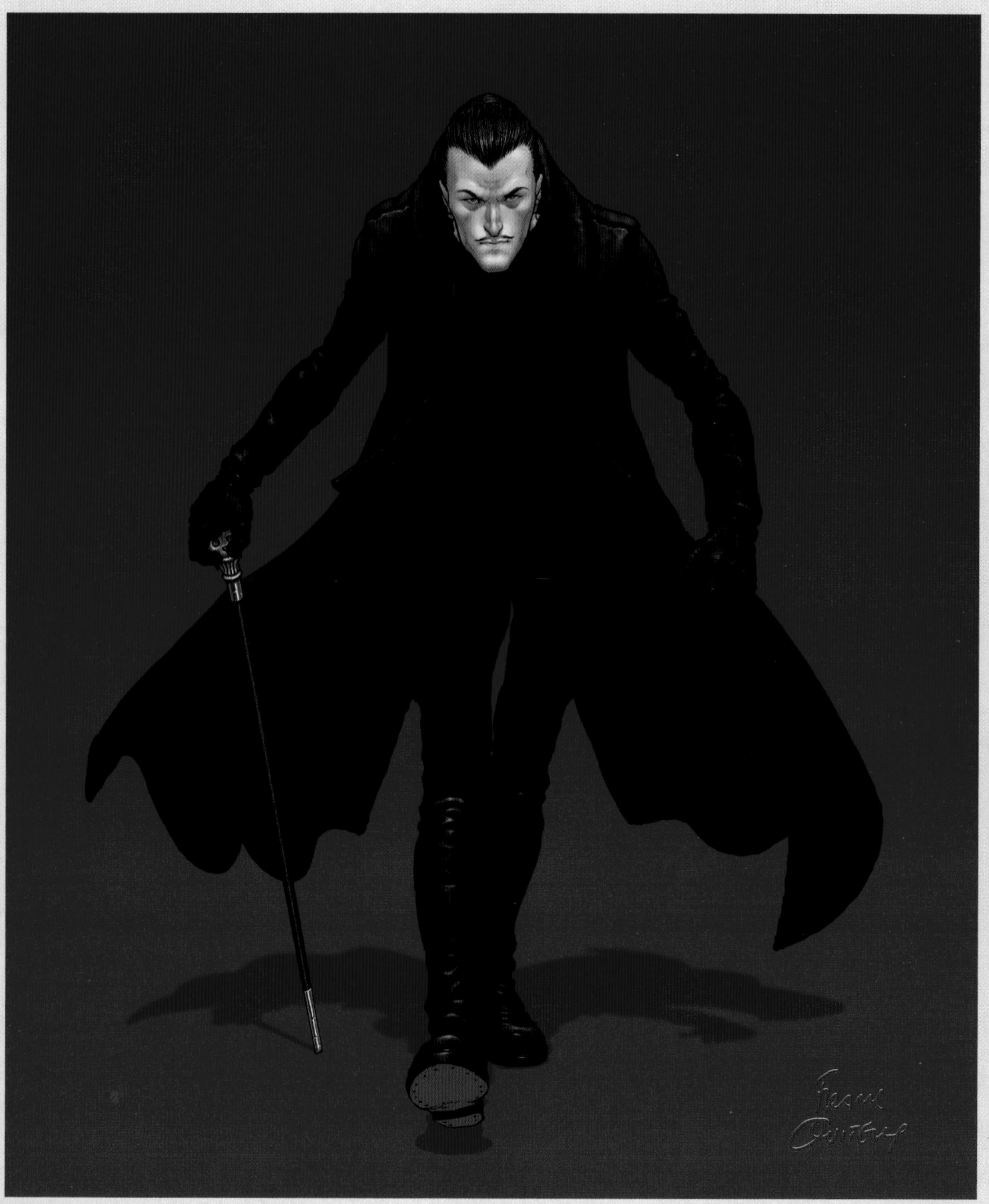

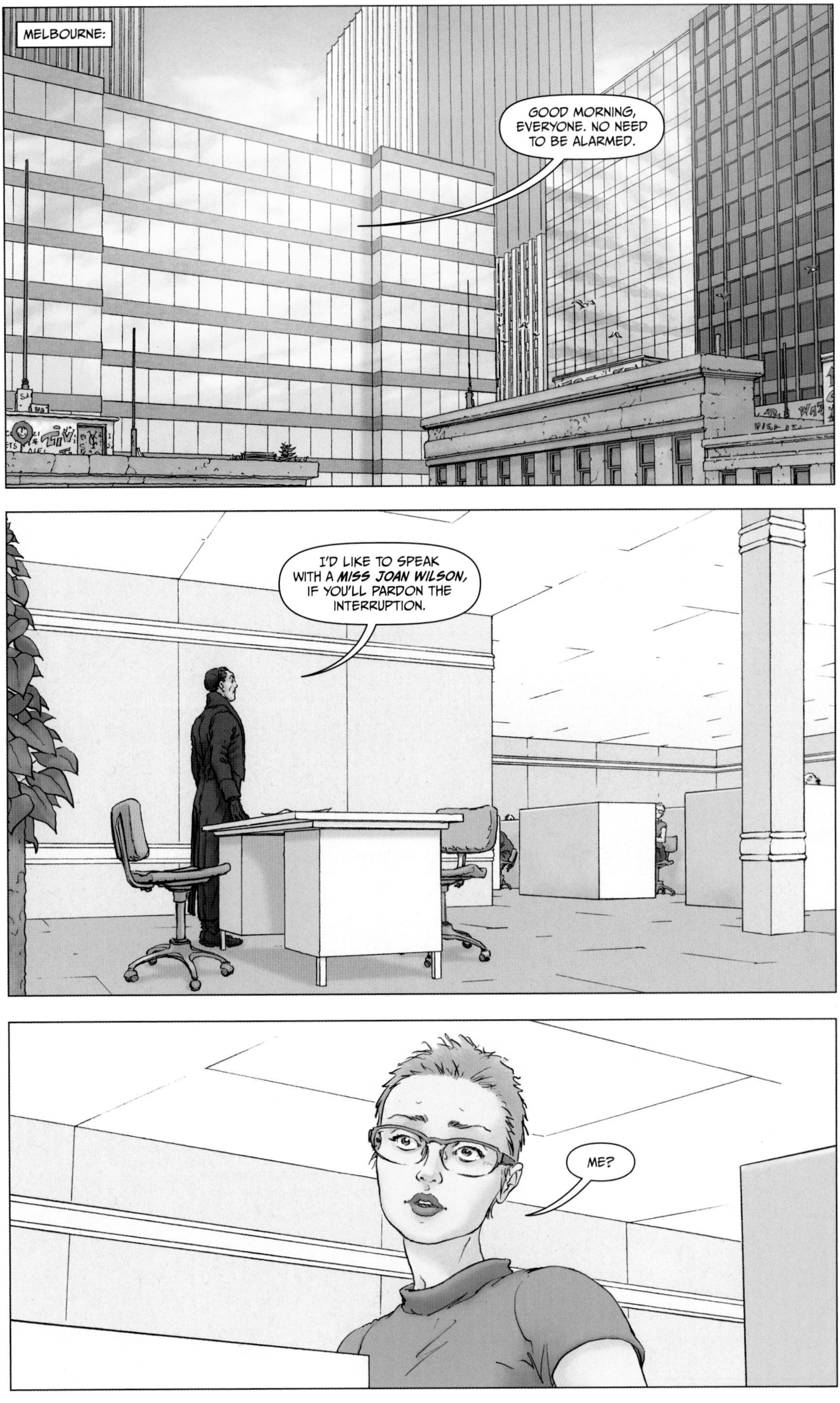
MELBOURNE:
GOOD MORNING, EVERYONE. NO NEED TO BE ALARMED.
I'D LIKE TO SPEAK WITH A MISS JOAN WILSON, IF YOU'LL PARDON THE INTERRUPTION.
ME?

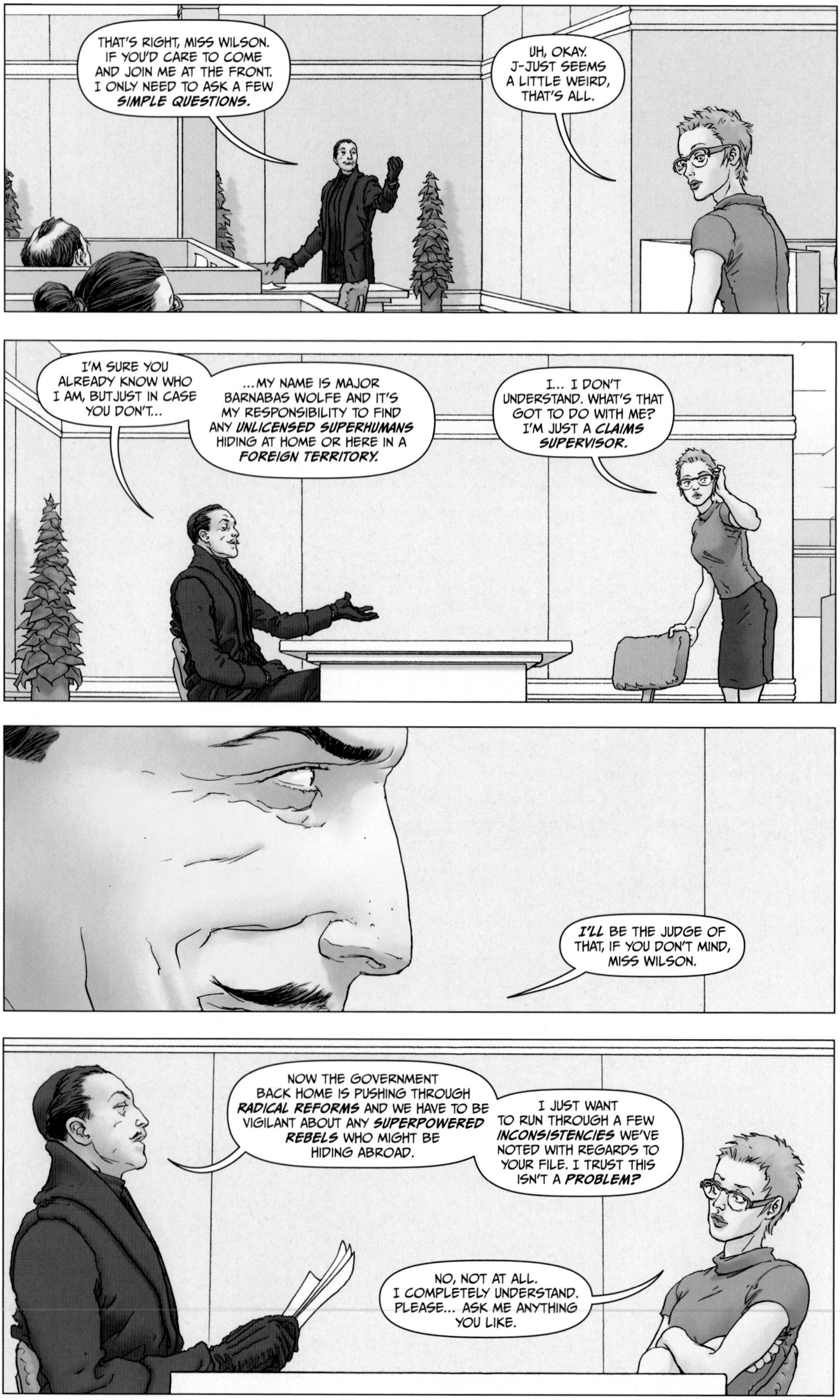
THAT'S RIGHT, MISS WILSON. IF YOU'D CARE TO COME AND JOIN ME AT THE FRONT. I ONLY NEED TO ASK A FEW *SIMPLE QUESTIONS.*
UH, OKAY. J-JUST SEEMS A LITTLE WEIRD, THAT'S ALL.
I'M SURE YOU ALREADY KNOW WHO I AM, BUTJUST IN CASE YOU DON'T...
...MY NAME IS MAJOR BARNABAS WOLFE AND IT'S MY RESPONSIBILITY TO FIND ANY *UNLICENSED SUPERHUMANS* HIDING AT HOME OR HERE IN A *FOREIGN TERRITORY.*
I... I DON'T UNDERSTAND. WHAT'S THAT GOT TO DO WITH ME? I'M JUST A *CLAIMS SUPERVISOR.*
I'LL BE THE JUDGE OF THAT, IF YOU DON'T MIND, MISS WILSON.
NOW THE GOVERNMENT BACK HOME IS PUSHING THROUGH *RADICAL REFORMS* AND WE HAVE TO BE VIGILANT ABOUT ANY *SUPERPOWERED REBELS* WHO MIGHT BE HIDING ABROAD.
I JUST WANT TO RUN THROUGH A FEW *INCONSISTENCIES* WE'VE NOTED WITH REGARDS TO YOUR FILE. I TRUST THIS ISN'T A *PROBLEM?*
NO, NOT AT ALL. I COMPLETELY UNDERSTAND. PLEASE... ASK ME ANYTHING YOU LIKE.

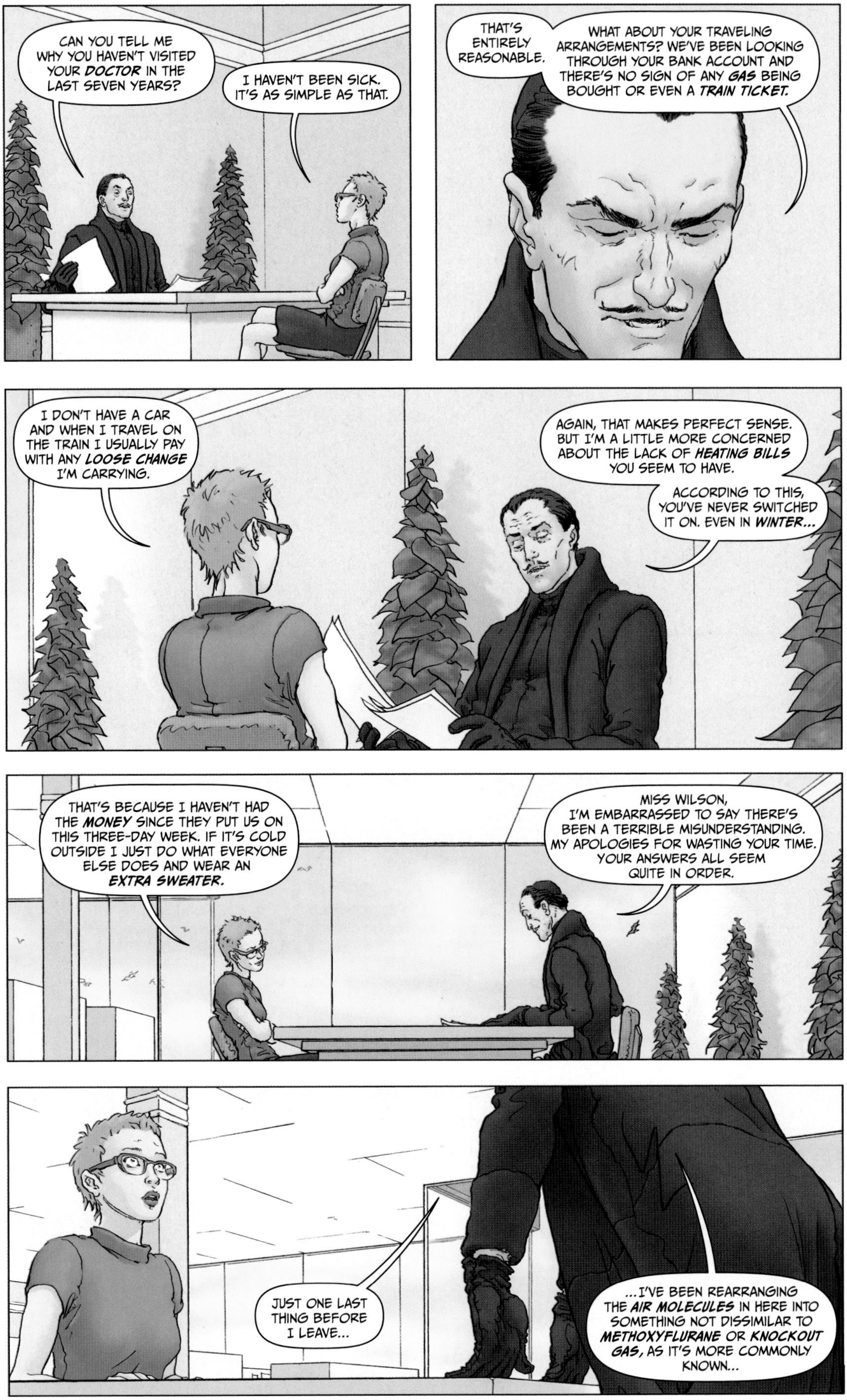
CAN YOU TELL ME WHY YOU HAVEN'T VISITED YOUR DOCTOR IN THE LAST SEVEN YEARS?
I HAVEN'T BEEN SICK. IT'S AS SIMPLE AS THAT.
THAT'S ENTIRELY REASONABLE.
WHAT ABOUT YOUR TRAVELING ARRANGEMENTS? WE'VE BEEN LOOKING THROUGH YOUR BANK ACCOUNT AND THERE'S NO SIGN OF ANY GAS BEING BOUGHT OR EVEN A TRAIN TICKET.
I DON'T HAVE A CAR AND WHEN I TRAVEL ON THE TRAIN I USUALLY PAY WITH ANY LOOSE CHANGE I'M CARRYING.
AGAIN, THAT MAKES PERFECT SENSE. BUT I'M A LITTLE MORE CONCERNED ABOUT THE LACK OF HEATING BILLS YOU SEEM TO HAVE.
ACCORDING TO THIS, YOU'VE NEVER SWITCHED IT ON. EVEN IN WINTER...
THAT'S BECAUSE I HAVEN'T HAD THE MONEY SINCE THEY PUT US ON THIS THREE-DAY WEEK. IF IT'S COLD OUTSIDE I JUST DO WHAT EVERYONE ELSE DOES AND WEAR AN EXTRA SWEATER.
MISS WILSON, I'M EMBARRASSED TO SAY THERE'S BEEN A TERRIBLE MISUNDERSTANDING. MY APOLOGIES FOR WASTING YOUR TIME. YOUR ANSWERS ALL SEEM QUITE IN ORDER.
JUST ONE LAST THING BEFORE I LEAVE...
...I'VE BEEN REARRANGING THE AIR MOLECULES IN HERE INTO SOMETHING NOT DISSIMILAR TO METHOXYFLURANE OR KNOCKOUT GAS, AS IT'S MORE COMMONLY KNOWN...

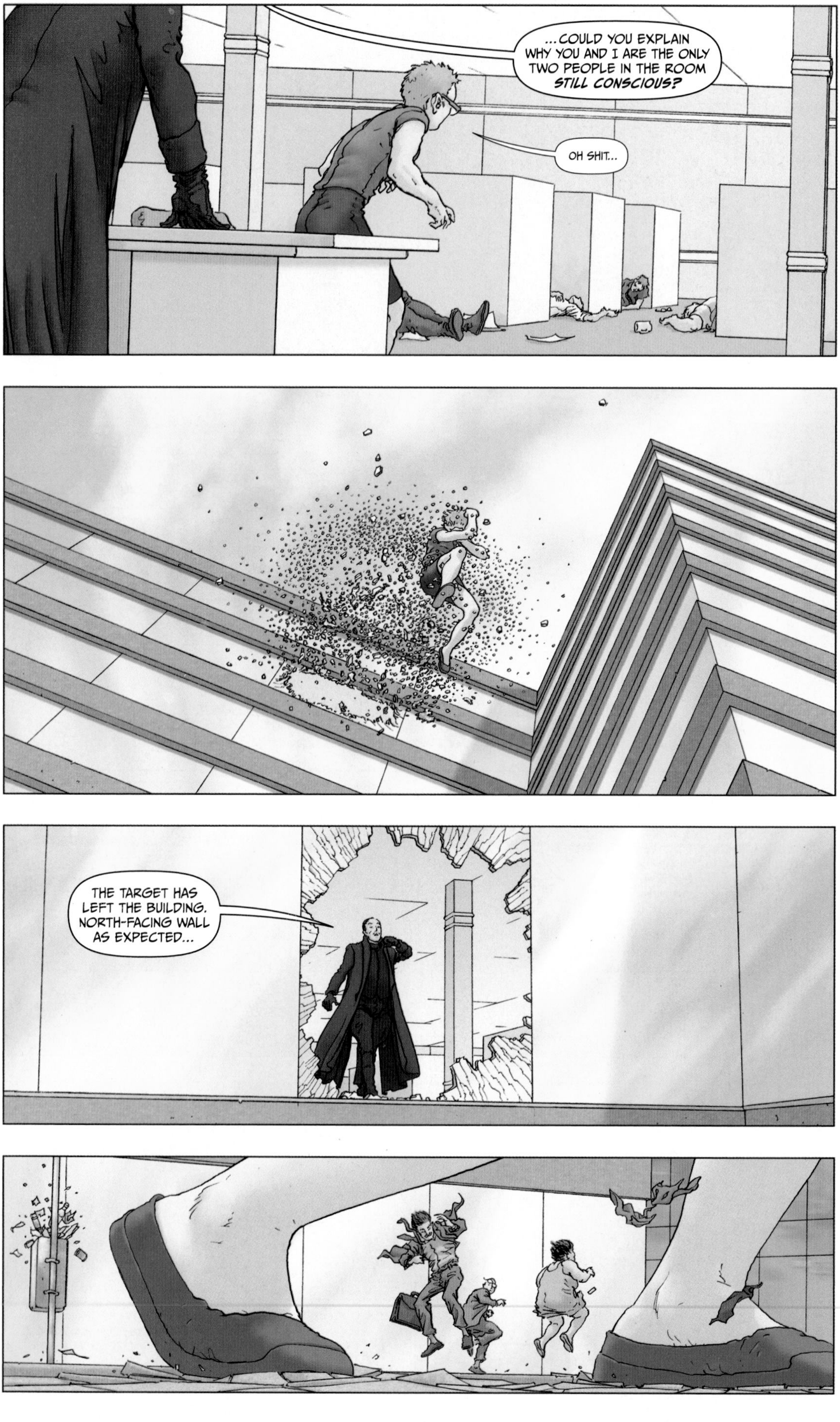
...COULD YOU EXPLAIN WHY YOU AND I ARE THE ONLY TWO PEOPLE IN THE ROOM STILL CONSCIOUS?
OH SHIT...
THE TARGET HAS LEFT THE BUILDING. NORTH-FACING WALL AS EXPECTED...

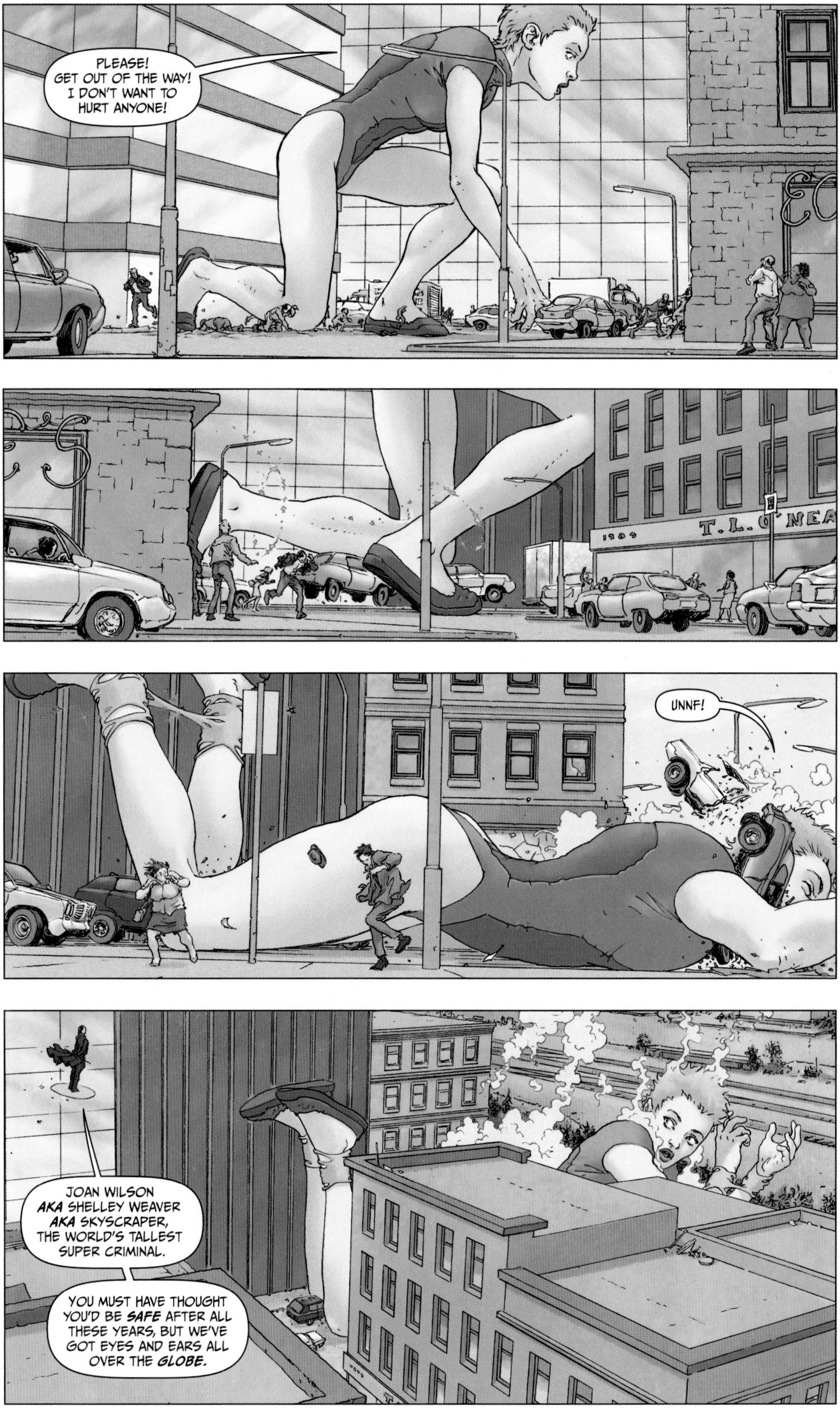
PLEASE! GET OUT OF THE WAY! I DON'T WANT TO HURT ANYONE!
UNNF!
JOAN WILSON **AKA** SHELLEY WEAVER **AKA** SKYSCRAPER, THE WORLD'S TALLEST SUPER CRIMINAL.
YOU MUST HAVE THOUGHT YOU'D BE ***SAFE*** AFTER ALL THESE YEARS, BUT WE'VE GOT EYES AND EARS ALL OVER THE ***GLOBE.***

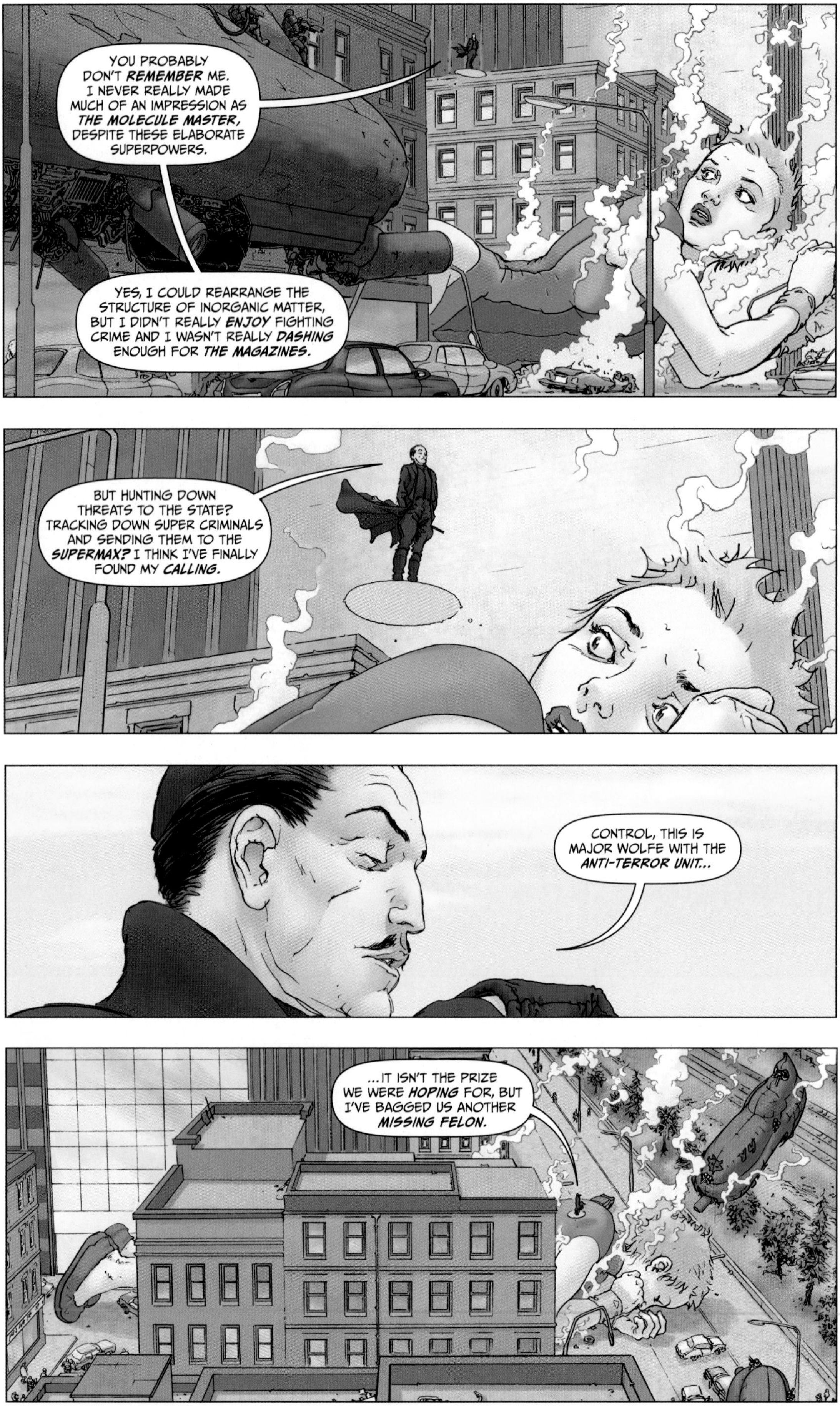
YOU PROBABLY DON'T REMEMBER ME. I NEVER REALLY MADE MUCH OF AN IMPRESSION AS THE MOLECULE MASTER, DESPITE THESE ELABORATE SUPERPOWERS.
YES, I COULD REARRANGE THE STRUCTURE OF INORGANIC MATTER, BUT I DIDN'T REALLY ENJOY FIGHTING CRIME AND I WASN'T REALLY DASHING ENOUGH FOR THE MAGAZINES.
BUT HUNTING DOWN THREATS TO THE STATE? TRACKING DOWN SUPER CRIMINALS AND SENDING THEM TO THE SUPERMAX? I THINK I'VE FINALLY FOUND MY CALLING.
CONTROL, THIS IS MAJOR WOLFE WITH THE ANTI-TERROR UNIT...
...IT ISN'T THE PRIZE WE WERE HOPING FOR, BUT I'VE BAGGED US ANOTHER MISSING FELON.

I LOVE COMING UP WITH SILLY EXCUSES TO GET OUT OF SCHOOL AND HELP WITH *EMERGENCIES.*

PRETENDING TO GET SEASICK WHILE READING *MOBY-DICK* GAVE ME A CHANCE TO RESCUE A *SKY DIVER* AND PULL A TROUBLED *CRUISE SHIP* INTO SAFER WATERS.

I DON'T REALLY MIND THE OTHER KIDS THINKING I'M A WET BLANKET.

A CLUMSY ALTER EGO IS A USEFUL TOOL FOR ANY SUPERHERO AND IF MY *GRANDFATHER* DIDN'T MIND TRIPPING OVER HIS SHOELACES, I DON'T SEE WHY IT SHOULD BOTHER *ME.*

BESIDES, NOT HAVING ANY FRIENDS TO HANG OUT WITH MEANS I CAN SPEND MY LUNCH BREAKS UP HERE WORKING ON MY *SECRET PROJECT.*

I'VE GOT MY FLIGHT TIME HERE AND BACK DOWN TO *NINETEEN MINUTES* AS OF YESTERDAY. THAT'S *PLENTY* OF TIME TO GET BACK FOR THE FIRST CLASS OF THE *AFTERNOON.*

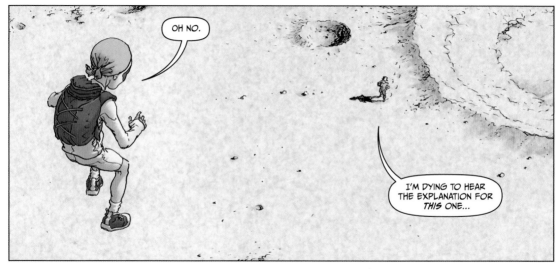

OH NO.

I'M DYING TO HEAR THE EXPLANATION FOR *THIS* ONE...

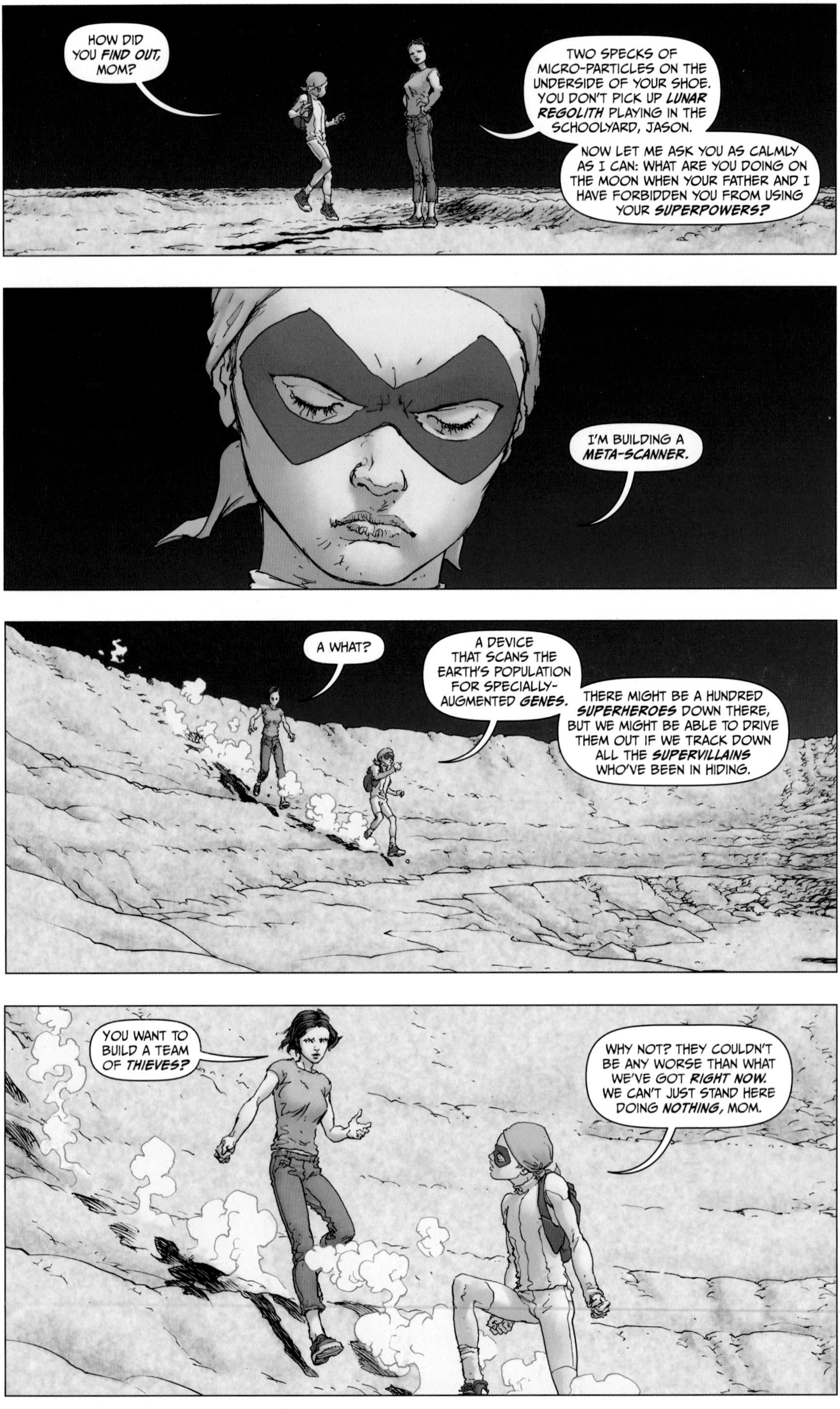
HOW DID YOU FIND OUT, MOM?
TWO SPECKS OF MICRO-PARTICLES ON THE UNDERSIDE OF YOUR SHOE. YOU DON'T PICK UP LUNAR REGOLITH PLAYING IN THE SCHOOLYARD, JASON.
NOW LET ME ASK YOU AS CALMLY AS I CAN: WHAT ARE YOU DOING ON THE MOON WHEN YOUR FATHER AND I HAVE FORBIDDEN YOU FROM USING YOUR SUPERPOWERS?
I'M BUILDING A META-SCANNER.
A WHAT?
A DEVICE THAT SCANS THE EARTH'S POPULATION FOR SPECIALLY-AUGMENTED GENES.
THERE MIGHT BE A HUNDRED SUPERHEROES DOWN THERE, BUT WE MIGHT BE ABLE TO DRIVE THEM OUT IF WE TRACK DOWN ALL THE SUPERVILLAINS WHO'VE BEEN IN HIDING.
YOU WANT TO BUILD A TEAM OF THIEVES?
WHY NOT? THEY COULDN'T BE ANY WORSE THAN WHAT WE'VE GOT RIGHT NOW. WE CAN'T JUST STAND HERE DOING NOTHING, MOM.

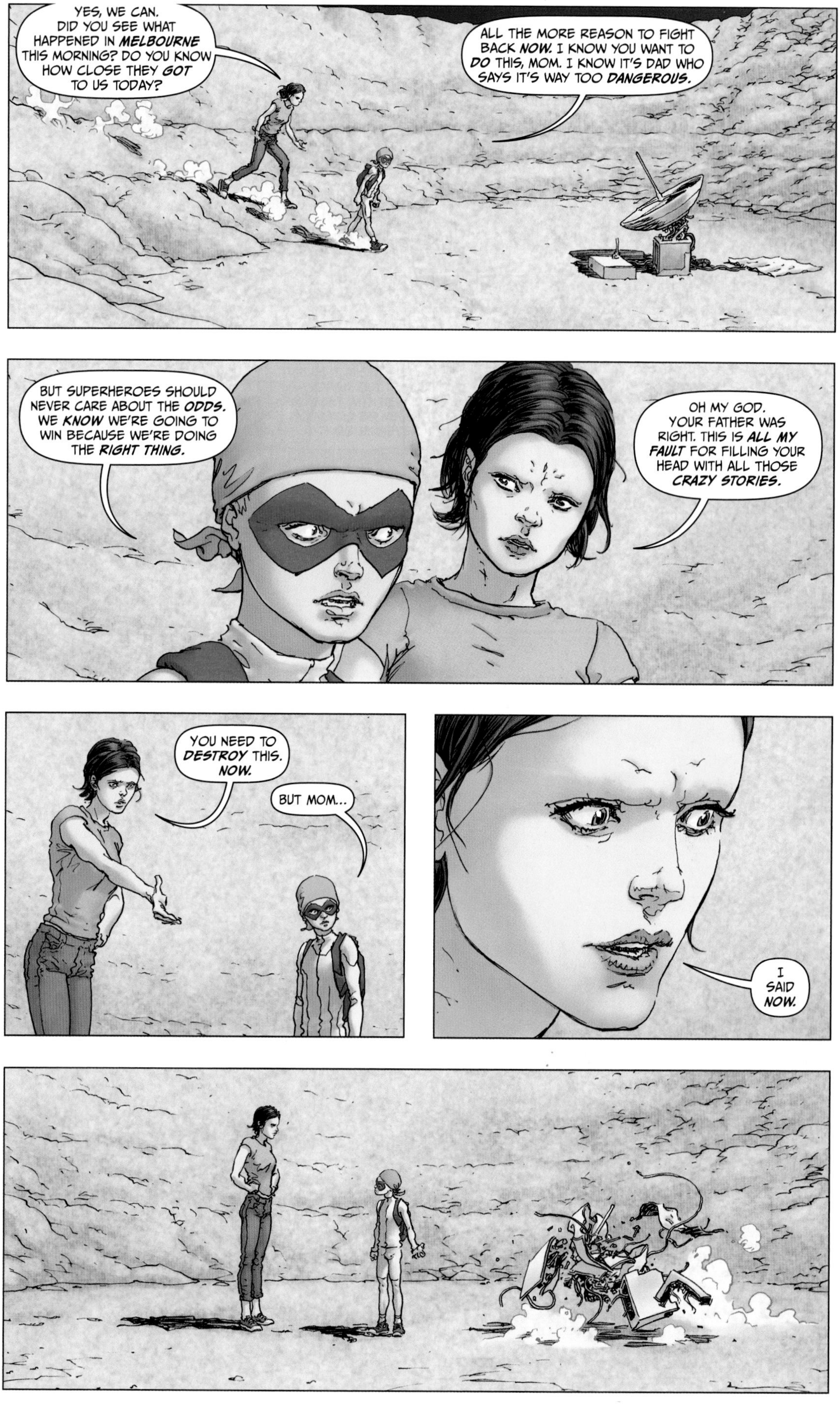
YES, WE CAN. DID YOU SEE WHAT HAPPENED IN MELBOURNE THIS MORNING? DO YOU KNOW HOW CLOSE THEY GOT TO US TODAY?
ALL THE MORE REASON TO FIGHT BACK NOW. I KNOW YOU WANT TO DO THIS, MOM. I KNOW IT'S DAD WHO SAYS IT'S WAY TOO DANGEROUS.
BUT SUPERHEROES SHOULD NEVER CARE ABOUT THE ODDS. WE KNOW WE'RE GOING TO WIN BECAUSE WE'RE DOING THE RIGHT THING.
OH MY GOD. YOUR FATHER WAS RIGHT. THIS IS ALL MY FAULT FOR FILLING YOUR HEAD WITH ALL THOSE CRAZY STORIES.
YOU NEED TO DESTROY THIS. NOW.
BUT MOM...
I SAID NOW.

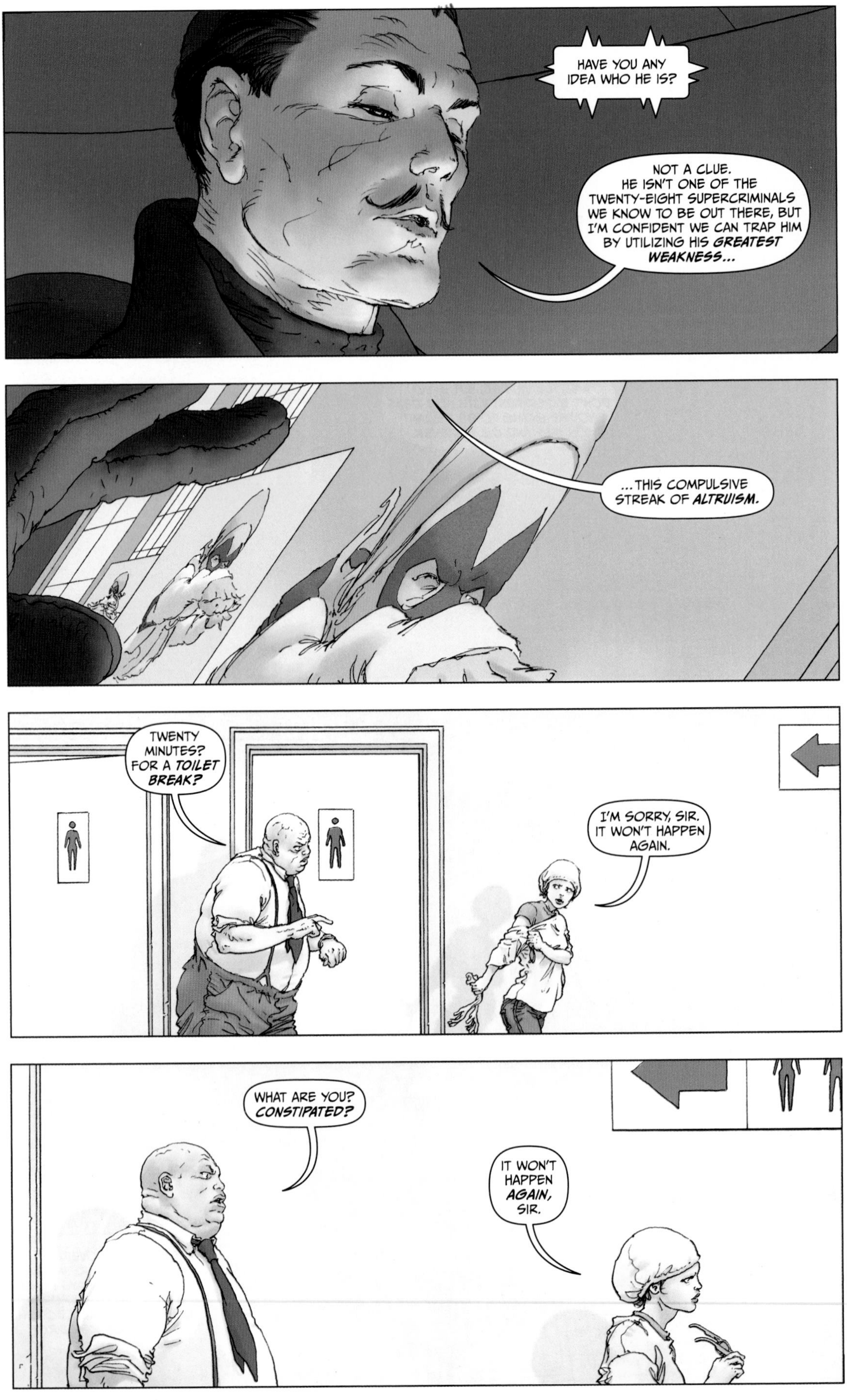
HAVE YOU ANY IDEA WHO HE IS?
NOT A CLUE. HE ISN'T ONE OF THE TWENTY-EIGHT SUPERCRIMINALS WE KNOW TO BE OUT THERE, BUT I'M CONFIDENT WE CAN TRAP HIM BY UTILIZING HIS GREATEST WEAKNESS...
...THIS COMPULSIVE STREAK OF ALTRUISM.
TWENTY MINUTES? FOR A TOILET BREAK?
I'M SORRY, SIR. IT WON'T HAPPEN AGAIN.
WHAT ARE YOU? CONSTIPATED?
IT WON'T HAPPEN AGAIN, SIR.

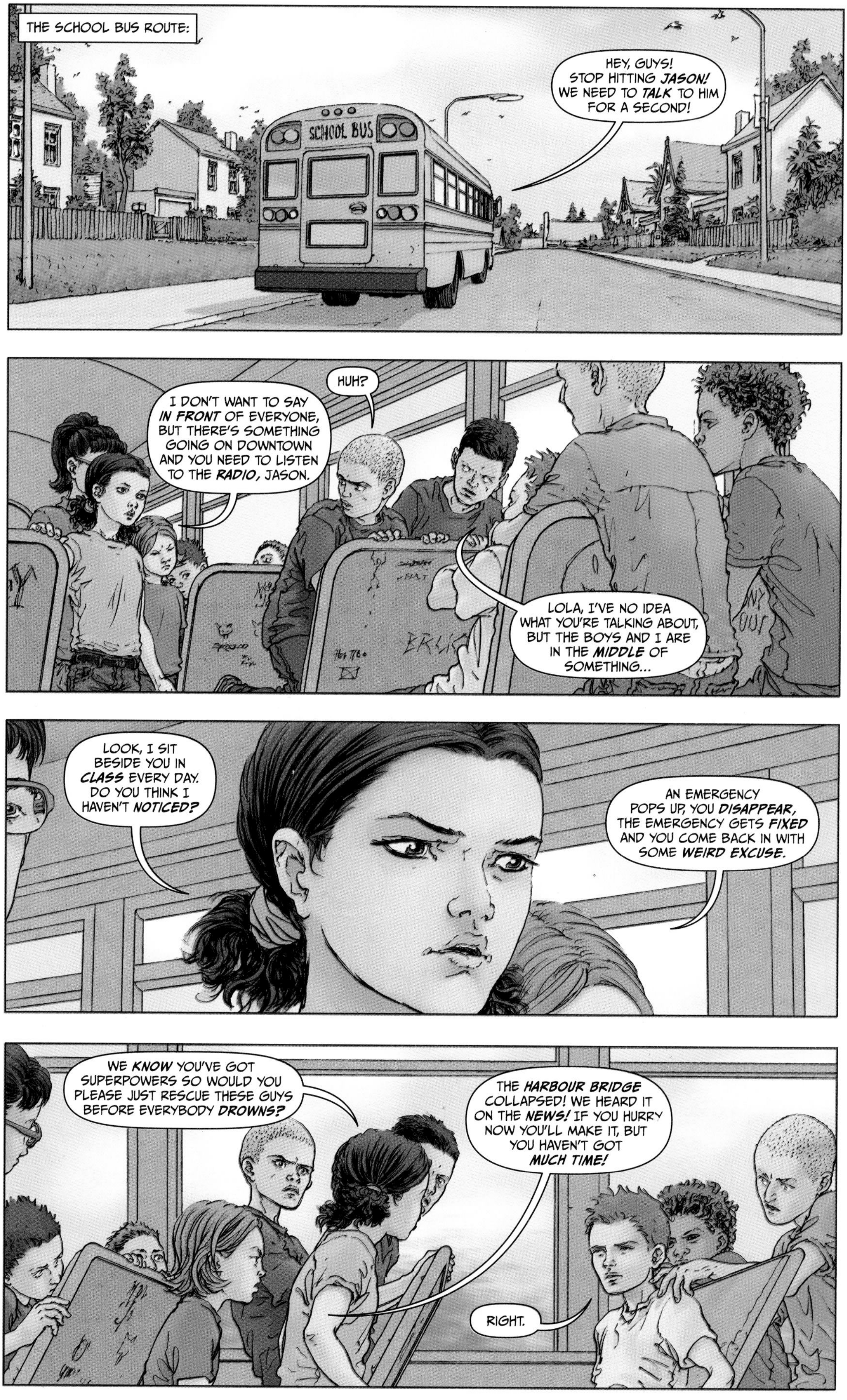
THE SCHOOL BUS ROUTE:
SCHOOL BUS
HEY, GUYS! STOP HITTING JASON! WE NEED TO TALK TO HIM FOR A SECOND!
I DON'T WANT TO SAY IN FRONT OF EVERYONE, BUT THERE'S SOMETHING GOING ON DOWNTOWN AND YOU NEED TO LISTEN TO THE RADIO, JASON.
HUH?
LOLA, I'VE NO IDEA WHAT YOU'RE TALKING ABOUT, BUT THE BOYS AND I ARE IN THE MIDDLE OF SOMETHING...
LOOK, I SIT BESIDE YOU IN CLASS EVERY DAY. DO YOU THINK I HAVEN'T NOTICED?
AN EMERGENCY POPS UP, YOU DISAPPEAR, THE EMERGENCY GETS FIXED AND YOU COME BACK IN WITH SOME WEIRD EXCUSE.
WE KNOW YOU'VE GOT SUPERPOWERS SO WOULD YOU PLEASE JUST RESCUE THESE GUYS BEFORE EVERYBODY DROWNS?
THE HARBOUR BRIDGE COLLAPSED! WE HEARD IT ON THE NEWS! IF YOU HURRY NOW YOU'LL MAKE IT, BUT YOU HAVEN'T GOT MUCH TIME!
RIGHT.

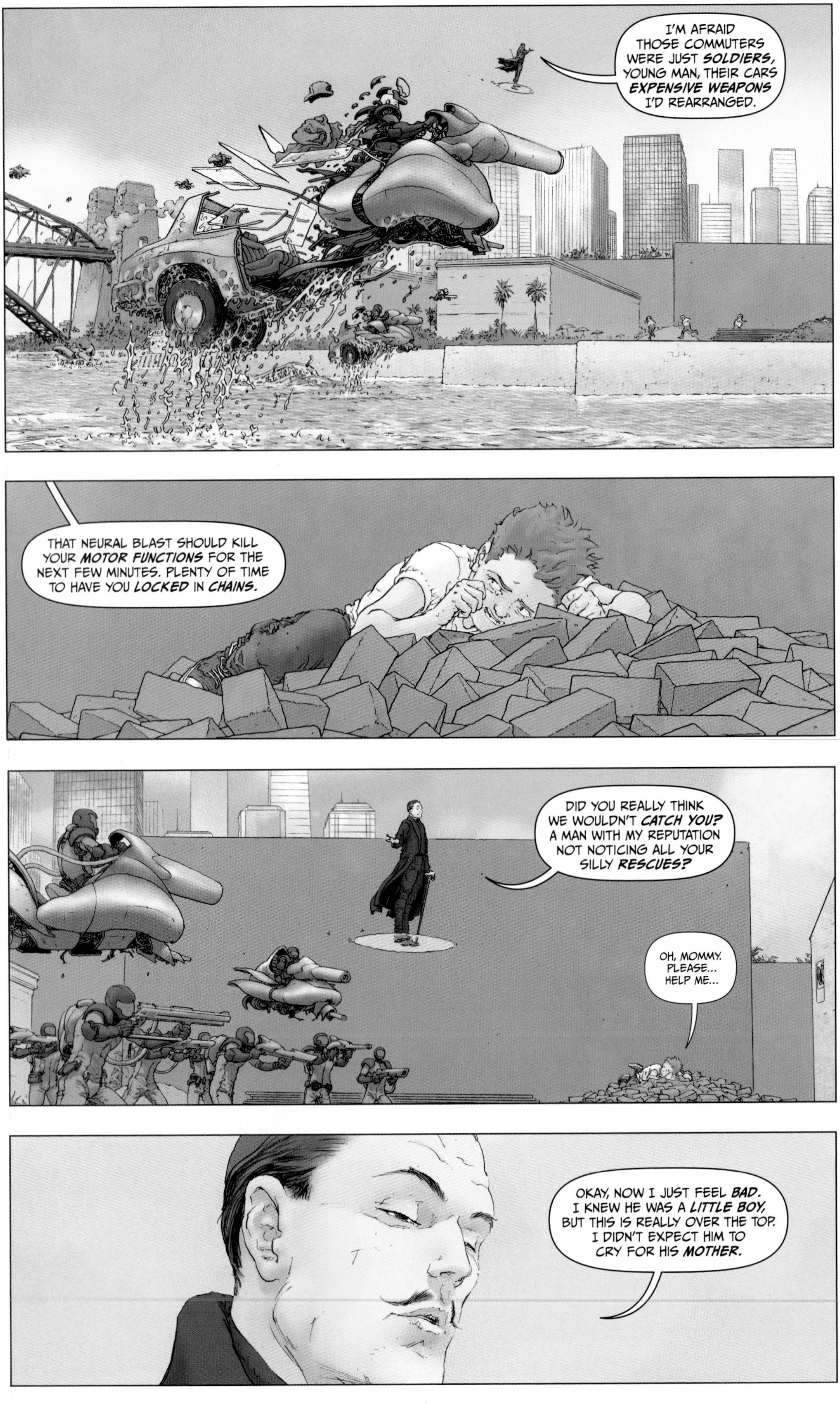
I'M AFRAID THOSE COMMUTERS WERE JUST SOLDIERS, YOUNG MAN, THEIR CARS EXPENSIVE WEAPONS I'D REARRANGED.
THAT NEURAL BLAST SHOULD KILL YOUR MOTOR FUNCTIONS FOR THE NEXT FEW MINUTES. PLENTY OF TIME TO HAVE YOU LOCKED IN CHAINS.
DID YOU REALLY THINK WE WOULDN'T CATCH YOU? A MAN WITH MY REPUTATION NOT NOTICING ALL YOUR SILLY RESCUES?
OH, MOMMY. PLEASE... HELP ME...
OKAY, NOW I JUST FEEL BAD. I KNEW HE WAS A LITTLE BOY, BUT THIS IS REALLY OVER THE TOP. I DIDN'T EXPECT HIM TO CRY FOR HIS MOTHER.

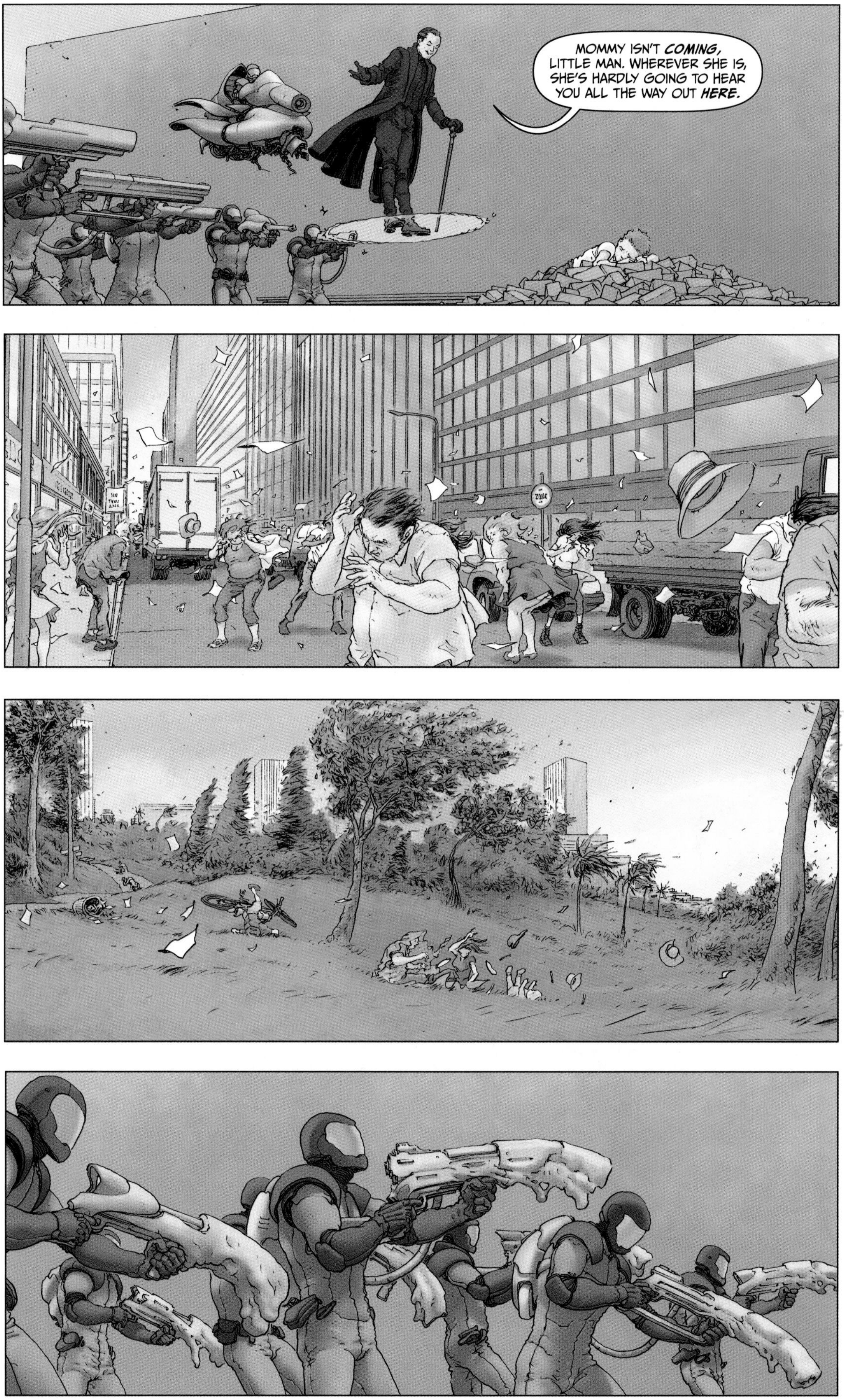
MOMMY ISN'T *COMING,* LITTLE MAN. WHEREVER SHE IS, SHE'S HARDLY GOING TO HEAR YOU ALL THE WAY OUT *HERE.*

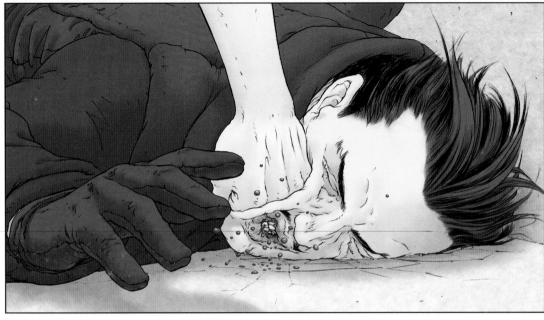

ALPHA TEAM! THREE ROUNDS ON MY COMMAND!

DON'T WORRY, MOM. THEY'LL HAVE TO GET THROUGH *ME* FIRST.

THIS KID'S *HILARIOUS.*

WEAPONS CHARGED, BOYS!

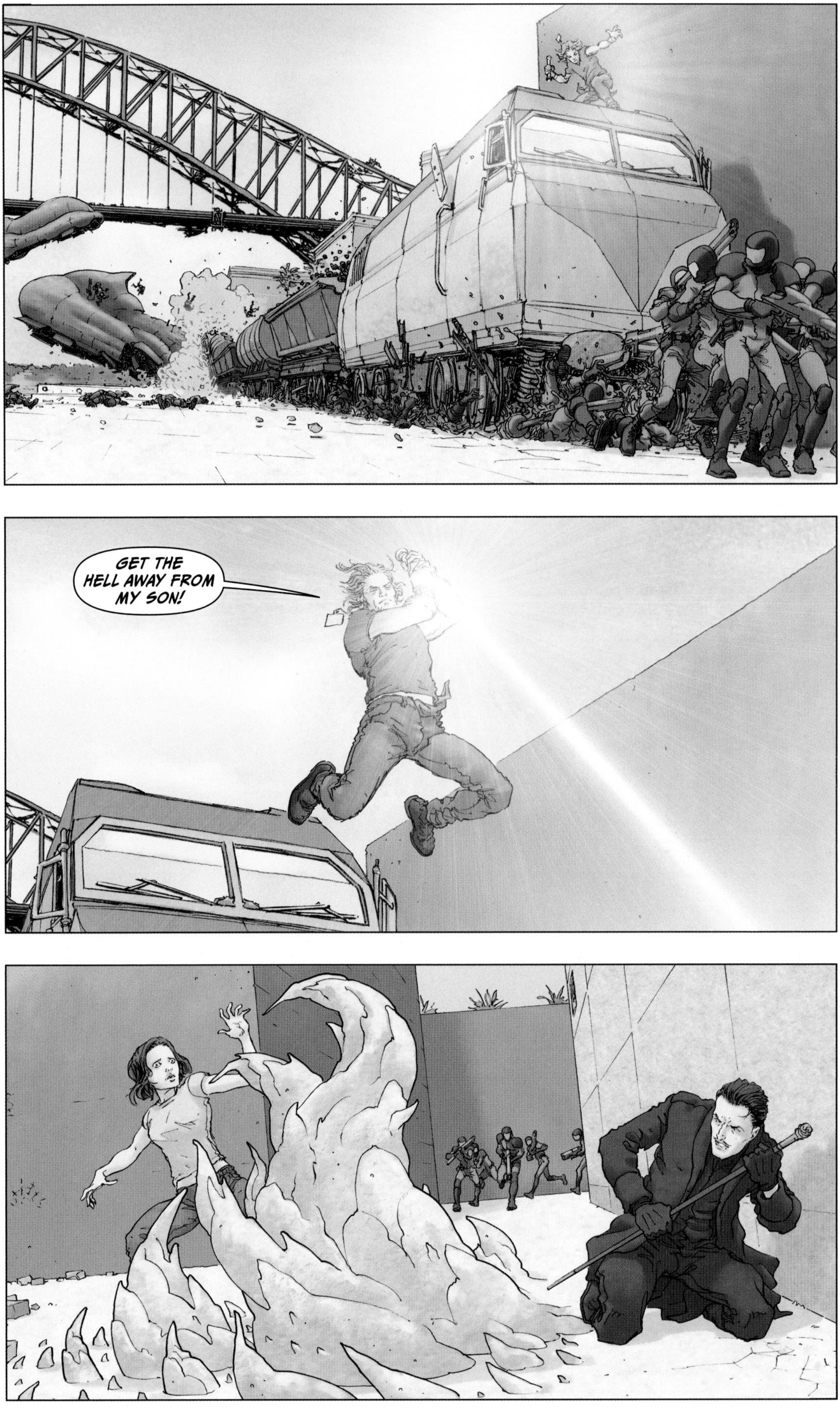
GET THE HELL AWAY FROM MY SON!

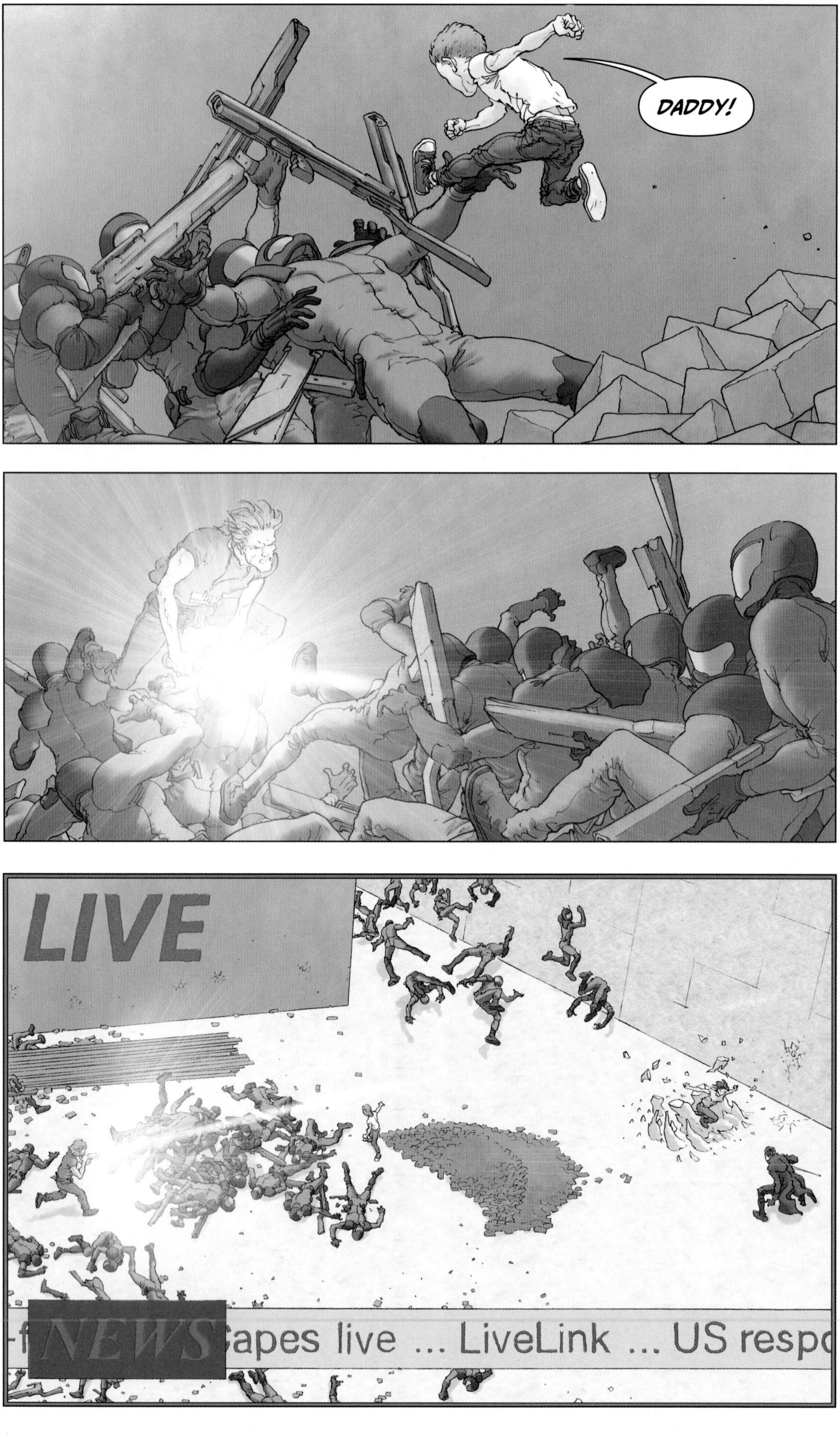
DADDY!
LIVE
NEWS
Capes live ... LiveLink ... US respo

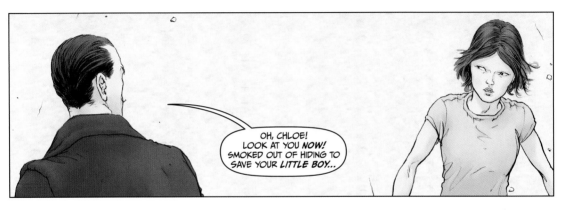

OH, CHLOE! LOOK AT YOU *NOW!* SMOKED OUT OF HIDING TO SAVE YOUR *LITTLE BOY*...

WELL, IT LOOKS LIKE YOU'VE BITTEN OFF MORE THAN YOU CAN CHEW, MY DEAR.

THERE'S *HUNDREDS* OF US HERE AND MORE ON THE *WAY.* DO YOU REALLY THINK SOME USELESS PARTY GIRL STANDS A CHANCE AGAINST *US?*

THINGS HAVE *CHANGED,* BARNABAS. I'M NOT A *LITTLE GIRL* ANYMORE.

MY *MOM* WAS A SUPERHERO. MY *DAD* WAS A SUPERHERO...

...THAT MEANS I WON THIS FIGHT BEFORE YOU GOT OUT OF BED.

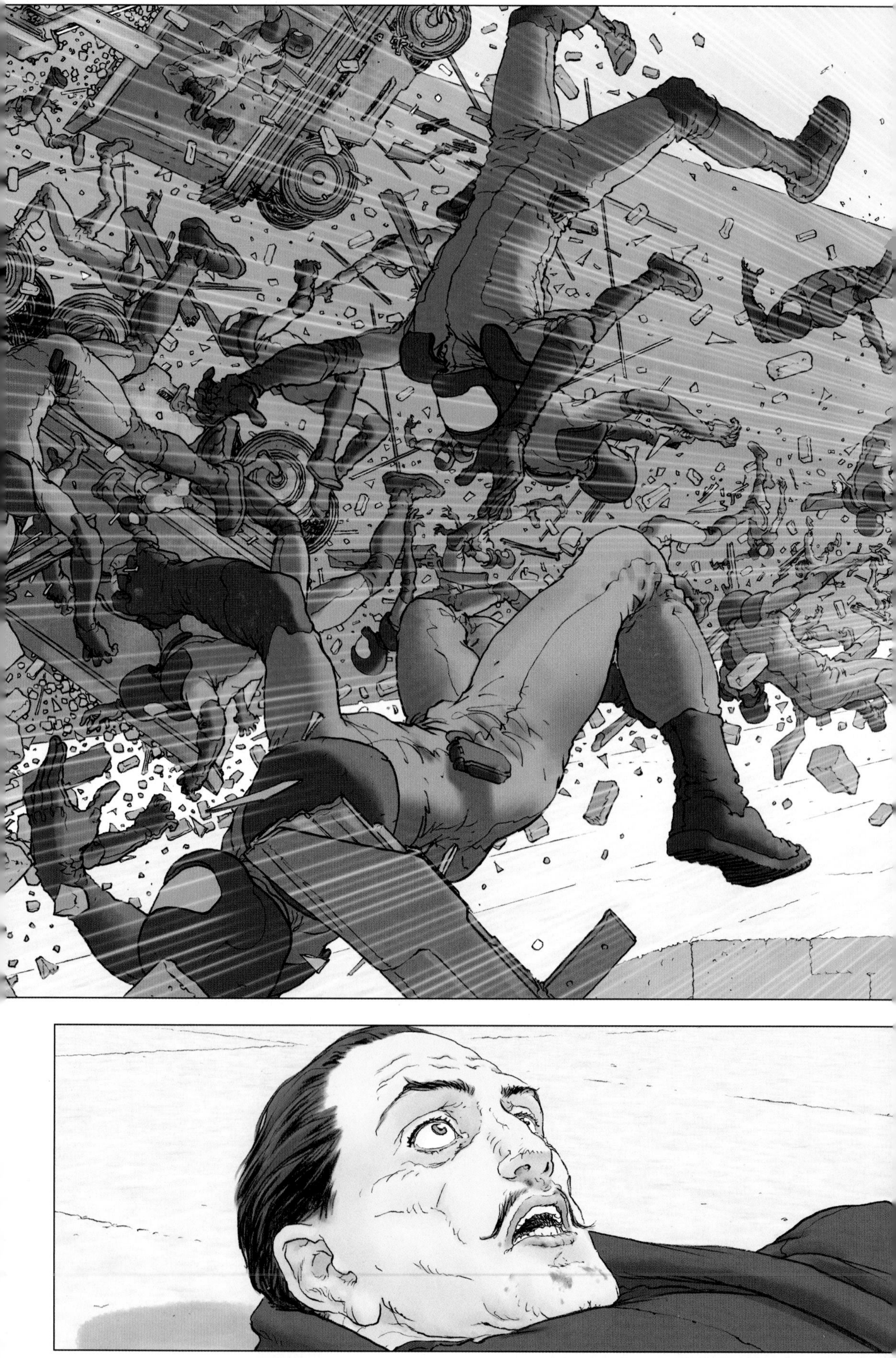

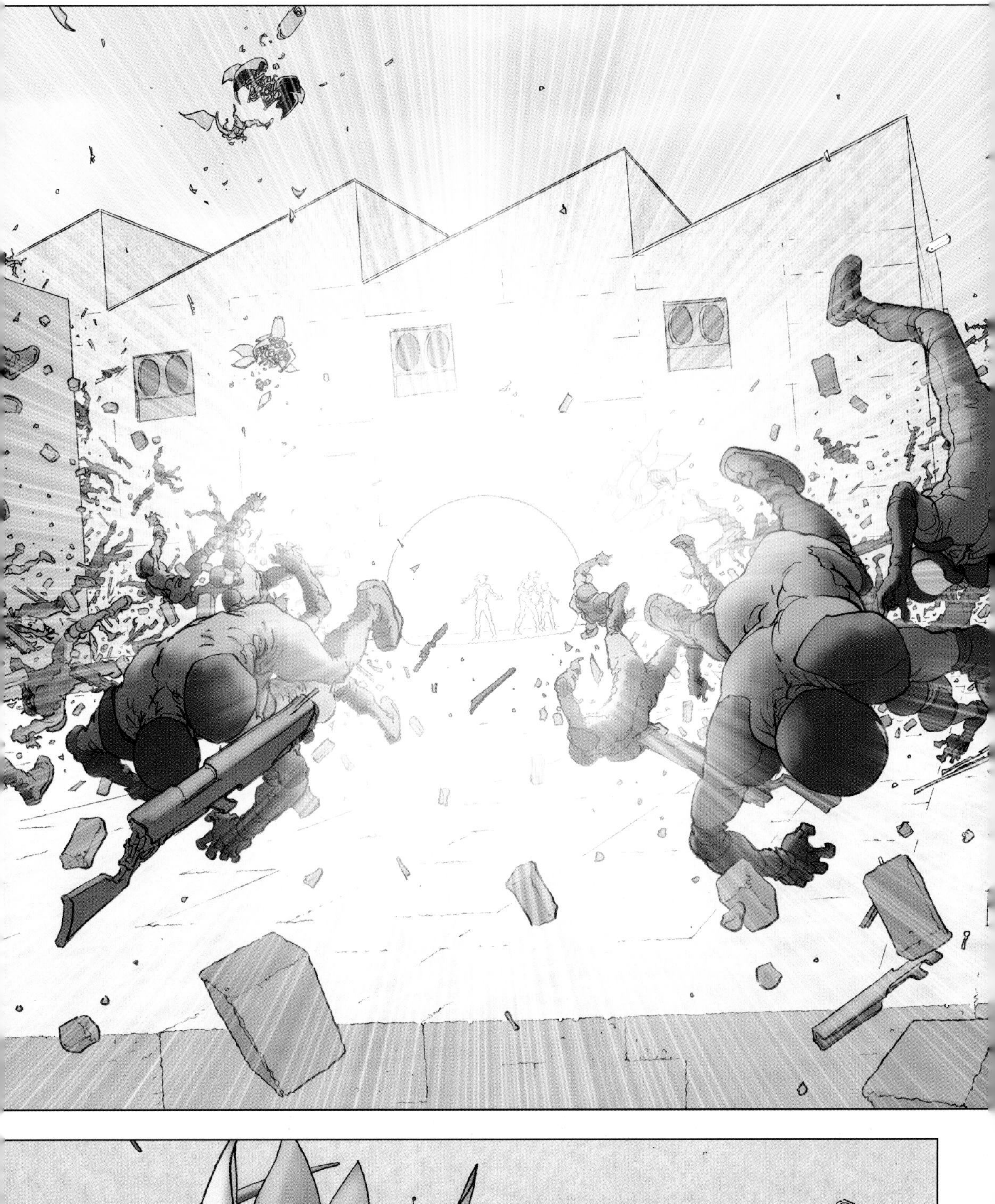

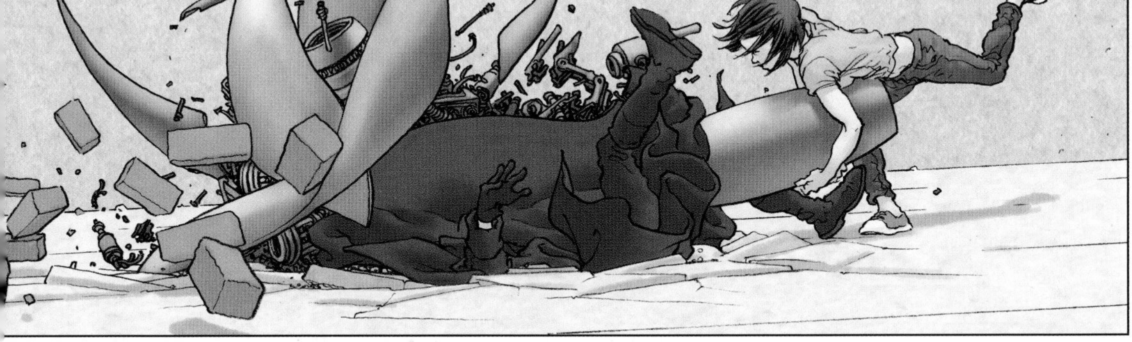

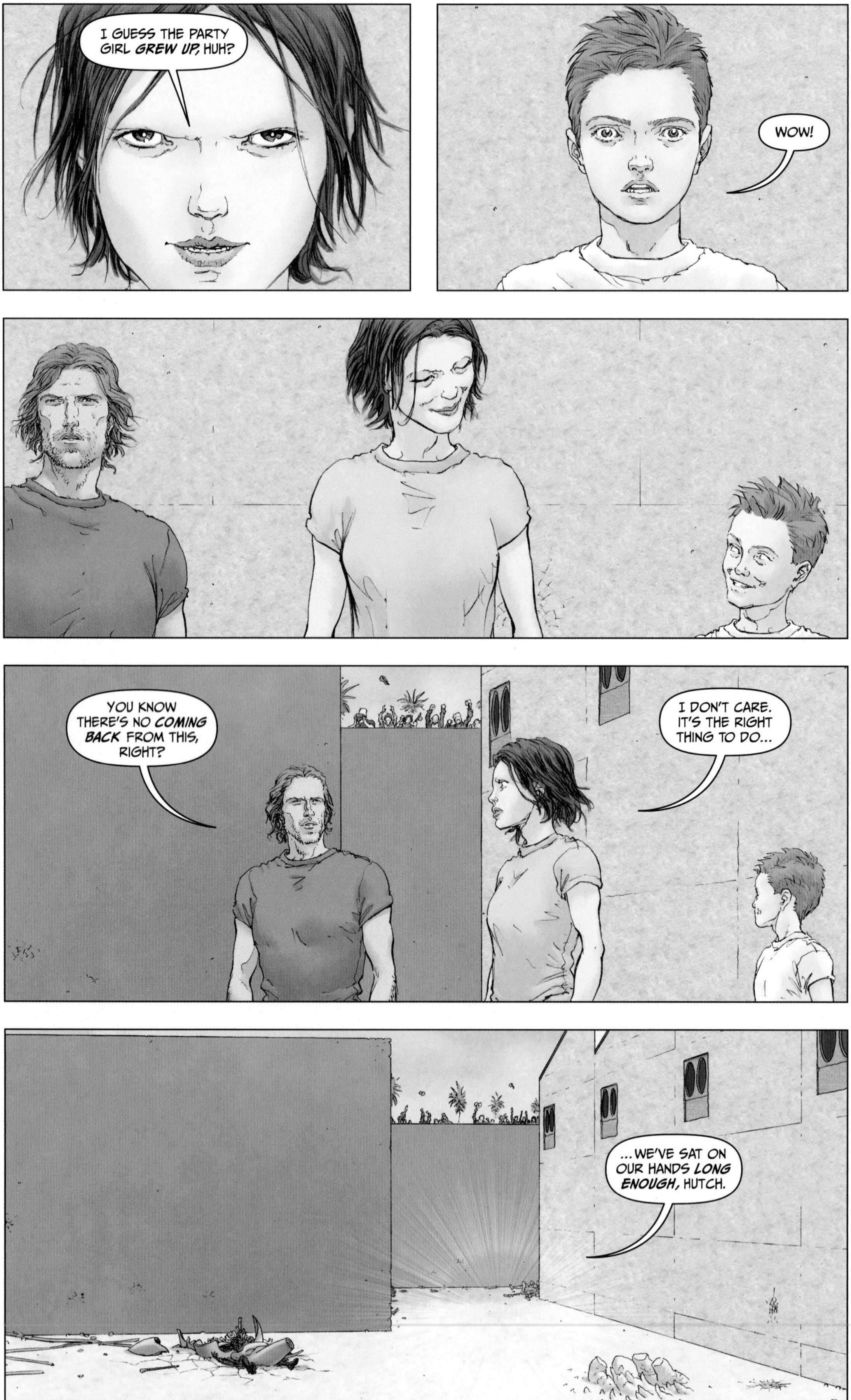
I GUESS THE PARTY GIRL GREW UP, HUH?
WOW!
YOU KNOW THERE'S NO COMING BACK FROM THIS, RIGHT?
I DON'T CARE. IT'S THE RIGHT THING TO DO...
...WE'VE SAT ON OUR HANDS LONG ENOUGH, HUTCH.

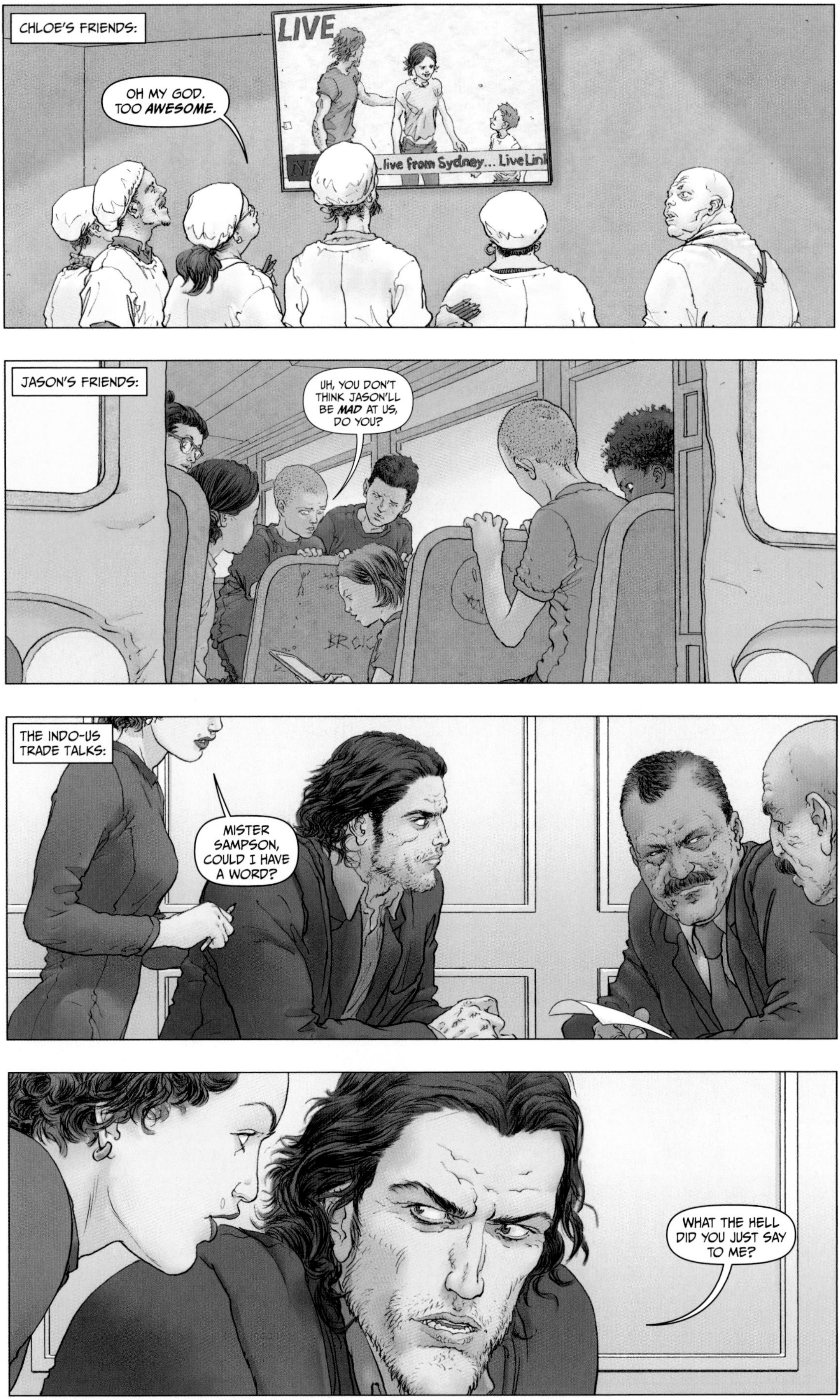
CHLOE'S FRIENDS:
LIVE
...live from Sydney... LiveLink
OH MY GOD. TOO **AWESOME.**
JASON'S FRIENDS:
UH, YOU DON'T THINK JASON'LL BE **MAD** AT US, DO YOU?
THE INDO-US TRADE TALKS:
MISTER SAMPSON, COULD I HAVE A WORD?
WHAT THE HELL DID YOU JUST SAY TO ME?

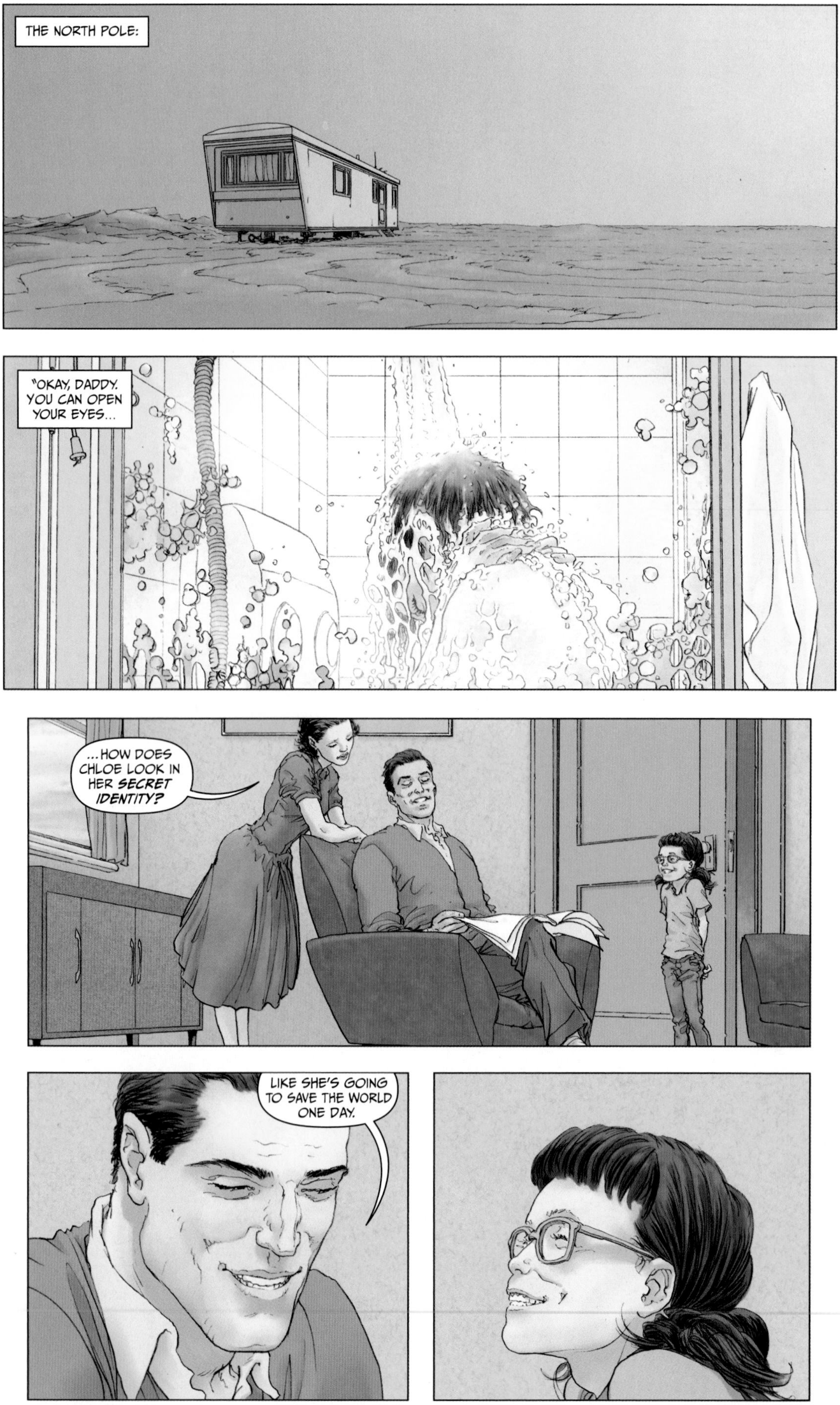
THE NORTH POLE:
"OKAY, DADDY. YOU CAN OPEN YOUR EYES...
...HOW DOES CHLOE LOOK IN HER *SECRET IDENTITY?*
LIKE SHE'S GOING TO SAVE THE WORLD ONE DAY.

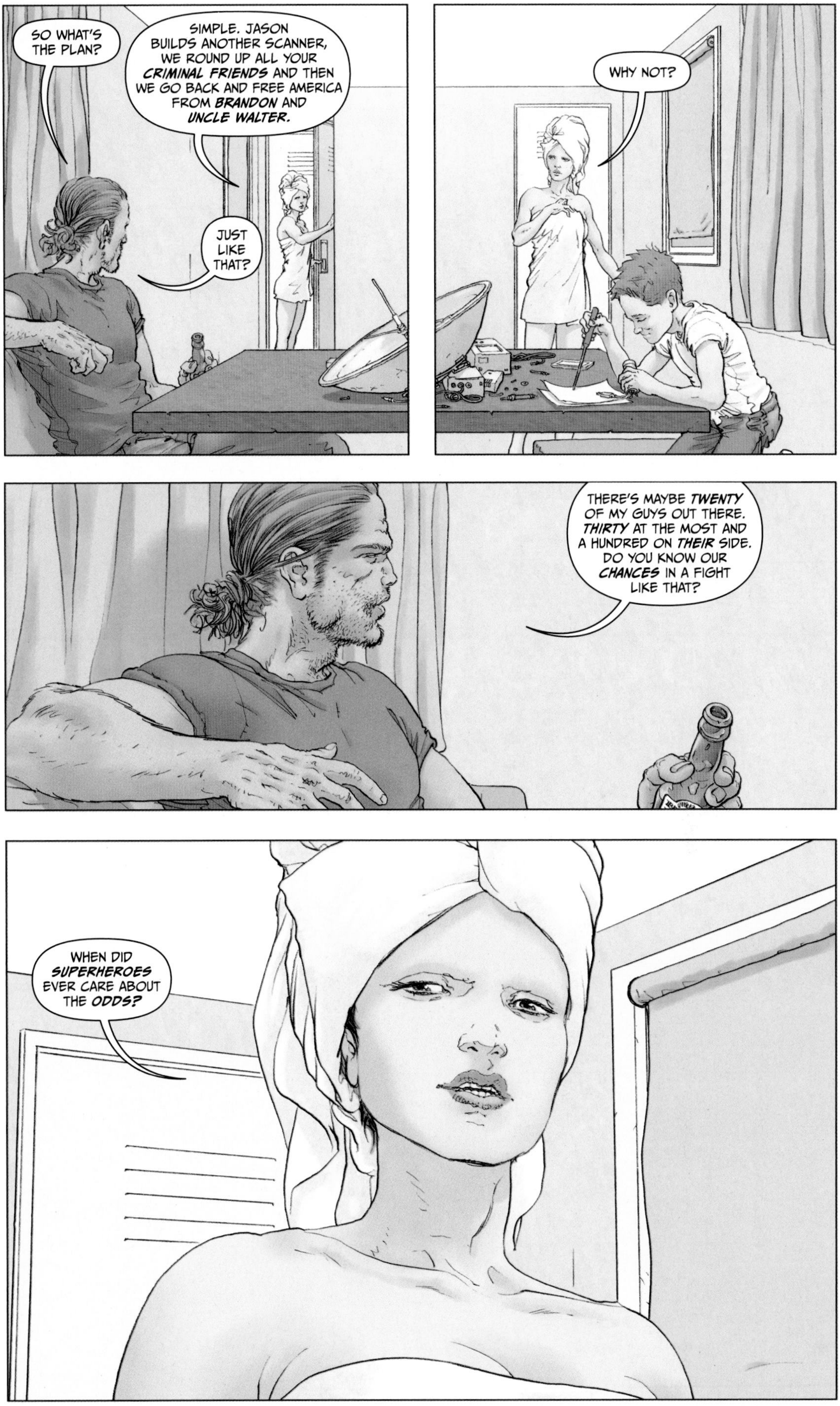
SO WHAT'S THE PLAN?
SIMPLE. JASON BUILDS ANOTHER SCANNER, WE ROUND UP ALL YOUR CRIMINAL FRIENDS AND THEN WE GO BACK AND FREE AMERICA FROM BRANDON AND UNCLE WALTER.
JUST LIKE THAT?
WHY NOT?
THERE'S MAYBE TWENTY OF MY GUYS OUT THERE. THIRTY AT THE MOST AND A HUNDRED ON THEIR SIDE. DO YOU KNOW OUR CHANCES IN A FIGHT LIKE THAT?
WHEN DID SUPERHEROES EVER CARE ABOUT THE ODDS?

END OF
BOOK ONE

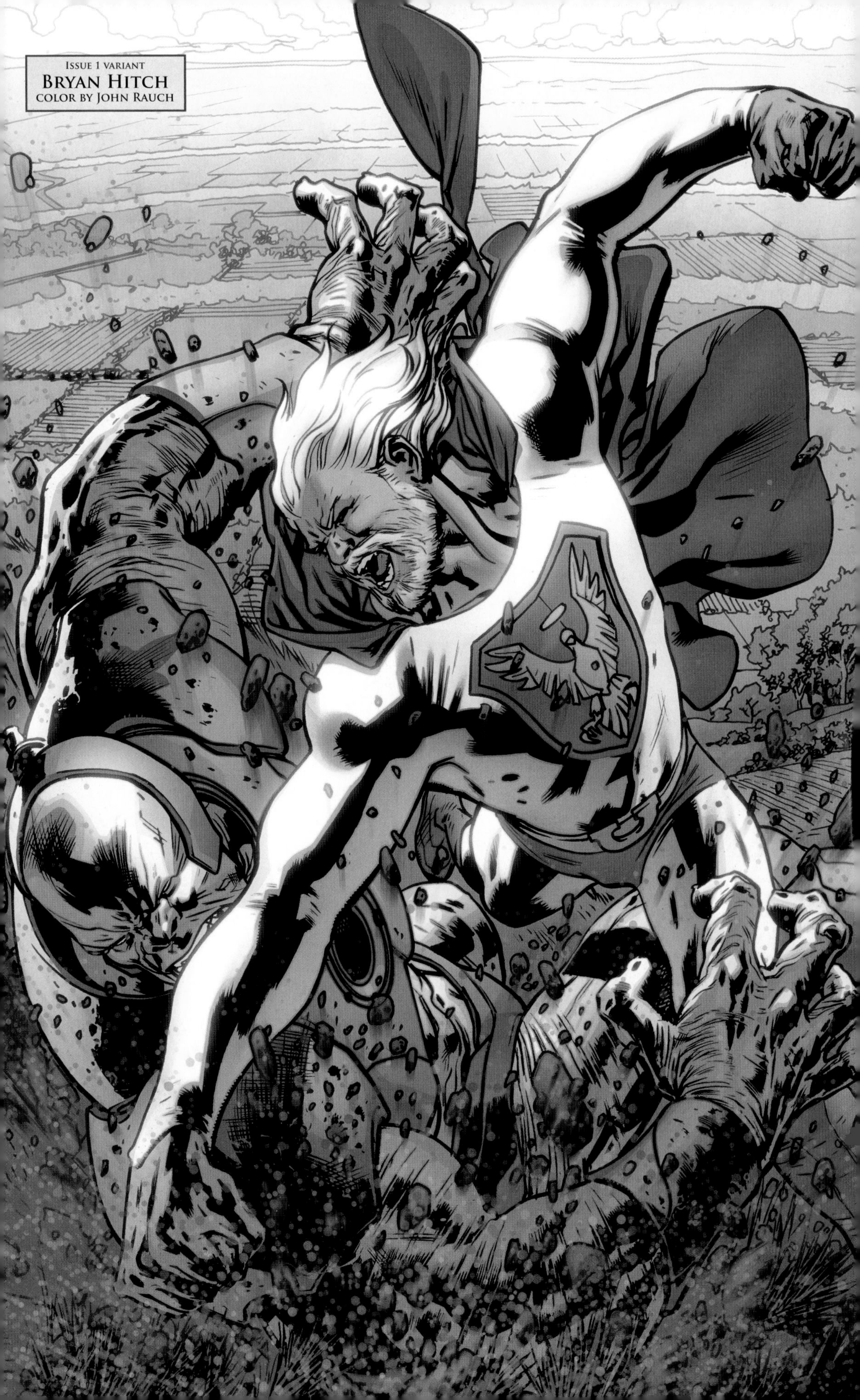
ISSUE 1 VARIANT
BRYAN HITCH
COLOR BY JOHN RAUCH

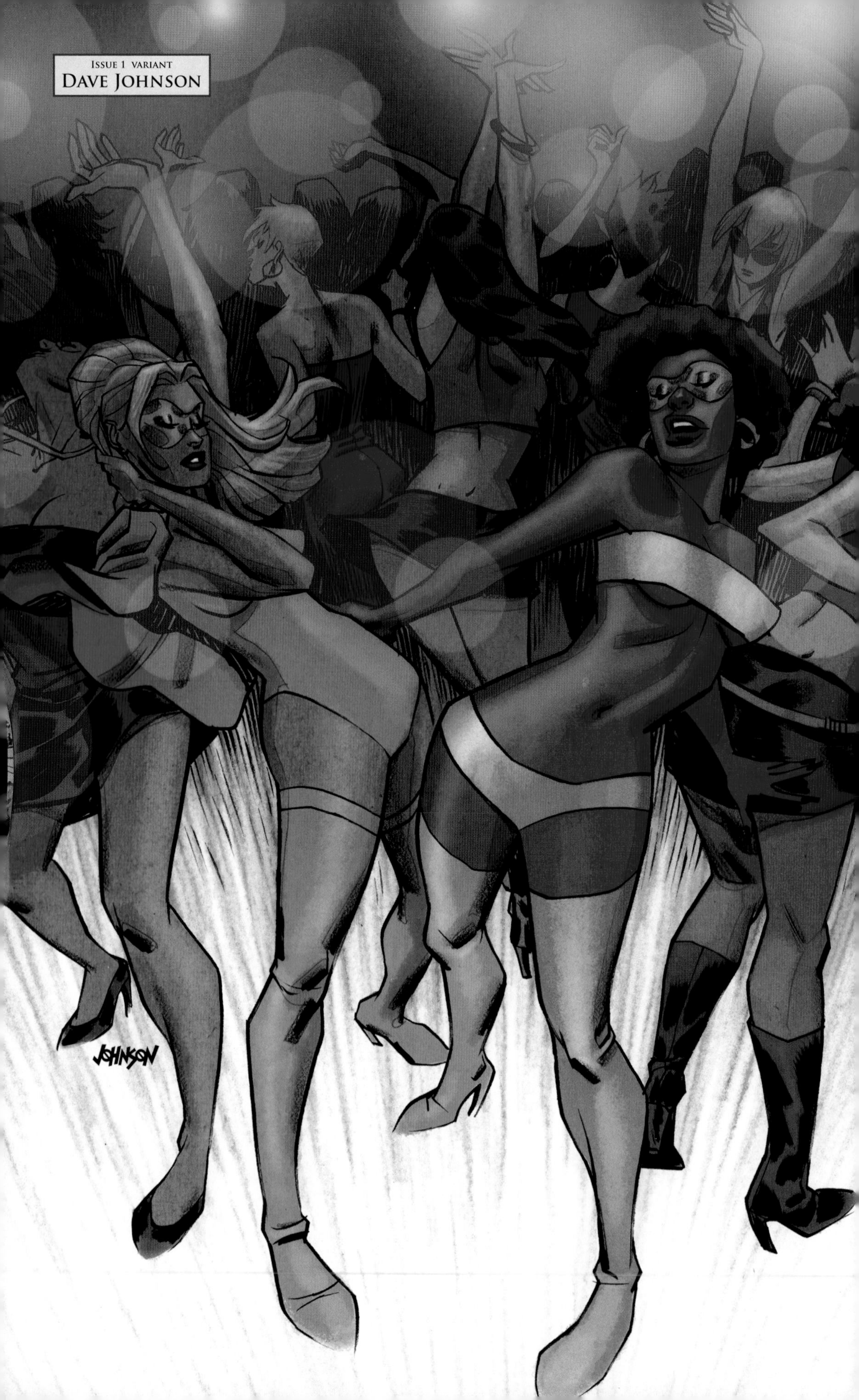
JOHNSON

ISSUE 1 VARIANT
DAVE JOHNSON

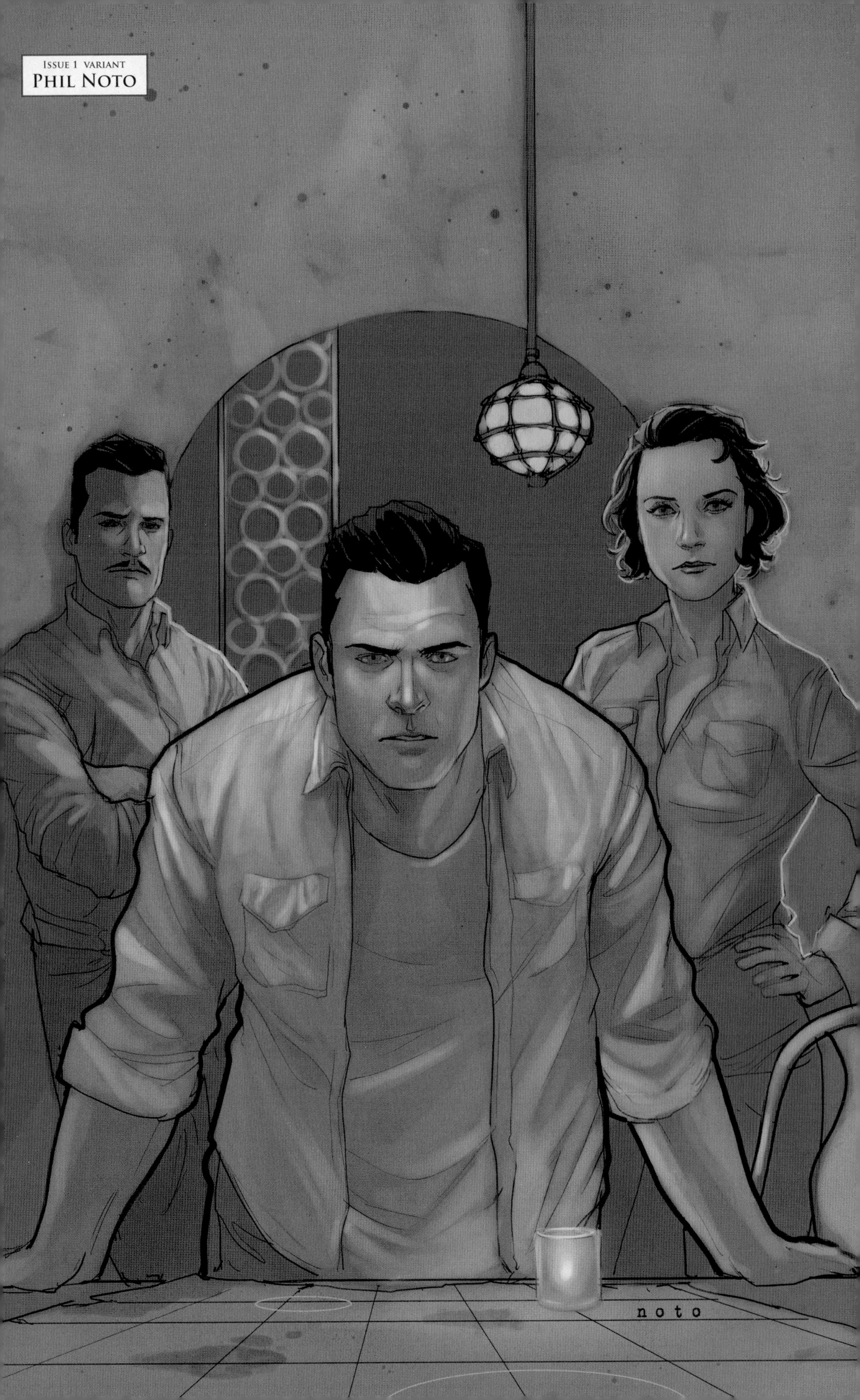
noto

ISSUE 1 VARIANT
PHIL NOTO

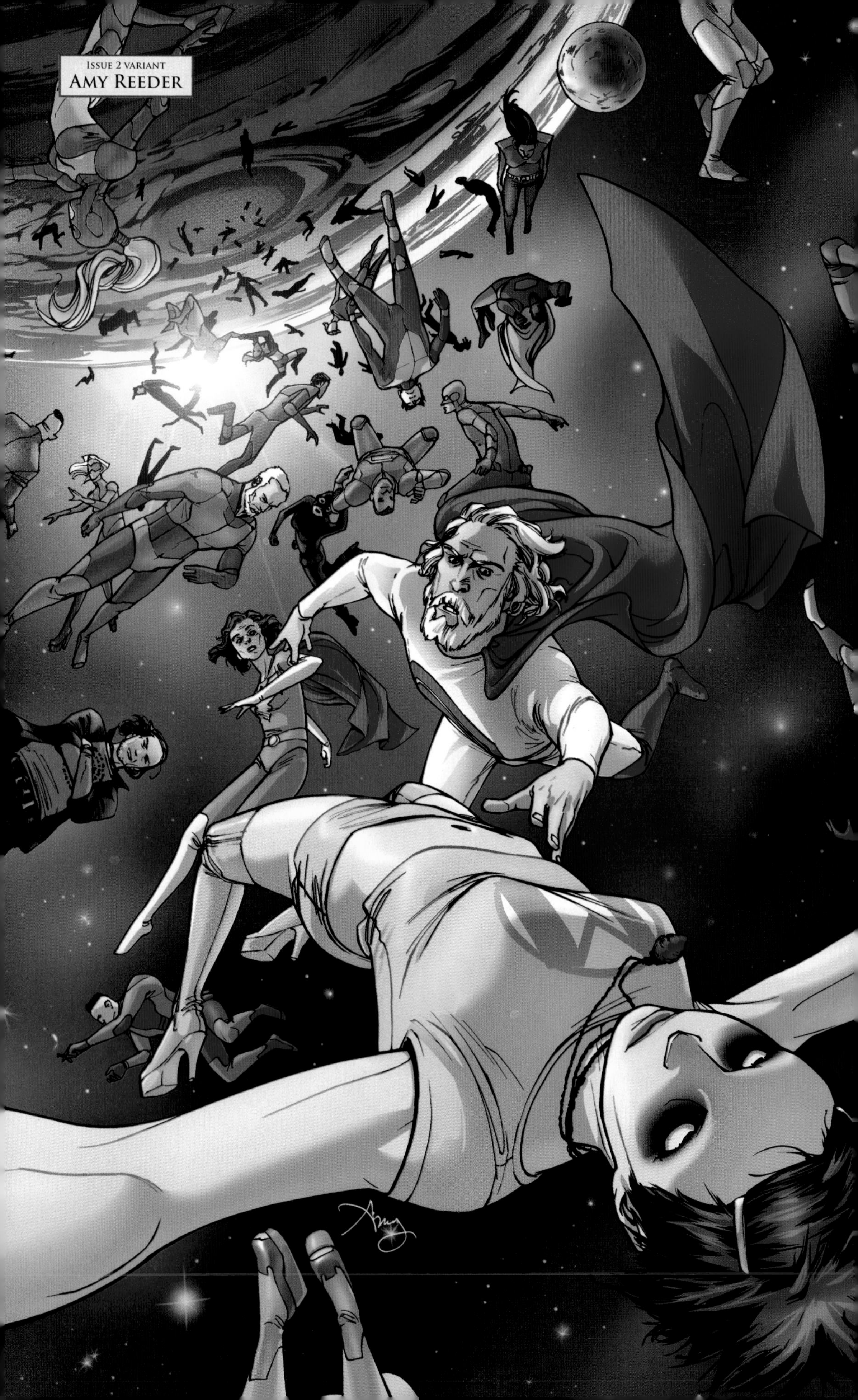

Issue 2 variant
Amy Reeder

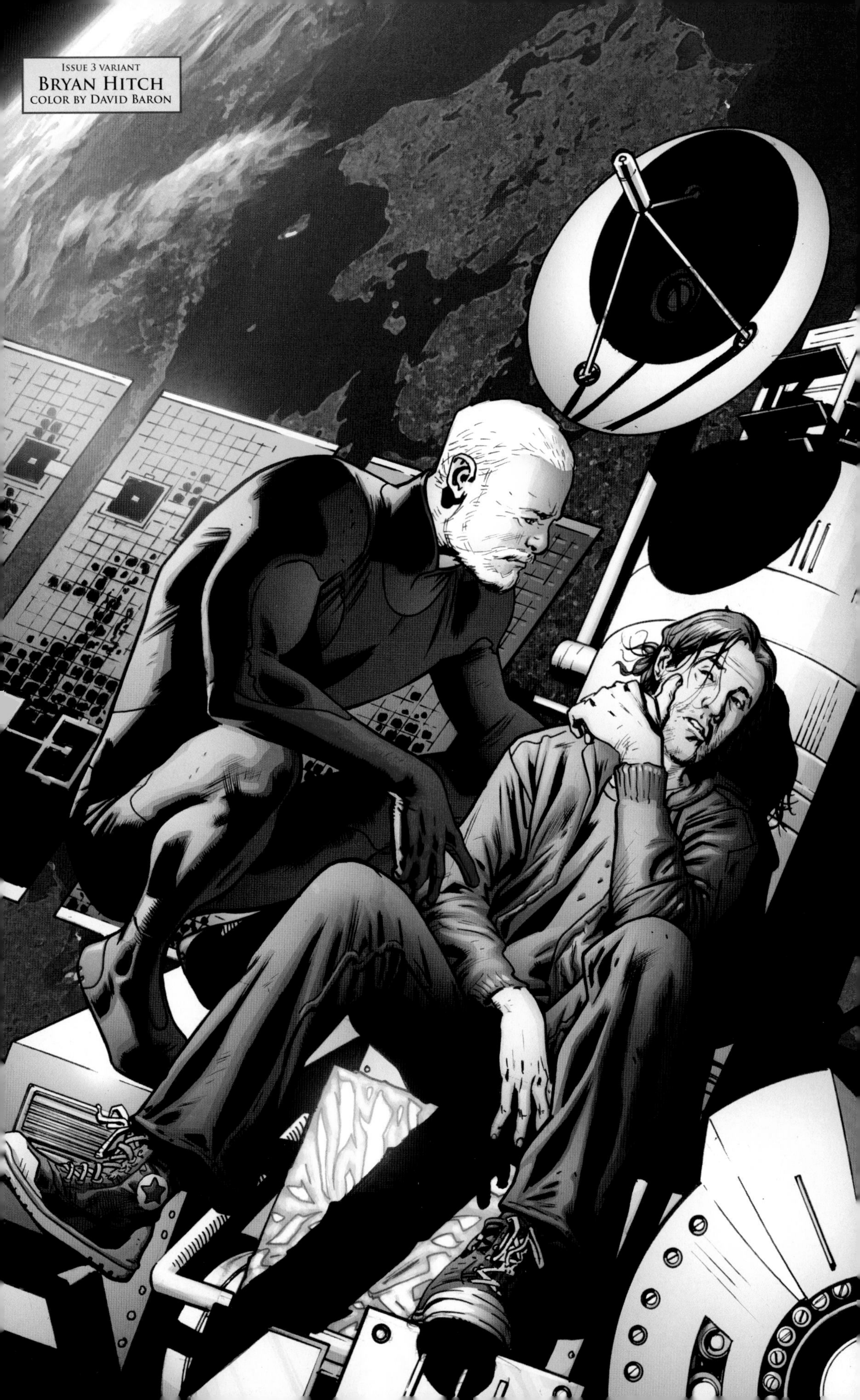

Issue 3 variant
Bryan Hitch
Color by David Baron

ISSUE 3 VARIANT
SEAN PHILLIPS

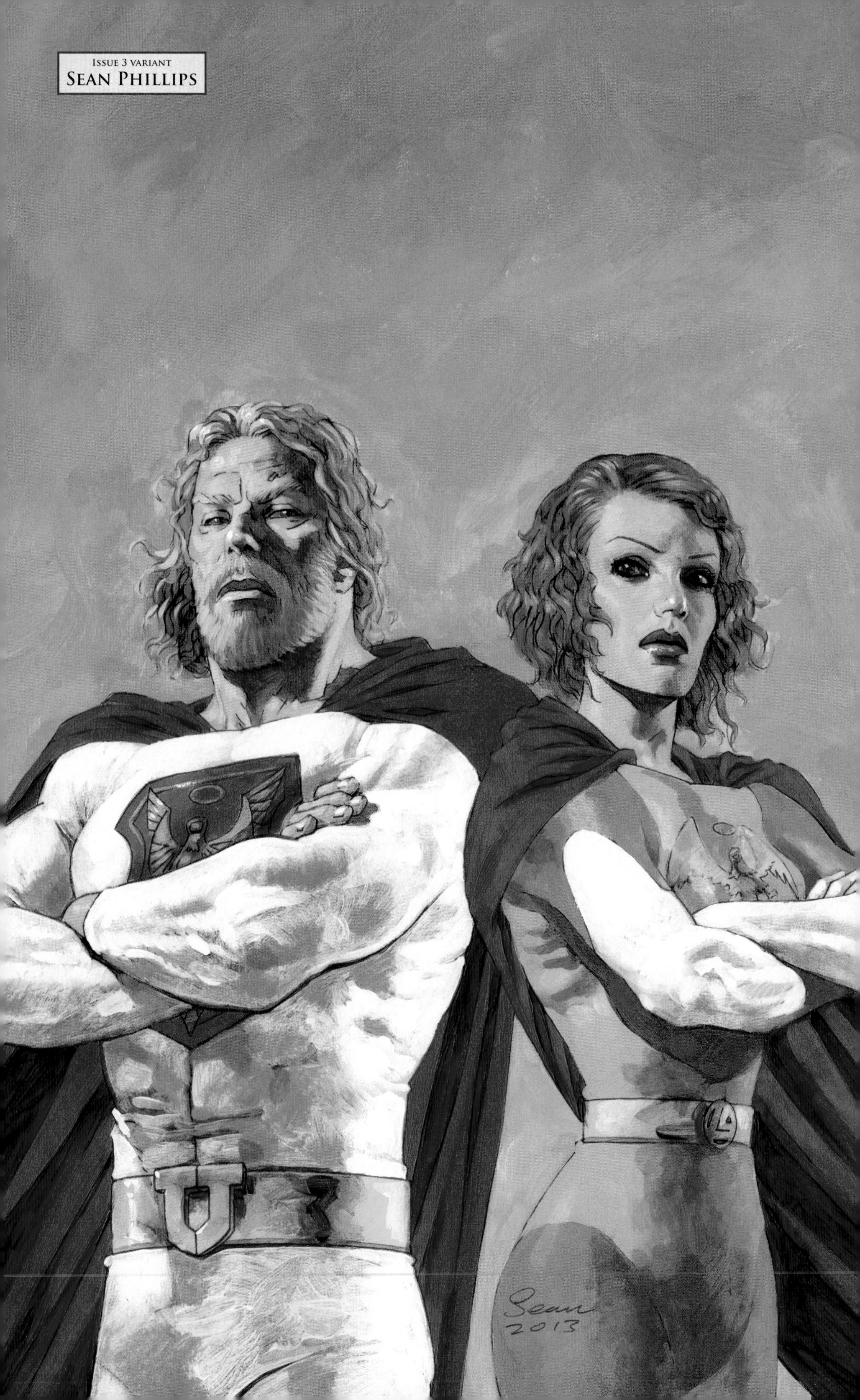
Sean
2013

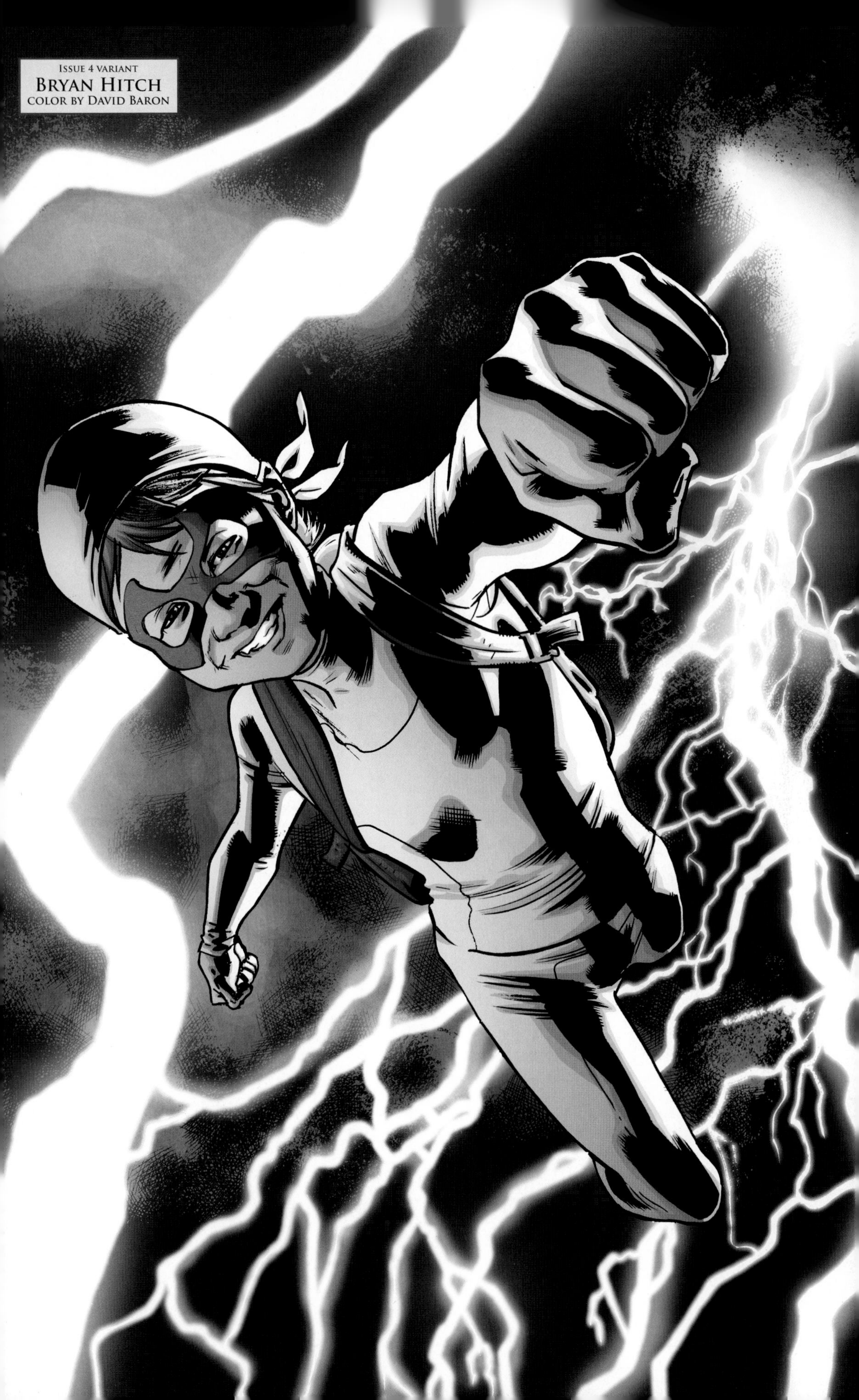

Issue 4 variant
Bryan Hitch
color by David Baron

Issue 4 variant
IAN McQUE

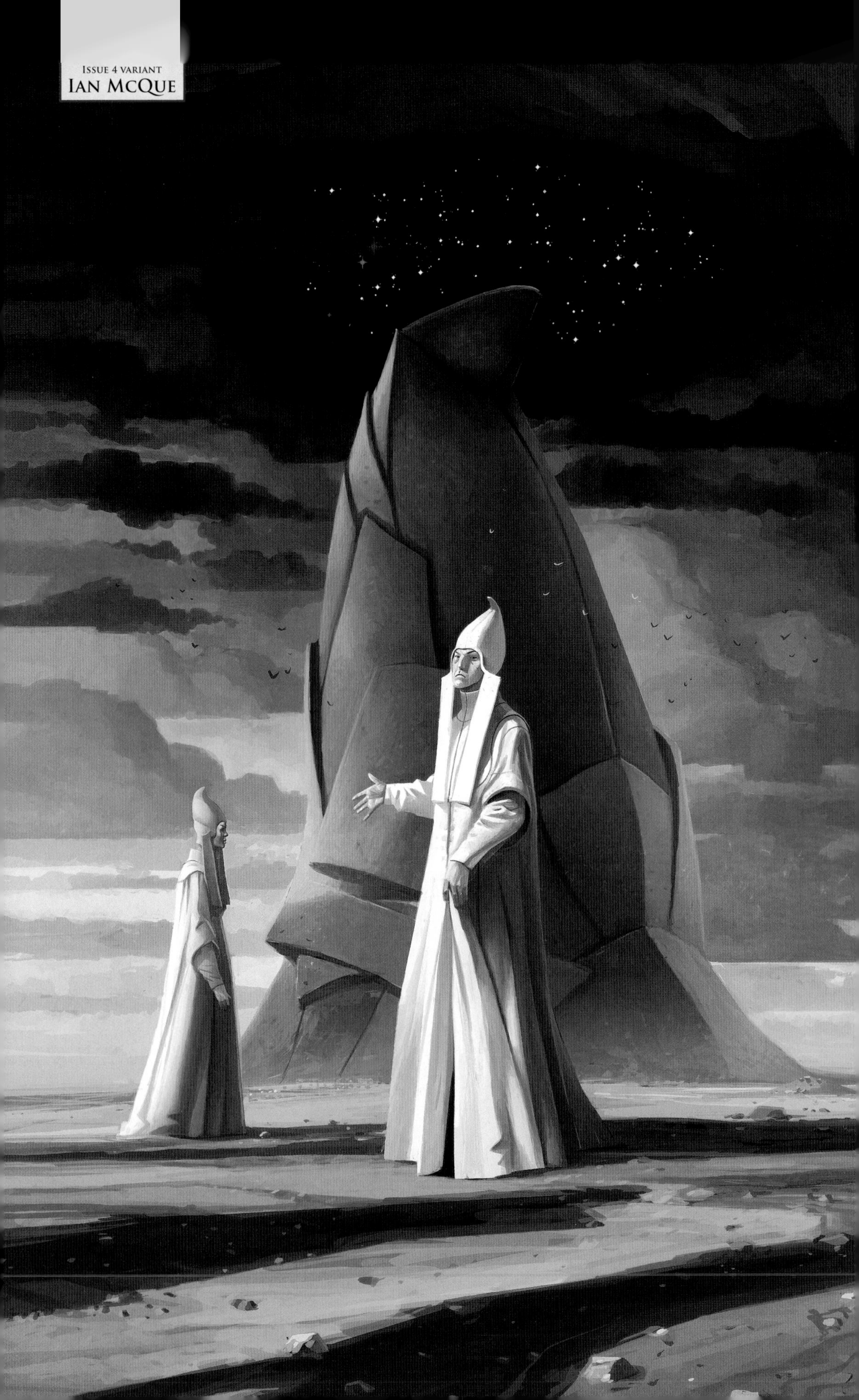

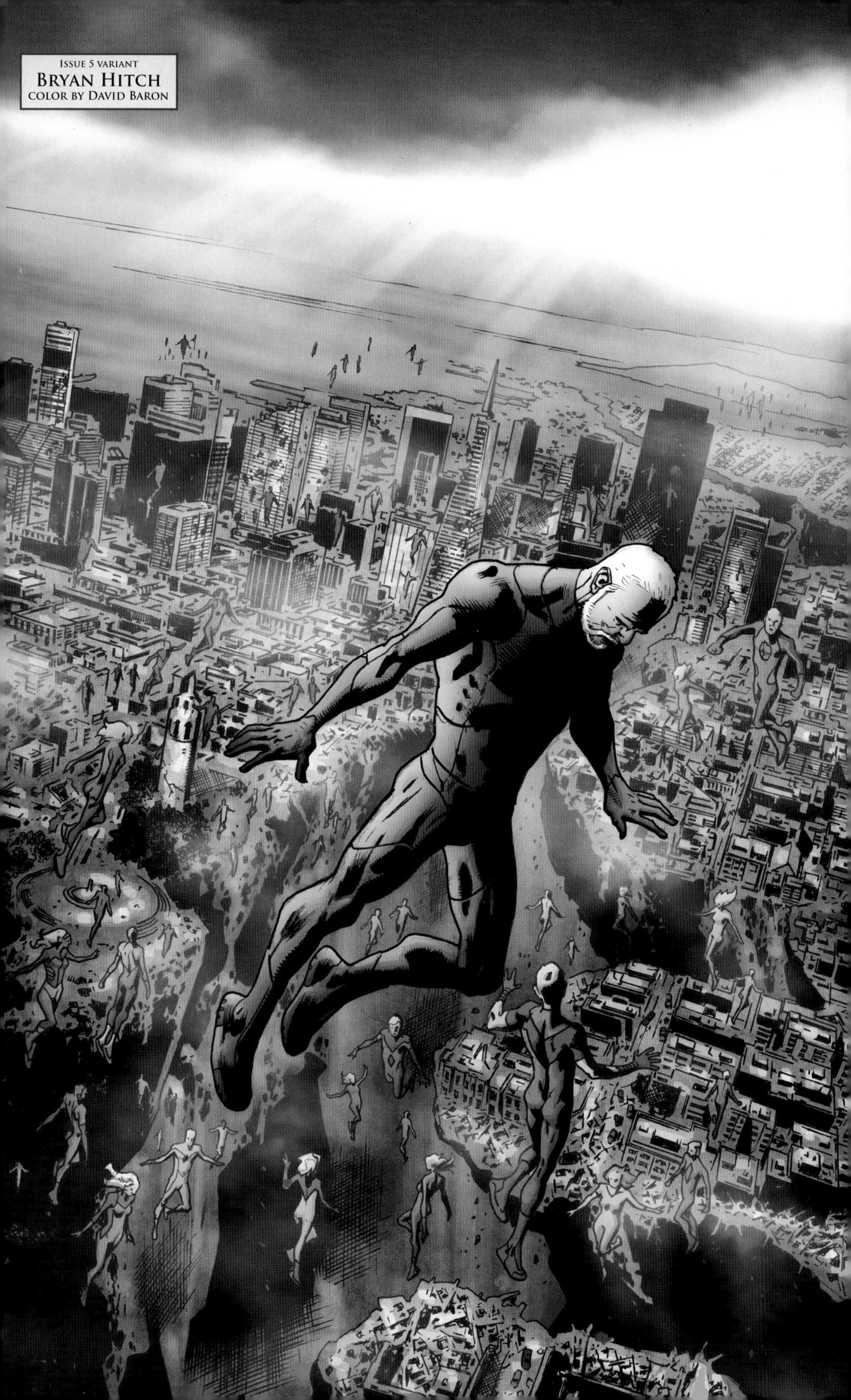

Issue 5 variant
Bryan Hitch
color by David Baron

Issue 5 variant
DUNCAN FEGREDO
color by Peter Doherty

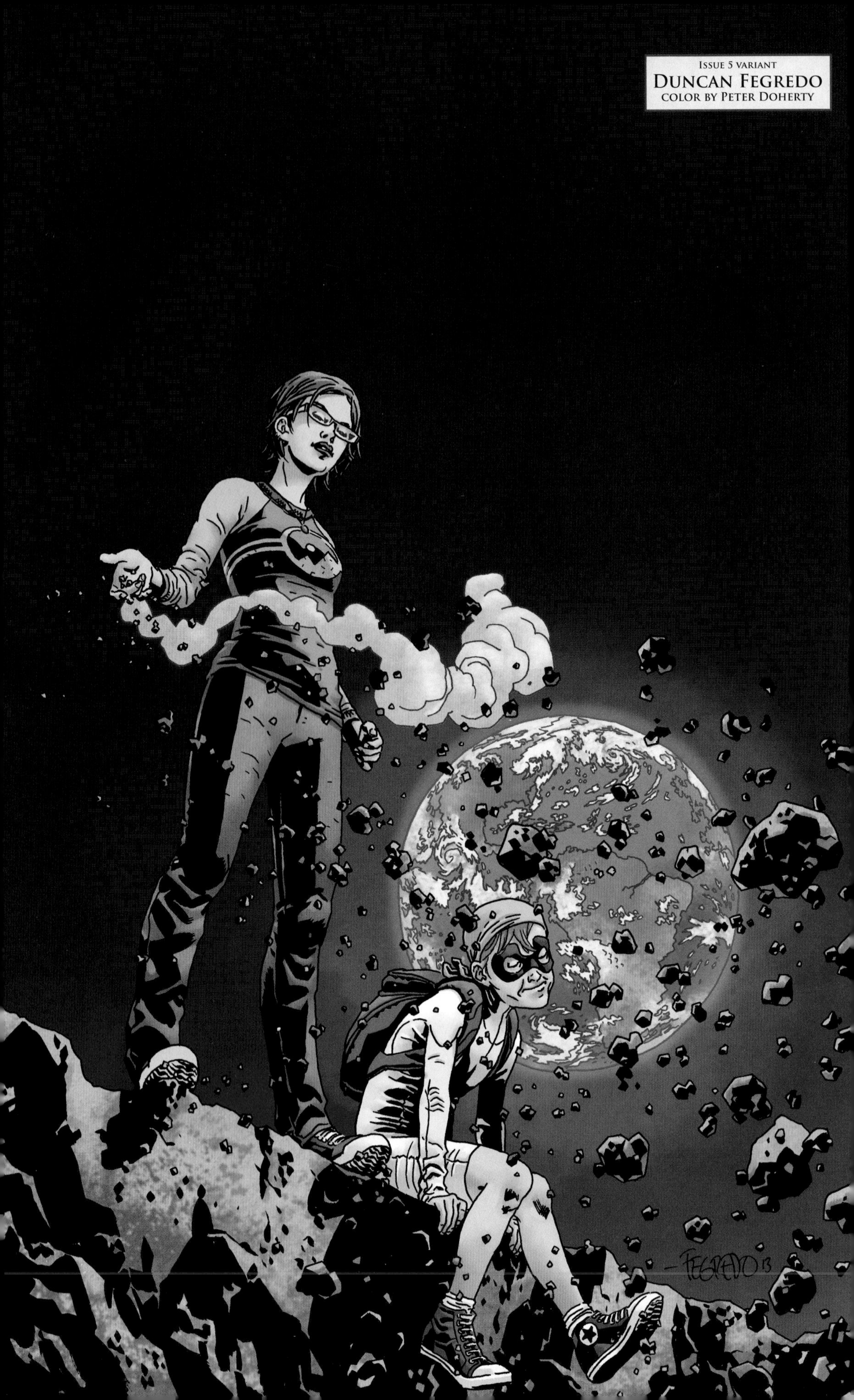
FEGREDO 13

Giant Size Edition
JOHN CASSADAY
COLOR BY PETER DOHERTY

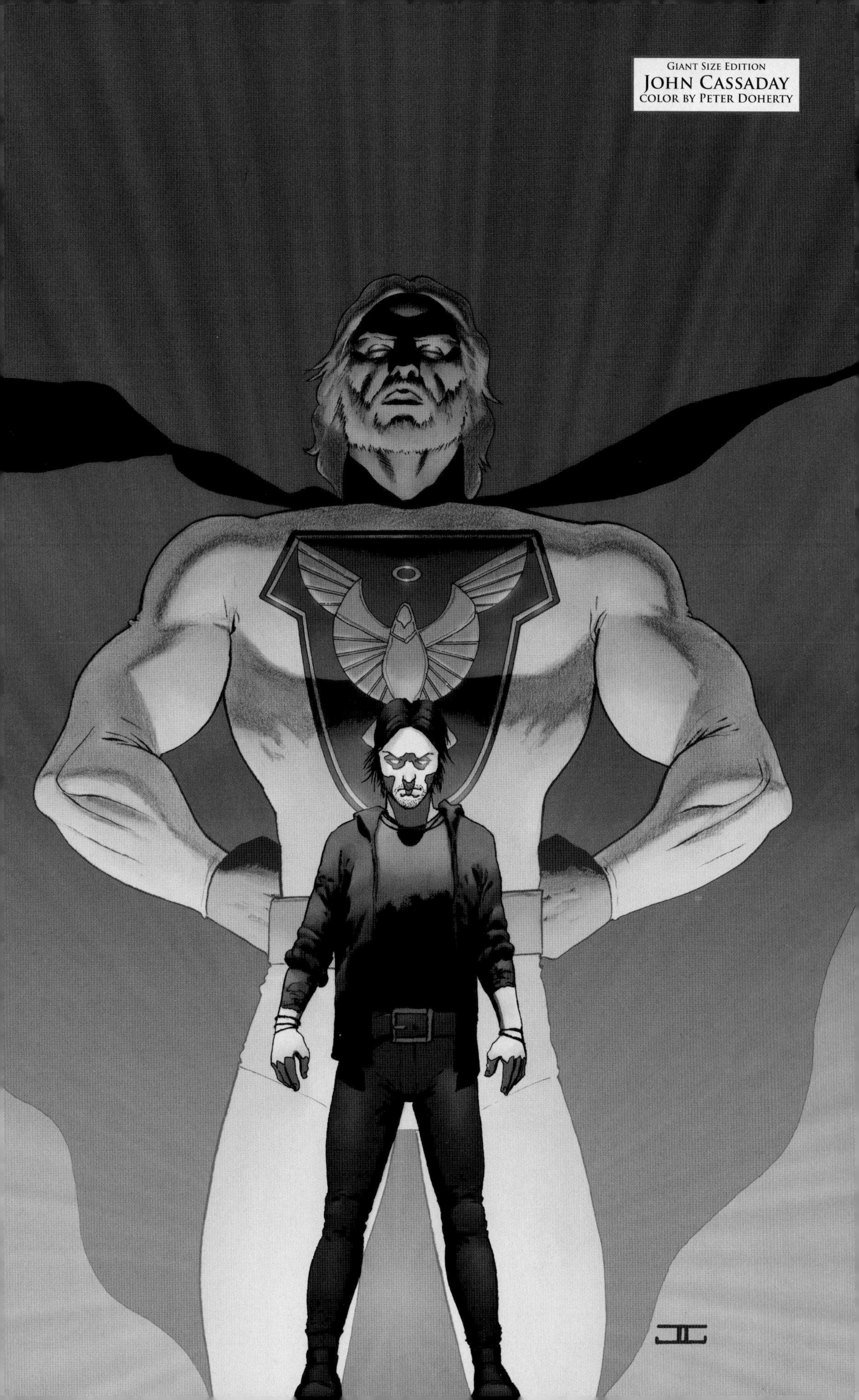

MARK MILLAR

Mark Millar is the *New York Times* best-selling writer of *Wanted*, the *Kick-Ass* series, *The Secret Service*, *Jupiter's Legacy*, *Nemesis*, *Superior*, *Super Crooks*, *American Jesus*, *MPH*, *Starlight*, and *Chrononauts*. *Wanted*, *Kick-Ass*, *Kick-Ass 2*, and *The Secret Service* (as *Kingsman: The Secret Service*) have been adapted into feature films, and *Nemesis*, *Superior*, *Starlight*, *War Heroes* and *Chrononauts* are in development at major studios.

His DC Comics work includes the seminal *Superman: Red Son*, and at Marvel Comics he created *The Ultimates* – selected by *Time* magazine as the comic book of the decade, *Wolverine: Old Man Logan*, and *Civil War* – the industry's biggest-selling superhero series in almost two decades.

Mark has been an Executive Producer on all his movie adaptations and is currently creative consultant to Fox Studios on their Marvel slate of movies. His autobiography, *The Man With the Golden Brain*, will be published next year.

FRANK QUITELY

Frank Quitely is a Scottish comic book artist. He is best known for his frequent collaborations with Grant Morrison on titles such as *New X-Men*, *We3*, *All-Star Superman*, and *Batman and Robin*, as well as his work with Mark Millar on *The Authority* and *Jupiter's Legacy*.

Frank Quitely spent the first three years of his comic book career in the independently-published Scottish adult humor anthology *Electric Soup*, learning the basics of writing, drawing and lettering his own black and white strip, *The Greens*.

Leaving the writing behind, he spent a further two years painting the futuristic western *Missionary Man* and Japanese sci-fi strip *Shimura*, both for the poular UK anthology *Judge Dredd Megazine*.

The next five years were mostly spent at DC, producing ten black and white strips for Paradox Press' *The Big Books*, six shorts and two mini-series for Vertigo, including *Flex Mentallo*, and a selection of one-shots, original graphic novels and ongoing series at DCU and Wildstorm, including *Batman*, *JLA* and *The Authority*.

After two years on *New X-Men* at Marvel, he headed back to Vertigo for a fully painted *Sandman* short, and the creator-owned mini-series *We3*, followed by *All-Star Superman*, *Batman and Robin*, *New Gods*, and *Pax Americana*, all for DC Comics.

When not digitally painting covers or dabbling in small press ventures, he's occasionally to be found designing characters for animation, and producing artwork for CD covers and Posters.

He currently has *Jupiter's Legacy* Volume Two and several smaller creator-owned projects in the pipeline.

PETER DOHERTY

Peter's first work in comics was during 1990, providing painted artwork for the John Wagner-written *"Young Death: The Boyhood of a Super-fiend"*, published in the first year of the *Judge Dredd Megazine*. For the next few years he painted art for a number of Judge Dredd stories.

During the closing years of the 90s he worked for several comics publishers, most notably DC/Vertigo, and branched out into illustration, TV, and movie work.

A year as an in-house concept artist at a games company revealed to Peter that he didn't much like having bosses, and he returned to freelancing. Working digitally for the first time opened the door to coloring work, firstly on the Grant Morrison/Cameron Stewart *Seaguy,* and with Geof Darrow on his creation *The Shaolin Cowboy .*

Over the last decade he's balanced working on projects both as the sole artist and as a coloring collaborator with other artists, most recently with his old friends, Frank Quitely and Duncan Fegredo, on the Millarworld projects *Jupiter's Legacy* and *MPH,* respectively.

ROB MILLER

Since stumbling onto the Glasgow comic scene in 2005 (via architecture and the underground title *Khaki Shorts*), Rob Miller has been fortunate enough to assist Frank Quitely on his recent genre-defining works with Mark Millar and Grant Morrison.

Working from Jamie Grant's highly regarded Hope Street Studios has allowed him to collaborate with other Scottish comics professionals, including Alan Grant and Alex Ronald, as well as providing the opportunity to publish prized collections of some of his very favorite local underground artists – Dave Alexander, Hugh "Shug '90" McKenna and John Miller – under his own Braw Books imprint.

NICOLE BOOSE

Nicole Boose began her comics career as an assistant editor for Harris Comics' *Vampirella,* before joining the editorial staff at Marvel Comics. There, she edited titles including *Cable & Deadpool, Invincible Iron Man,* and Stephen King's *Dark Tower* adaptations, and oversaw Marvel's line of custom comic publications.

Since 2008, Nicole has worked as a freelance editor and consultant in the comics industry, with editorial credits that include the Millarworld titles *Superior, Super Crooks, Jupiter's Legacy, MPH, Starlight,* and *Chrononauts*. Nicole is also Communications Manager for Comics Experience, an online school and community for comic creators.

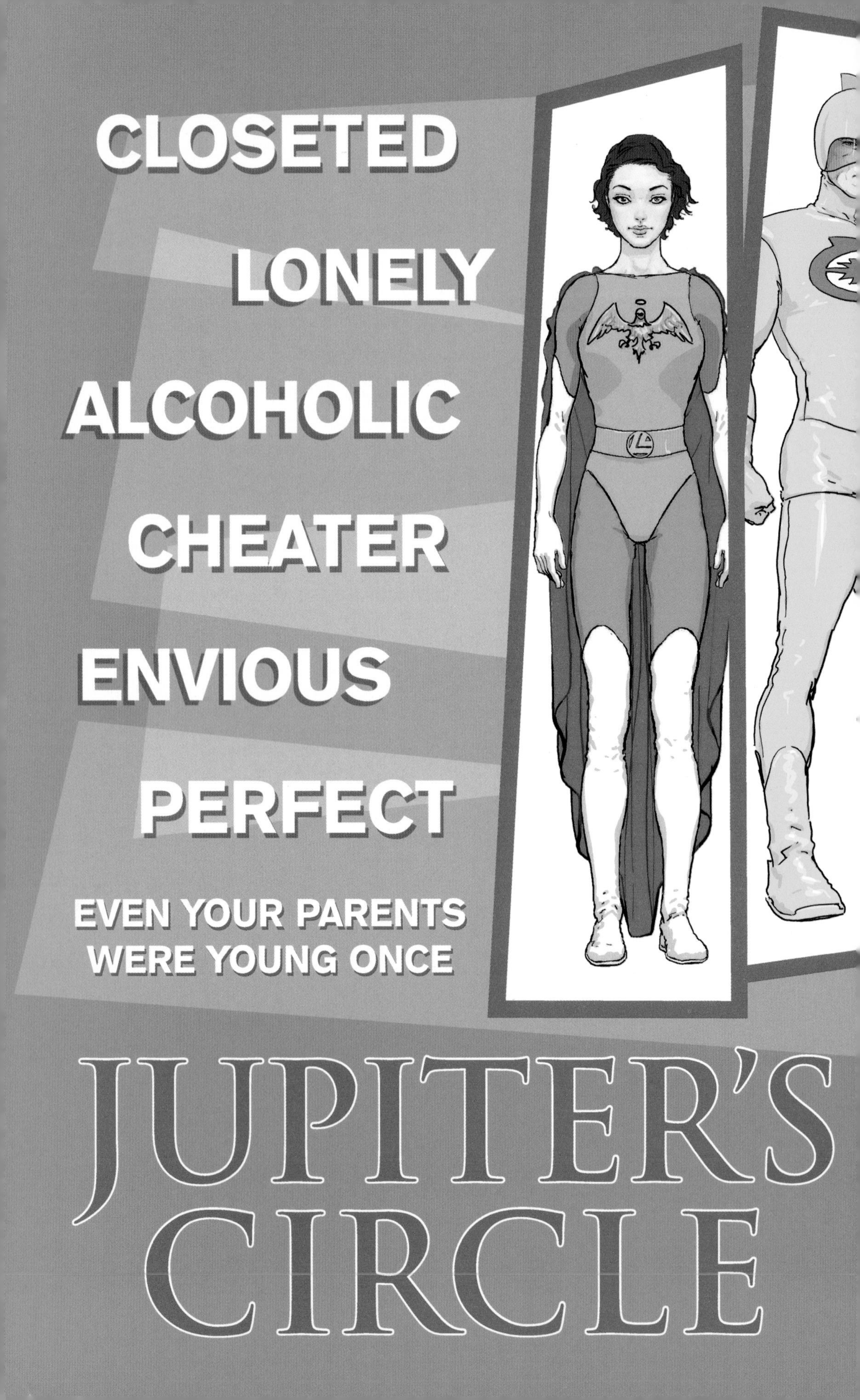
CLOSETED
LONELY
ALCOHOLIC
CHEATER
ENVIOUS
PERFECT
EVEN YOUR PARENTS WERE YOUNG ONCE
JUPITER'S CIRCLE

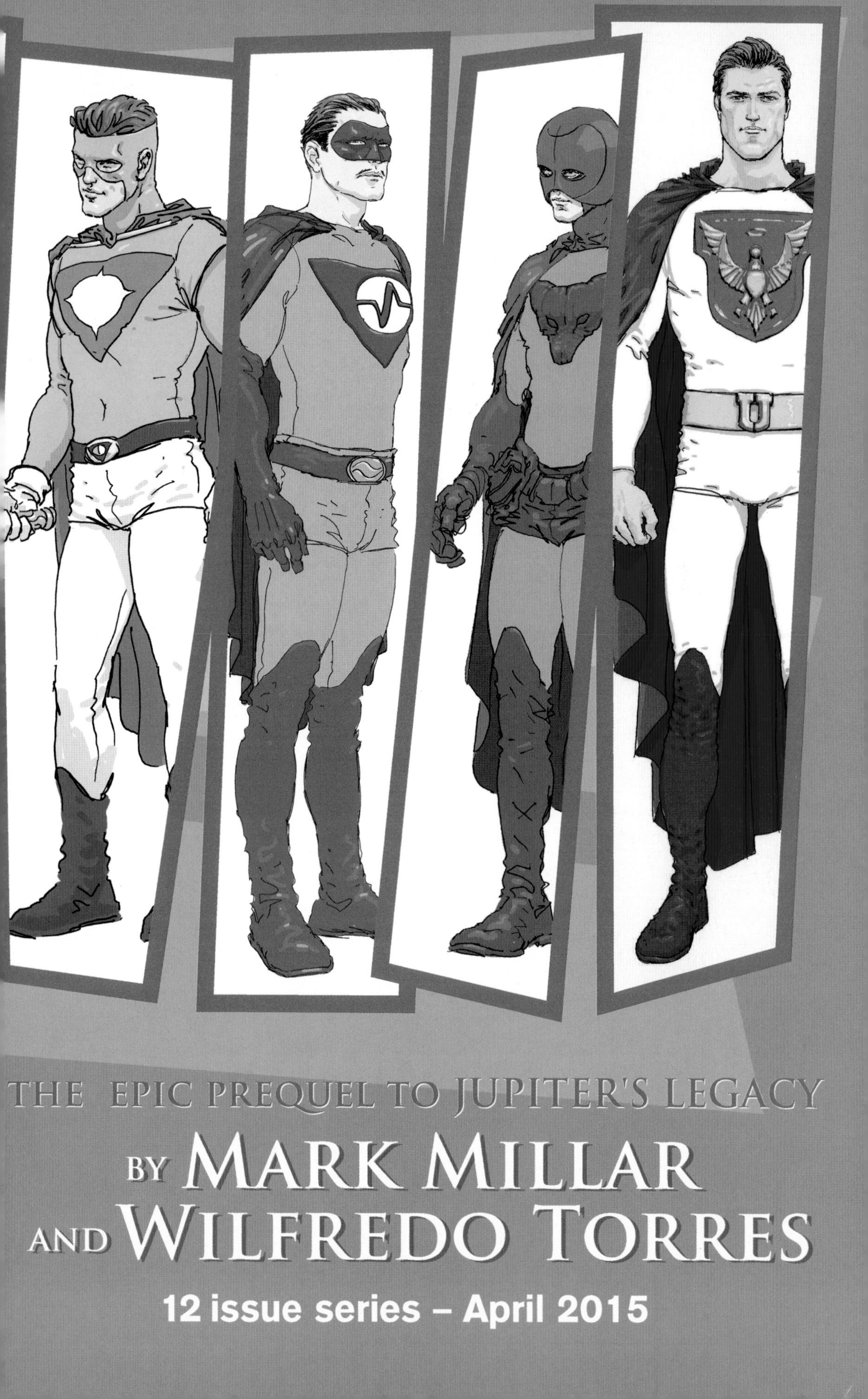

MILLARWORLD®

THE COLLECTION CHECKLIST

KICK-ASS
MARK MILLAR
JOHN ROMITA JR.

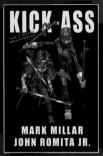

KICK-ASS
Art by John Romita Jr.

- [ ] Kick-Ass #1-8

KICK-ASS 2 PRELUDE:
HIT-GIRL
MARK MILLAR
JOHN ROMITA JR.
TOM PALMER AND DEAN WHITE

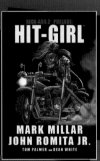

HIT-GIRL
Art by John Romita Jr.

- [ ] Hit-Girl #1-5

KICK-ASS 2
MARK MILLAR
JOHN ROMITA JR.

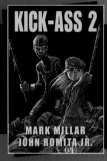

KICK-ASS 2
Art by John Romita Jr.

- [ ] Kick-Ass 2 #1-7

KICK-ASS 3
MARK MILLAR
JOHN ROMITA JR.

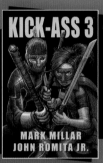

KICK-ASS 3
Art by John Romita Jr.

- [ ] Kick-Ass 3 #1-8

MILLAR MURPHY
CHRONONAUTS
#1
$3.50

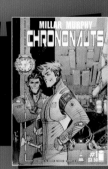

CHRONONAUTS
Art by Sean Gordon Murphy

- [ ] Chrononauts #1-4

MARK MILLAR DUNCAN FEGREDO
MPH

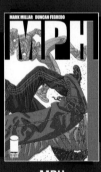

MPH
Art by Duncan Fegredo

- [ ] MPH #1-5

MARK MILLAR GORAN PARLOV
STARLIGHT

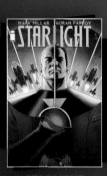

STARLIGHT
Art by Goran Parlov

- [ ] Starlight #1-6

MARK MILLAR DAVE GIBBONS MATTHEW VAUGHN
KINGSMAN
THE SECRET SERVICE

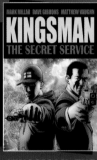

KINGSMAN: THE SECRET SERVICE
Art by Dave Gibbons

- [ ] The Secret Service #1-6

MARK MILLAR·WILFREDO TORRES
JUPITER'S
CIRCLE

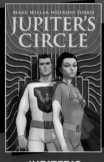

JUPITER'S CIRCLE
Art by Wilfredo Torres

- [ ] Jupiter's Circle #1-5

MARK MILLAR·FRANK QUITELY
JUPITER'S
LEGACY

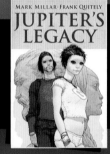

JUPITER'S LEGACY
Art by Frank Quitely

- [ ] Jupiter's Legacy #1-5

MARK MILLAR LEINIL YU
SUPER
CROOKS
THE HEIST

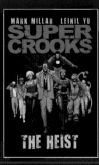

SUPER CROOKS
Art by Leinil Yu

- [ ] Super Crooks #1-4

MARK MILLAR & LEINIL YU
SUPERIOR
FROM THE
WRITER OF
KICK-ASS

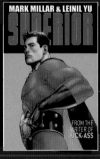

SUPERIOR
Art by Leinil Yu

- [ ] Superior #1-7

MILLAR & McNIVEN'S
NEMESIS

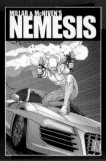

NEMESIS
Art by Steve McNiven

- [ ] Nemesis #1-4

WANTED
MARK MILLAR • JG JONES • PAUL MOUNTS
UNIVERSAL PICTURES

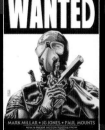

WANTED
Art by JG Jones

- [ ] Wanted #1-6

AMERICAN
JESUS
BOOK ONE : CHOSEN
MARK MILLAR ✦ PETER GROSS

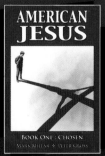

AMERICAN JESUS
Art by Peter Gross

- [ ] American Jesus #1-3